"Miranda, I think we should have a baby," Joe announced

Shock rippled through her, and along with it came a hysterical and overwhelming urge to laugh. She struggled against it, and she could feel her face turning red with the effort. Joe misinterpreted her reaction.

"I've insulted you. I know you have every right to haul off and belt me, but don't be angry, Miranda, please don't," he begged. "It's an outrageous thing to suggest, but at least take a moment to think it over." He reached across and took the hand clenched around a spoon on the tabletop, unfastened her fingers and held them.

"You don't believe in the whole ridiculous romantic charade," he went on. "You know, fall in love, make the other person responsible for your happiness. Now, the sensible approach is to treat the matter entirely as a business proposition."

"You're talking about marriage?" She realized she sounded stunned. She *felt* stunned. She was still trying to digest his version of love and happily ever after.

"Not right away—only if you do get pregnant. Then we'd *have to* marry. The child would be the Wallace heir—and the Irving heir, too, of course. Will you at least think it over?" he asked.

She swallowed hard. "I already have. I accept."

Dear Reader,

I became aware as I wrote this story of how fearful much of society is about the coming millennium. Friends spoke of storing water and food, and others were fearful for their investments. It occurred to me that we must all trust that everything will turn out all right.

It also occurred to me, as *The Baby Trust* changed drastically, in the writing of it, from my early vision, that a writer must trust in the process of creation. When my faithful computer collapsed while I was revising the manuscript, I tried not to panic but instead to trust that everything was on the floppy disk I'd carelessly updated every few days.

This entire book has been a lesson in trust for me, and I've attempted to convey my sense of confidence that everything would work out, as I wrote—and cried over—the final few pages.

The millennium is a wonderful new beginning for our beleaguered world, and I hope that in some small way this book relays that message.

Bobby Hutchinson

Books by Bobby Hutchinson

HARLEQUIN SUPERROMANCE
723—SIDE EFFECTS
753—THE BABY DOCTOR
797—FALLING FOR THE DOCTOR
844—FAMILY PRACTICE

THE BABY TRUST
Bobby Hutchinson

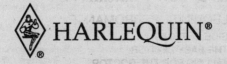

HARLEQUIN®

TORONTO • NEW YORK • LONDON
AMSTERDAM • PARIS • SYDNEY • HAMBURG
STOCKHOLM • ATHENS • TOKYO • MILAN • MADRID
PRAGUE • WARSAW • BUDAPEST • AUCKLAND

ISBN 0-373-70876-9

THE BABY TRUST

Copyright © 1999 by Bobby Hutchinson.

Visit us at www.romance.net

Printed in U.S.A.

THE BABY TRUST

PROLOGUE

London, June 16, 1900

"WHAT IN BLAZES is keeping her?"

For the third time in ten minutes, Harold Wallace drew his gold watch from the pocket of his waistcoat and held it at arm's length, squinting and scowling at the handsome Swiss timepiece as though it were deliberately playing tricks on him.

What could be delaying Cordelia? She was now thirty-three minutes late for their two o'clock appointment. In the sixteen years he'd been her solicitor, Harold had never known Cordelia to be this tardy.

And damnation, it was hot. London was suffering through an early heat wave, and although his office was the finest in the building—he was, after all, one of the founding partners of Wallace and Houmes— not the faintest trace of a breeze stirred the draperies at the open windows.

Harold ran a finger under his high white collar and patted the sweat from his forehead with the crumpled handkerchief he kept in his top desk drawer for just that purpose, so as to leave pristine the fine linen one tucked discreetly into the breast pocket of his favorite suit.

Cordelia had once remarked that she admired good grooming and attention to detail in a gentleman's livery, and Harold had never forgotten it.

The fact was, he remembered almost everything Cordelia had said to him from the very first moment she'd appeared in his much-smaller office in Chancery Lane all those years ago. He'd been thirty-four, struggling to establish himself as a solicitor both brilliant and reliable enough to attract London's elite.

The first thing that had struck him that morning was her beauty. Dark-eyed, dark-haired, tall and graceful, she was dazzling. It had bothered him only slightly to learn she was nine years his senior, with a grown daughter, Geneva, already twenty-three.

The second thing he'd noted that first day was Cordelia's force of will. She was newly widowed, to her great relief—indeed, rumor had it she had poisoned him!—from a man who'd forced her to live a penurious existence in the midst of wealth, refusing her and her daughter all but the barest necessities of life. As a result, she was determined to manage her own financial affairs henceforth—an unusual situation in England in 1884.

With the turn of the century, of course, everything had changed, Harold mused. Women were now demanding emancipation, but back then Cordelia's insistence on reverting legally to her maiden name, Irving, and becoming knowledgeable about every detail of her deceased husband's small fortune, had been highly unusual.

When Harold had inquired about male relatives who might intervene and refute Cordelia's decision—according to English law, inheritance always passed to the nearest male relative on either the husband's side or the wife's; women were not considered capable of managing business affairs—she'd said that fortunately she was an only child. There were two uncles, both in their dotage, but no immediate relatives on her husband's side. Dark eyes flashing, she'd pointed out that a sizable portion of her husband's estate had belonged to her family, turned over, under the terms of inheritance law, to her husband on the death of her parents. She was only reclaiming what was rightfully hers, she'd stated in her low melodious voice. She was wise enough to realize that she needed an excellent lawyer to assist her. *Was* he an excellent lawyer?

Harold had smiled at her naiveté and assured her he was. And it wasn't arrogance on his part to say that he'd done a first-class job over the years. But then, she'd been an apt pupil, her business instincts uncannily sound and sure. Her investments prospered and her fortune grew. She was now an extremely wealthy woman.

Cordelia had accepted his invitation to dinner that first evening, and within a month they'd become passionate secret lovers. But it had taken him half a year to admit that he was *in* love with her, and another six months to propose, because he knew his family would find her unsuitable—too old, too opinionated, not from an impressive family, not rich enough.

He'd been astonished, insulted and deeply hurt when Cordelia had turned him down, but he'd been unable to stop loving her. He'd proposed dozens of times since, with the same result. Cordelia's first marriage had been disastrous, and she steadfastly insisted she would never marry again. She didn't want to bear any more children; she enjoyed her independence. She admitted freely that she loved him—and he knew she did—but she wouldn't marry him.

Over the years, Harold had raged, pleaded, threatened. He'd even suggested they flout social convention and simply live together, but Cordelia had never wavered. She would be his lover, never his mistress or his wife.

Fifteen years had slipped by. Cordelia hired tutors to provide the education Geneva had longed for and been denied by her stingy father. The young woman became a doctor, a brave and unusual thing for a woman to attempt, but then, Geneva was truly her mother's daughter in every way.

Last summer, Cordelia had sold her grand house in London and moved to the country, to Bethel Farm, a comfortable, secluded estate in the Cotswolds, in the heart of central England. Bethel Farm had been part of her inheritance, the place where she'd spent the happiest times of her childhood.

The move had made his life exceedingly awkward, but Harold visited her there as often as his practice allowed, and her infrequent trips down to London were occasions he greatly anticipated.

He'd turned fifty last month, and it was a blow to realize he was no longer young. Fortunately, he had a brother who'd provided his aging father with an heir, but at times Harold found himself thinking wistfully of a family of his own, of someone besides Bucky, his golden retriever, waiting for him when he arrived home at night. Those thoughts went right out of his head, however, when he was with Cordelia. His love for her had only grown stronger with the years.

He pulled out his watch to check the time again, but just as he did there was a tap on the door. A young clerk sidled in and smiled ingratiatingly.

"Miss Irving is here, sir."

"Well, hurry up and show her in, Ruscombe."

Harold patted his thinning hair into place and hastily mopped his forehead once more. He heard the rustling of her silk dress an instant before she glided in.

The moment the door closed behind her, he gathered her into his arms and kissed her. As always, she smelled of roses and tasted of mint, and he marveled at how little she'd changed over the years. Her hair had a few white strands, but it was still luxuriously thick, drawn up in a heavy chignon on her neck. Her skin was soft and smooth, with only a few lines around eyes and mouth. She was a trifle stouter, which vexed her, but he always insisted it only added to her beauty.

She returned his kiss warmly, holding him close for a moment longer than he expected. They smiled into each other's eyes with the familiarity that comes through years of intimacy.

"You're very late, my dear," he chided. "Because you're usually so prompt, I was becoming worried."

"I'm sorry, Harold. I missed the early train. Baby has a summer complaint and she fretted all night, and just as I was about to leave at dawn there was an emergency. Geneva had to treat one of the stable boys—a horse kicked him and broke his ribs. So I stayed with baby until Geneva was free."

The baby, whose given name was Pearl, was Cordelia's adored granddaughter. Harold had to struggle with conflicting emotions each time she mentioned the child. They might have had a grandchild together, if only...

Geneva had borne Pearl out of wedlock two months ago. Like Geneva, the father was a doctor. True to Irving form, Geneva had refused to marry him before he left England to fight the Boer War, where he had been tragically killed. Although Cordelia never would admit it, Geneva's scandalous pregnancy was the reason they'd moved out to Bethel Farm.

Harold envied Cordelia this grandchild more than he'd ever thought possible, yet at the same time he was secretly appalled by Geneva's irresponsible behavior—although he'd never tell Cordelia so.

He looped an arm around her waist now and led the way over to his desk. "Come, my dear, have a seat and we'll dispense with whatever business matters there are, then we'll go out for tea. I managed to get us tickets for the musical tonight at Albert Hall.''

"How wonderful, Harold." She settled herself into his most comfortable chair, and he took the seat behind his desk, as he always did.

"What's first on the agenda, Cordelia?"

She didn't respond immediately, and suddenly Harold realized something was amiss. Normally the most composed of women, Cordelia was fiddling with her handbag, touching the ivory cameo at her throat, nervously smoothing the skirt of her lilac frock. She wouldn't meet his gaze, and alarm filled him.

"What is it, my dear? Is something wrong?"

She drew in a long deep breath, and then in a quiet but certain voice said, "I need your help and your expertise, Harold. I want you to set up a trust."

"What sort of trust, Cordelia?"

"One that will ensure Irving women will always have a home and an income of their own. Bethel Farm must always remain their property, but I also want it designated as a haven for women with nowhere else to go, who need shelter and are willing to work on a farm to earn their bed and board."

The words tumbled out, and he could make little sense of them.

She hurried on. "Of course it will be available to any female Irving descendant who wants or needs to live there, but in the event that Irvings aren't in residence, then it will be used as a shelter. At the discretion of the Irving heir, of course. I wish it to pass from mother to daughter, but the trust must guarantee that no one can ever mortgage the property or sell it or endanger it in any way. Bethel Farm is profitable, as you know, but I also intend to deposit a significant amount of money into an account on the trust's behalf, which will be invested prudently.'' She opened her handbag, extracted several handwritten sheets of notepaper and thrust them across the desk at him. "There are a number of considerations I want included. I've listed them here. I know you will make certain that every legal loophole is covered, Harold. This trust must be inviolate.''

With a puzzled frown, Harold took the proffered papers. "But my dear Cordelia, I don't understand. You already have a will, leaving Bethel Farm to Geneva, who undoubtedly will leave it to Pearl. As for its becoming a shelter for impoverished women, surely you can't want such individuals living with you.''

She smiled a little at the horror in his voice. "No, no, not living with me. I want it to be available to women who find themselves in situations similar to the one I was in when I was married. There was nowhere for me to go, Harold, no one to turn to. I was absolutely my husband's prisoner. I've never forgotten how that felt. I never will.'' Then she looked him straight in the eye and said in an even tone, "You see, I won't be living much longer at Bethel Farm. Geneva and I have discussed it at great length, and we...we've decided to immigrate. To America, to the city of Seattle. Geneva has a friend there, a lady doctor who's invited her to join a medical practice. I've already booked our passage. We'll be sailing in August.''

The shock he felt was overwhelming. For a moment, he couldn't speak. In spite of the heat, he felt icy cold. At last he stammered, ''Immigrate? To America?'' He realized he sounded like a simpleton, parroting her words, but he couldn't seem to formulate a coherent sentence of his own.

All he could think was that she was leaving him as certainly as if she'd announced she was dying. He knew that if she went to America he'd likely never see her again. To his shame, he felt tears gather in his eyes. He hurriedly got to his feet and stumbled across to the window, his back to her. When he could control his voice, he asked, ''Why, Cordelia? Why are you doing this?''

''Oh, my darling, I'm sorry. I've so dreaded telling you.'' She sounded almost as miserable as he felt, but he didn't turn around—and she didn't come to him.

''It's because of Pearl.'' Her voice was subdued and very sad. ''Even out at the farm there's gossip. They whisper about her in the village, labeling her illegitimate. It will only get worse as she grows. It will affect her life. She will never be accepted by society here in England, you know that. She will always be an outcast. And Geneva and I love her. We can't risk her happiness that way.''

He wanted to roar at her, *What about our happiness? What about us?* But he didn't. Instead, he clamped his jaw and pulled the draperies back to stare out at the busy London street. Below the window a family walked past, the woman's hand tucked into the crook of the man's elbow, a small boy in a blue suit riding high on his father's shoulders.

The woman tipped her bonneted head and smiled up lovingly at her husband. Pain shot through Harold's chest, and it was terribly difficult for him to retain his composure.

He understood that in this moment his life was being changed forever, and he couldn't see any future at all.

Cordelia was speaking again; he forced himself to listen, to focus on business instead of the ache in his heart.

"I know the wisest thing would be to sell Bethel Farm, but for sentimental reasons I simply can't part with it. It's where I was happiest as a child, Geneva loves it there and now it's Pearl's birthplace. You will act as trustee, Harold. When you retire, you must appoint someone from this firm, someone in whom you have the utmost confidence, to take over that responsibility. You will, of course, be paid out of the income from the trust."

"That could be expensive over time. Have you considered how long you wish this trust to continue?" Concentrating only on the legal details helped. By doing so, he was able after a moment to turn from the window and take a seat again behind his desk.

He lifted his pen from the well and began to make notes on a sheet of vellum. His hand trembled, and he hoped she wouldn't notice. "It's customary that a trust expire at some point," he stated.

"Must it expire?"

"It would be best to have a certain period of time in mind, yes. Situations change. Even the law changes with time. If at the designated date it seems feasible to continue, then the entire matter can be reviewed and a new document drawn up."

She thought for a moment. "One hundred years, then. We'll make it for a hundred years, until the year 2000."

He laid down his pen, shocked at the date. "That appears rather excessive, Cordelia. It's impossible to predict what the world will be like in a century. Consider the massive changes that have occurred these past hundred years. Why, any document drawn up in 1800 is likely hopelessly outdated now that 1900 has arrived."

She shook her head. "Money and property never go out of style, Harold. And Pearl comes from good strong English stock. She could conceivably live a hundred years. I hope and pray that she will. But even if she doesn't, even if no Irving women survive the century, I'm certain there will still be females needing refuge throughout the coming years. I've suggested on those sheets that the trust pass from mother to eldest daughter when the daughter reaches the age of twenty-one. If no Irvings are born, Bethel Farm will continue as a shelter for as long as it remains self-supporting."

"And what if the Irving progeny are male? Are boys to be excluded, discriminated against simply because of their gender? Would you love Pearl less if she'd been a boy?"

She looked at him for several moments, and then a small smile played across her lips, acknowledgment that his argument was valid. "You're right, Harold. It's unfair to limit the trust to females."

"We'll simply say 'progeny,' then. And what do you envision at the termination of the trust, in the year, uh, 2000?" It seemed the height of madness to him to contemplate a time that far in the future, but he knew it was fruitless to argue with Cordelia once her mind was set on a thing.

She sat in deep thought for a while. "The farm will go to the youngest Irving offspring under the age of twenty-one. If there are no young Irvings, the property will be sold and the profits, after expenses, distributed among any and all descendants. If there are no Irvings alive, then Bethel Farm will be sold and the money donated to a deserving charity." Her chin came up and she shot him a challenging look. "A charity for women only, Harold. I concede reluctantly on the gender issue of inheritance, but I can't find it in my heart to trust that even in a hundred years there will be equality."

The words explained their entire relationship. Her absolute trust was what she'd been unable to give, not just to him but any man. It was the reason she'd refused to marry him or live with him. Her marriage had damaged her irreparably, and her wound would never heal.

"I'll do my very best for you, Cordelia."

She looked at him, and he could see the sadness in her eyes. "I know you will, Harold. You always have, and I'm grateful."

The trust would go on long after they were both gone from the earth. In some strange fashion, that gave him comfort. It would be their brainchild, the only progeny Harold Wallace and Cordelia Irving would ever produce together, formed in part from the ashes of his dead dreams.

CHAPTER ONE

December 31, 1998

MIRANDA JANE IRVING squinted through her glasses at the snow blowing straight into her windshield and decided not to chance the steep driveway down to the house.

She bravely aimed her new red Jeep into a high snowdrift at the top of the hill, where a parking space hid beneath billows of white, and sighed with relief when the sturdy vehicle found traction. She backed up a little to make sure she wasn't stuck, then straightened the wheels and turned off the motor.

It was early afternoon on New Year's Eve, and Seattle was experiencing one of the worst snowstorms in recent years. The road crews were working hard, but they couldn't keep up with the storm, and driving home from the city, the last few miles had been treacherous.

It was good to be home. Miranda assured herself it was also good to know she wouldn't be going out again until after the New Year. She and Gram would celebrate together, cozy and warm and safe.

She sat for a moment in the Jeep's toasty interior,

relishing the new smell. The vehicle was a lavish birthday present to herself, and she loved it. She'd just picked it up yesterday afternoon from the dealer, and she was still getting used to it. Driving into the city and back in a snowstorm today had been a challenge, but her friend and fellow teacher, Alma Hamilton, had invited her for a birthday brunch, and Miranda wouldn't have missed it for anything. She glanced at the oversize floral gift bag on the seat beside her and grinned. Alma had given her a funny card, a basket overflowing with dainty soaps and lotions and containers of bubble bath, and she'd even baked a chocolate birthday cake and decorated it with candles and whipped-cream roses—all in Miranda's honor.

"Getting born on New Year's Eve has to be a rotten deal," Alma had declared when Miranda blew out her candles. "People already have parties to go to, and they've spent most of their money on Christmas, so you're shortchanged all the way 'round. Getting born today wasn't the best planning you ever did, honey."

Alma was right. Twenty-eight years before, Miranda mused, she'd missed being a New Year's baby by a scant ten minutes, and it often struck her that her first missed opportunity had come to epitomize her life. She always seemed to be slightly out of synch with the universe.

She sighed, grabbed her gift bag and climbed out of the Jeep, pulling her down coat around her as she shivered in the icy wind that blew up from the water. Living by the ocean was wonderful, but on days like this it was also freezing cold. Her glasses frosted over, and she shoved them down her nose.

She fumbled in the mailbox, then stuffed the fistful of envelopes she'd retrieved into her outsize handbag, before she slipped and skidded down the icy driveway to the house.

Somehow she managed not to fall, and she burst through the front door in a flurry of snowflakes, grateful for the blast of warmth and the delicious smells that greeted her.

"Hey, Gram!" she hollered, tugging off her mittens and struggling out of her boots and coat, smiling as Pearl came from the kitchen to welcome her.

"Something smells good. What're you cooking?" She spoke in a loud voice because her grandmother was getting very deaf and refused to wear a hearing aid. At ninety-eight, she didn't have to do any damn thing she didn't want to do, Pearl Irving insisted, and Miranda agreed with her.

"I made us good thick stew and another loaf of fresh bread." Pearl's tiny frame was enveloped in a voluminous denim apron, and she had a smudge of flour on one wrinkled cheek. Miranda bent way down to give her a hug, and their eyeglasses collided.

"Heavens to Betsy, you're ice-cold, girl. How was your brunch?"

"Fantastic." Miranda described the effort Alma had gone to, and showed Pearl her card and gifts.

"I figured she'd bake you a cake, so I didn't. I made bread pudding with apples for dessert. We'll stick some candles on it so you can blow them out."

Miranda had bought Gram a bread maker for Christmas, and she was beginning to regret it. Pearl was so thrilled with the machine that they'd had fresh bread every day, as well as Gram's creative solutions with the last day's leftover crusts: French toast for breakfast, thick sandwiches for lunch, more croutons than salad at dinner, bread pudding, bread everything. Could a person develop a bread allergy?

"Is Solange still here?" Miranda knew her mother had a date.

Pearl jerked a thumb at the stairs. "Getting ready to go out with the reverend. She seems certain that fool of a man will get through the snow to pick her up."

"The main road's plowed, but our side road's a disaster. If he makes it, he'll have to park at the top of the driveway the way I did."

But even as she said the words, Miranda heard a vehicle right outside the door. Pearl went to the window and pulled back the curtain.

"Wouldn't you know it. He's driven right down. He's gonna get stuck for certain."

The doorbell pealed, and Pearl ignored it. She hurried back into the kitchen, leaving Miranda to answer.

"Happy New Year, and many happy returns, Miranda." Leon Baillie billowed through the door, a black wide-brimmed fedora on his head, an ankle-length sheepskin-lined coat bulking around his rotund frame. With a flourish he handed her a single red rose, which had already started wilting from the frost.

"May God bless you with all the worldly things your heart desires in this coming year."

The sentiment was kind, but Baillie's mellifluous voice grated on Miranda's nerves. The man always sounded as if he were addressing a huge congregation from a pulpit. He did have a following, but Miranda figured it wasn't large enough to merit the size of his voice.

"Nasty weather, nasty, nasty." He rubbed his hands together and shuddered dramatically. "But we must remember, as Shelley so eloquently wrote, 'If winter comes, can spring be far behind?'" Baillie smiled at his own erudition, revealing large perfect teeth in a ruddy face that was undeniably handsome. He had his own program on a local Seattle TV station once a week, and even Pearl had to grudgingly admit that he filmed well. "Even though he's as phony as a three-dollar bill," she always concluded with a snort.

"Maybe you should have left your van at the top of the hill, Leon," Miranda suggested. "It's pretty icy out there."

"We Canucks are used to ice and snow." Baillie always made a big deal out of being from the rugged north. "And how are you, my dear?"

"Fine, Leon." *And I'm definitely not your dear.* "Take your coat off and sit down. Solange is upstairs. I'll get her." Miranda escaped up the stairs, hurrying to her mother's bedroom on the second floor of the large old house.

Solange was standing in front of her dresser, staring at her image in the tilted mirror. Her lush body was enrobed in a swirl of scarlet chiffon, and the untidy heap of discarded silky dresses on the bed attested to how difficult the choice had been. Her newly gilded hair was like a coppery helmet, fitted close to her sleek narrow skull. At fifty-six, she was as beautiful as any magazine illustration, and she looked and dressed twenty years younger than her age.

She had a different earring in each ear. "What do you think, sweetie pie?" She smiled at Miranda through the glass. "Droopy silver or classic pearl?"

"Silver." Miranda didn't have any preference, but she knew sounding decisive was the fastest way to move Solange along. "Leon's waiting."

Solange removed the pearl teardrop and replaced it with silver. "You're right. Silver's best. How do I look? Is this dress okay? I'd almost decided on the black sheath, but we're going to a hotel, very formal, dinner with dancing, and black's so predictable. I also needed a bit of skirt. It's too awkward to dance when the dress is narrow all the way down." The one she wore flared dramatically just above the knee.

"You look beautiful." Miranda figured those had probably been her first spoken words. She'd certainly been telling her mother that for as long as she could remember.

Solange never tired of hearing it. Beaming, she wafted over to her daughter and stood on tiptoe to press a kiss on Miranda's cheek, surrounded as always by a musky cloud of My Sin, her favorite perfume. "Happy birthday, sweetie. I can hardly believe you're twenty-eight. And every year, I swear you look more like your father.''

Miranda knew that wasn't exactly a compliment; her looks were understated, her body lean and rangy. Her father had bequeathed her his good bones, his large, nearsighted, deep-set blue eyes, and the tall body that was strong and slender instead of sensually rounded, the way Solange's was.

And there were the freckles that generously dusted her nose and cheeks; Solange, with her perfect ivory skin, had once labeled them ''unfortunate.''

Even Miranda's curly hair was an unremarkable color, a light ordinary brown, which Solange had given up on persuading her to brighten.

It was just as well she hadn't inherited Solange's dramatic looks, Miranda always concluded. She understood that her mother needed to be acknowledged as the beauty in the family. There wasn't room for two butterflies. Not that Miranda had ever considered herself a butterfly; she was more a worker bee, like her father, she assured herself now, and she was proud of it.

John Graham had been a fine man, a steady man, whose only madness was Solange, and there were times, like right now, as she watched her mother prepare for a spectacular evening, that Miranda wished her own life could be touched by at least a little madness.

Solange flitted over to the bed and dug beneath the discarded dresses for a tissue-wrapped box, which she handed to Miranda.

"Open it, sweetie. I just know you're going to love it."

Miranda carefully peeled off the tissue and lifted the lid on the elegant box. Inside was a deep blue satin nightgown with tiny straps and a matching peignoir, sensual, elegant, seductive...and about the last thing Miranda would ever use.

"Oh, it's beautiful." Miranda stroked the fabric. It *was* beautiful; it just wasn't anything she would ever have occasion to wear. "Thank you so much, Solange." She'd learned years before not to let her disappointment ever show, not to upset her mother.

"Here, hold it up to you." Solange pulled the gown out and draped it across Miranda. "It's bias-cut. It'll make the most of your figure, cling in all the right places, sweetie." Solange winked, delighted with herself. "I just knew it was you when I saw it. Try it on, darling."

Miranda wanted to avoid that. "There isn't time. Leon's waiting for you downstairs."

"Oh, pooh, let him wait. It's good for him." But with typical inconstancy, Solange forgot about the nightgown. She slid her feet into high strappy sandals and leaned toward the mirror to make last-minute adjustments to her makeup.

"Just between you and me, darling, I think Leon's going to propose tonight. I have a strong premonition about these things, you know."

Miranda frowned at her mother's back, and set the gift box carefully on a chair. A feeling of uneasiness came over her. "But you'd never marry him, would you, Solange?"

Solange didn't answer. Instead, she dug in a drawer and drew out a red satin shoebag and a small black velvet evening bag, then stuffed the bag with tubes and pots and a small bottle of scent. "I'm so tired of this snow and having to carry my heels and wear boots all the time, aren't you, sweetie?"

"You really aren't thinking of marrying Baillie, are you?" Miranda suddenly needed to hear her mother laugh at such a silly notion and deny it. After all, legions of men had proposed before, and Solange had always refused.

"None of the Irving women ever marry. You wouldn't think of breaking a tradition like that, would you?" Miranda tried for a light humorous note, praying Solange would say, *Of course not. Don't be silly. Me get married?*

But she didn't. She shrugged.

"Certainly I wouldn't the first time he asks. You have to make men pursue you, Miranda. It drives them mad. It's what women do best."

"But you're not actually considering marrying him? You'd never really marry Leon Baillie, would you?" Apprehension made Miranda's voice louder than she'd intended, and Solange frowned and pressed a cautionary finger to her lips.

"Shhhh, we don't want him to hear us." She moved to the mirror again, pulling at a strand of hair that wasn't behaving, touching her pouty mouth with a lip pencil, narrowing her eyes at her reflection. When she answered, her tone was serious. "I haven't decided, Miranda. I've never tried marriage, you know. Your father wanted to, but of course that bitch of a wife of his wouldn't ever divorce him, and then he died so young. Technically I'm a spinster, and I'm not sure I want to be an old one. Maybe it's time.''

Miranda was speechless with horror, but Solange didn't seem to notice. She was hanging up the dresses on the bed, carefully smoothing them out before she placed them in the well-ordered closet.

''There, I'm ready. Let's go.'' She preceded Miranda down the stairs, conscious as always of making an entrance.

Leon was sitting near the fireplace. He'd removed his coat and hung it over the back of the sofa, but the outsize hat was still on his head. When he caught sight of Solange, he leaped to his feet, swept off the hat and bowed dramatically, accidentally revealing a bald spot on the top of his head that he usually kept well hidden with strategically combed hair.

Solange waved her fingers at him and giggled. ''Leon, you maniac. Where did you get that crazy hat? It's straight out of a western movie.''

Miranda could see by the crestfallen expression on the reverend's face that that wasn't exactly the response he'd been hoping for.

Leon recovered quickly, however, gallantly holding out his arm to steady Solange as she pulled on her fashionable boots. Then he helped her don her furry coat.

''Bye, sweetie pie.'' Solange wiggled her gloved fingers at Miranda, raising her voice to call, ''Bye, Mother.''

In the kitchen a pot banged into the sink, but other than that, there was no response from Pearl.

''I wish she'd give in and get a hearing aid,'' Solange said in an exasperated tone. ''Hollering at her all the time drives me nuts.''

''Now, darling, be charitable. We all get stubborn as we get older,'' Baillie said unctuously as he opened the door, letting in a blast of cold air and a whirl of snowflakes.

Miranda, still thinking about her mother's disturbing disclosure, vaguely heard the van doors open and slam shut, the motor engage and the sound of tires slipping on ice.

Pearl came and stood at the window, and Miranda moved over beside her. Together they watched as the van slid from side to side, violently yawed backward and forward, and finally halted halfway up the drive. Baillie began backing down, and the motor whined as he took another run at the hill.

Pearl shook her head in disgust. ''He's creating a proper mess, the darn fool,'' she commented as the van slithered to the bottom again, the motor protesting as Baillie stepped hard on the gas and tried once more. ''And he's never gonna make it up. I'm scared we're gonna have him hanging around all evening and probably most of tomorrow, as well, because it's plain that nothing's going up that driveway until the snow melts.''

Pearl was obviously right, but Leon took several more futile runs at the incline before he finally gave up.

At last the van came to rest, its back end stuck in a deep snowdrift at the bottom of the hill.

Solange stormed inside the house, with Leon close behind her. She was furious at this change in plans, and evidently she'd been telling Baillie so. He was blustering, making certain no one thought the fault was his.

"It's this marine snow, honey. Terrible stuff—heavy and wet. Any reasonable kind of snow and my van would just walk up that hill," he insisted. "I'll phone for a taxi."

But several calls all resulted in the same message: because of the storm, none of the cab companies would chance dispatching their cabs to such a remote address.

"We've gotten soft," Baillie expounded as he hung up after the last call. "A little snow and the system breaks down. What would happen if we had a real emergency? What's going to happen when Y2K arrives and disaster strikes? We'll be totally unprepared. You mark my words."

It was his favorite subject. Exasperated, Pearl scowled at him. "Y2K and your words be damned. Anybody with half a brain would have left that van at the top of the hill, the way Miranda did her Jeep."

Miranda watched as Baillie's angry expression turned to calculation. Suddenly, with a sinking sensation in her gut, she knew what was coming.

CHAPTER TWO

"I DON'T SUPPOSE you'd let us use your vehicle, my dear Miranda? I can guarantee no harm would come to it. I'm an excellent driver—one had to be in the RCMP," Baillie had the nerve to say, just as if they hadn't all seen him being totally inept only moments before.

Solange stopped pouting and clasped her hands to her chest, her green eyes beseeching. "Oh, sweetie pie, please say yes. My heart's set on going out tonight. It's New Year's Eve. I'd just feel trapped and desperate here with all this snow and no orchestra."

Miranda glanced at Pearl. The old woman was shaking her head vehemently, but Miranda realized there really was no choice. She didn't want the reverend around for New Year's Eve any more than Pearl did, and there was only one way to avoid it.

"All right. Go ahead and take the Jeep." She knew she sounded anything but gracious. "I need it back tomorrow at noon." She didn't have anywhere to go, but they didn't have to know that. Feeling resentful, and trapped herself, she got her keys from her handbag and handed them to Solange. "I'd rather you drove," she said. Baillie shot her a hostile look that changed miraculously to an ingratiating smile when she looked straight at him.

When they were finally gone, Pearl said in a reproving tone, "You shouldn't have done it, Miranda. Wouldn't surprise me that idiot wrecks your brand-new vehicle. You know Solange won't drive in this snow."

It wouldn't surprise her, either, Miranda thought with a sigh. "Well, at least you and I can have a quiet dinner and a nice New Year's Eve, Gram."

The stew was delicious, but Miranda's appetite wasn't as hearty as usual. She kept thinking over what Solange had said about marrying Baillie. Apart from the fact that both she and Gram abhorred the man, such an event would present very real practical problems. The house and a small income from investments were common property. Great-grandmother Geneva had stipulated in her will that Pearl and Solange share whatever inheritance she left, and when Miranda turned eighteen, they'd legally added her to the unorthodox arrangement. Solange had never taken the slightest interest in their investments, but it was all too probable Baillie would.

Even worse was the very real possibility that Solange and Baillie would choose to live here. Baillie apparently had an apartment in downtown Seattle. Solange held equal rights to the house. Miranda knew she'd want to move out if Baillie moved in.

But what about Gram? She'd been born in England, at Bethel Farm, but she'd been brought to this house as a baby, and apart from the war years, she'd lived here all her life. At ninety-eight, there was no way she could move. Which meant Miranda couldn't, either; she'd never abandon her grandmother.

The whole thing was a disaster. Miranda longed to talk over the matter with Gram, but she told herself there was no point in both of them losing their appetites.

They moved to the living room for dessert and coffee, and Miranda blew out the candles Gram had arranged on the pudding. Gram's birthday gift brought tears to Miranda's eyes. It was an anthology of photos by famous female photographers, and Gram had written on the title page, For Miranda Jane. You'll be in the next edition.

"Gram, thank you. I love it." Miranda hugged her, aware of the frailty of Pearl's body.

"I meant what I said about you being in the next issue. You're a gifted photographer, Miranda."

"Thanks." She was flattered that Gram thought she had talent, but Miranda had concluded years ago that photography probably wouldn't earn her a living. It would always be her hobby; teaching elementary school was far more practical.

Pearl settled into her favorite recliner, and a New Year's special called *Ancient Prophecies,* which predicted cataclysmic disasters when the millennium dawned.

"They should have had Baillie on here, with his nonsense about Y2K," Gram commented. "My mother used to tell me about the fanatics in London who gave away all their possessions and went up on hillsides the night the last century changed. Morning came, nothing happened—and they had to go down and start over again.''

Miranda cleaned up the kitchen. When she returned to the living room, Pearl had fallen asleep somewhere between Nostradamus and Mother Shipton.

Miranda dug the mail out of her handbag, and sorted through flyers and bills, pausing when she came to a heavy ivory vellum envelope from Wallace and Houmes, the law firm that managed the trust. She slit it open, extracted several typewritten pages and skimmed through them. She read them again, more slowly, glancing over at Gram. This would upset her.

Gram awoke. "You get a love letter?" She grinned at Miranda and shoved her glasses back up her nose.

"Nope. This is about the trust." Gram had to know; it was best to get it over with sooner than later. "A U.S. manufacturing company that makes tractors is interested in buying Bethel Farm and turning it into a factory."

"A factory?" Gram was horrified. "But they'd tear down the buildings. The gardens would be ruined."

"This lawyer says the real-estate market in England is depressed, and if I try to sell the property as it is, I'll have to accept a much lower figure than I'd get from this company, because the buildings need a lot of money spent on them and that would affect the selling price."

Miranda was the legal heir, and the final decision would be hers, but Gram was the one who loved Bethel Farm.

"I was born there," Pearl sighed. "My grandmother Cordelia spent her childhood there. She loved the farm. I had Solange there. You're the only one who's never been to the farm, Miranda, never experienced the beauty of the English countryside, the tranquillity. Oh, I can't bear the thought of our family losing it. And certainly never to a tractor manufacturer."

As always when this subject arose, Miranda felt terrible; guilty, responsible, inadequate. The loss of Bethel Farm *would be* her fault. By not having produced a child to inherit the trust, she'd made the sale of the farm mandatory.

"The letter's from Gabriel Wallace?"

Miranda checked. "No. It's signed Joseph Wallace."

"Must be Gabriel's son. I never met him." It had been years since Pearl's last trip to England.

"He's included a financial statement." Miranda slipped it free and handed it to Gram. "The income from the farm barely meets expenses. If I add the legal fees, the farm's in the red. We're still paying off the expenses we had on this house last year—the plumbing bills and the rewiring. And because we're on the waterfront, our taxes are up again. Sentiment aside, it makes sense to sell the farm. At the very least, that would do away with lawyers' fees and the inconvenience of being an absentee landlord."

The Irvings had been wealthy until the stock market crash of '29; great-grandmother Geneva had been an excellent doctor, but not as wise in business matters as her mother. Cordelia, who'd died in the great flu epidemic of 1918, had been a firm and cautious advocate of diversification when it came to investments. Geneva, on the other hand, consolidated her mother's portfolio and put everything into stocks, with disastrous results.

"We just can't afford to pass up a generous offer, Gram. The money from the sale will be divided among us. Selling would make an enormous difference to our finances." They weren't poor, but they certainly weren't well off, either.

"I know it makes good financial sense. It's just that Bethel Farm has always been as much my home as this place is." The old woman's eyes were sad behind her glasses. "I always thought I might get back there for one more visit before I died, but I just got too old. It's too late now. I don't have time left."

"C'mon, Gram, you're a long way from dead." Miranda's tone was acerbic because it drove her nuts when Gram got in one of her "dying" moods. The best thing to do was give her something else to dwell on. Unfortunately, Miranda had just the thing.

"Solange is talking about marrying Baillie," she blurted out. "I couldn't believe it when she told me."

"She'd never do a thing like that. She's just trying to get a rise out of you." Gram sounded positive, but Miranda shook her head.

"I don't think so. I know when she's fooling and when she's not, and she's really considering it. She said he's gonna propose tonight."

Gram snorted. "Of course he is. All Solange's fancy men do sooner or later. And when they do, she loses interest."

Miranda nodded. "She always has before, but something's different this time. What is it about this guy, except that he's the most obnoxious in recent years?"

Gram thought it over and then shook her head. "I'm not sure. Maybe she's feeling her age," she said in a thoughtful tone. "She's only four years off sixty, and sixty makes a woman sit up and take notice of time flying past. I remember feeling my age when I turned sixty, thinking that maybe I didn't have that many years left." She snorted. "Fool that I was. Here I've gone nearly another lifetime." She grinned at Miranda. "Ninety-eight—now *that* makes a woman feel old, all right."

Miranda smiled, relieved that Gram was back on track. "You're still going strong, Gram. You aren't rushing out and marrying somebody just because of your age, either."

"No fear of that. There was only Jacques for me. I never wanted any other man. Come down to it, neither are you rushing into marriage, Miranda. And out of the three of us, you're the only one who should be."

"I'm as fussy as you, Gram." Miranda knew Pearl was subtly turning the subject back to Bethel Farm and the conditions of the trust, and she wanted

to avoid it. "You and I somehow have to keep Solange from making this mistake. Marrying Baillie
would be a disaster, for her and for us."

She outlined her concerns about their joint interests and the possibility of Baillie moving into the
house. "And getting her unmarried would cost a fortune," she added. "You pegged Baillie as a gold
digger when you first met him."

Gram nodded. "All that garbage about being in
the RCMP, winning the lottery, being called to the
pulpit. It's all hot air, if you ask me. If Leon Baillie's a reverend, then I'm the reincarnation of Mar-
ilyn Monroe. He sees us sitting here on valuable
waterfront property—Solange probably told him
about Bethel Farm. He thinks we've got money, or
prospects at least. He's a fortune hunter and a
phony, pure and simple. How any daughter of mine
can be so gullible is beyond me. What we should
do is tell him about the Irving curse."

Gram believed there was a curse on the men Irving women loved, placed there by the penurious
husband Cordelia was rumored to have poisoned.

Miranda didn't believe in it, but she didn't entirely disbelieve, either. All the men her female relatives loved *had* died in some tragic fashion: Pearl's
father, in the Boer War; her lover, Jacques Desjardins, in a plane crash when Pearl was first pregnant
with Solange; and Miranda's own father, in a flood.
And all of them had been young.

Pearl was still thinking about Solange. "How do
we stop her if she does decide to marry Baillie?

She's as stubborn as a Missouri mule, and head-strong to go with it.''

There were lots of other adjectives to describe her mother, Miranda thought with more than a trace of bitterness—selfish, promiscuous, childish, thought-less, monumentally self-centered—although she de-served credit for moving back to this house when Miranda's father, John Graham, had died. From the age of twelve Miranda had had Pearl at least to guide her during her growing-up years.

"What do you say we forget all our problems for now and have some champagne. It's after eleven. 1999 is almost here.'' Miranda got the dark bottle from the fridge and filled her grandmother's glass, then held her own brimming flute aloft. ''To the coming year, and to us, Gram. To Irving women. Long may we flourish.''

"Hear, hear," Pearl affirmed, drinking the wine in drawn-out sips. "I do intend to stay awake until midnight, but at my age, you never know when you'll be overcome, so maybe I should have another glassful now.''

"Smart thinking." Miranda refilled Pearl's glass and her own, and in companionable silence they sipped the fizzy liquid.

After a time, Gram said in a confident tone, ''Ir-ving women never marry their lovers. Solange won't, either.''

Miranda could only hope Pearl was right.

"If you'd married Jacques, Gram, would you have been happy?'' Miranda had never asked that before.

Gram thought it over and finally shrugged. "Who knows. It was wartime. We didn't meet under ordinary circumstances. I've often thought I had the ideal romance, because to me Jacques was perfect, and he thought I was, too. That would likely have changed if we'd known each other longer than we did. There just wasn't time to see each other's foibles." She looked at Miranda, then after a moment added quietly, "I still love him, you know. Even after nearly sixty years, hardly a day goes by I don't think of him. And when I die, I know he'll be waiting for me."

Gram's wistful words echoed in Miranda's mind as the elderly woman slipped into the easy sleep of old age and the storm outside worsened. What would it be like to love with such passion that the memory stayed fresh for a lifetime?

What would it be like to love at all? Miranda tucked another blanket around Pearl as the wind rattled the windowpanes and the old year ticked its final few moments away. Maybe there'd been a Jacques for her, but she'd just been in the wrong place at the wrong time and never met him.

At five minutes before midnight the phone rang.

Miranda snatched it up before it woke Pearl and hurried into the kitchen with it.

"Sweetie?" Solange's excited voice trilled over the line. "Guess what?"

A sense of impending disaster overcame Miranda. She struggled to keep her voice level. "What is it, Solange?"

"I wanted you and Mother to be the first to know.

Leon and I got engaged just now. Isn't that romantic?''

Miranda closed her eyes and fought against an almost overwhelming urge to scream at her mother.

"He's given me the most beautiful ring," Solange babbled. "A perfectly huge diamond with lots of chips around it. It looks so good on me. We're planning to get married at Easter. I've always thought that was a perfect time for a wedding, don't you agree, sweetie?''

Miranda swallowed hard, once and then again.

"Congratulations," she finally managed. She couldn't help adding, "Are you sure being married to him is what you really want?''

"What a thing to say! Of course it is. He's in love with me, and I'm very fond of him.'' Solange sounded suddenly testy. "Put Mother on. I want to tell her the news myself.''

Solange had to know how Pearl would react. It was vintage Solange, Miranda thought furiously, this need to upset the old woman.

"She's asleep. I'll tell her when she wakes up.''

Injured silence.

"You didn't have any problem driving the Jeep, did you, Solange?'' Miranda was almost afraid to ask.

"Oh, sweetie, I couldn't drive in that storm. You could barely see the road.''

"But Leon made it okay? No accidents?''

"Nothing major, just a teeny fender bender. The truck slid right into us. Leon got the guy's name. His insurance will cover it.'' The noise in the background increased. "I have to go. It's almost midnight. Happy New Year, Miranda Jane."

The connection ended, and Miranda felt like throwing the phone at the wall. She laid it down and stared blindly at the kitchen clock as the hands inched toward midnight.

When the moment came and passed, an enormous sense of sadness overtook her and her eyes filled with tears. The sound of the storm and the creaking of the big old house were eerie. And as her frustration and anger at Solange slowly faded, she was poignantly aware of being desperately lonely, now that the New Year had begun and the day of her birth was drawing to a close. She had to make a real effort not to burst into tears.

She was here at home by choice tonight, she reminded herself as she made her way back into the living room and slumped into a comfortable old armchair close to the fire.

Gram was still snoring softly, snug and warm in her cocoon of blankets.

Ian Roscoe, one of the other single teachers at Bayview Elementary, had invited Miranda to a party tonight, but Ian was recently divorced and spent a great deal of time talking about his ex and her faults. Spending the evening here with Gram wasn't a sacrifice at all.

She wasn't good at dating anyway, she told herself stoutly. The older she got, the less inclined she became to overlook annoying habits and character traits in the men she met.

Be honest, Miranda, her conscience prompted.

The older you get, the fewer men you meet. Alma, who changed lovers with breathtaking ease and speed, was always after her to get out more, come along to a bar, socialize, answer an ad on e-mail, subscribe to a dating service… Miranda never did.

The truth was, she had a shameful secret, and it grew more daunting with every year that passed.

CHAPTER THREE

HOW WOULD ALMA react if she knew that at the ripe old age of twenty-eight, Miranda was still a virgin? She probably wouldn't believe such a thing could be true in this day and age. And Miranda had misled her: after she'd had several dates the previous year with a man from a photography class, Alma had asked with casual interest, "Was he any good in bed?"

Miranda had said they weren't suited, which was the truth, as far as it went.

Never mind Alma—what would her *mother* say? Imagining Solange's shock and horror at such a revelation brought a wry grin to Miranda's lips. Sexuality and sensuality were so basic to Solange she would likely view her daughter's peculiar status as a personal insult and an aberration.

On that score, she wasn't at all like her mother, Miranda concluded. After John Graham's death—maybe even before it, who really knew?—Solange had always had a lover, and on several occasions she'd been known to have two at the same time.

Miranda had learned certain things about sex from Solange.

At fifteen, Miranda had had a steady boyfriend, a

boy named Andy. They'd kissed and done some heavy petting, and Miranda had enjoyed it. One afternoon, school had let out early and Miranda had invited him home, knowing the house would be empty, Solange and Pearl both at work.

They were in the living room when Miranda first heard the sounds from upstairs, her mother's screams, a man's voice crying out.

She'd raced up to Solange's room, convinced she was being murdered. The bedroom door was half open, and Solange and a man with thick dark hair all down his back were on the bed. It was the first time Miranda had seen two naked bodies joined in that way, and they were far too involved in what they were doing even to realize she was there.

She'd stared in horror and a kind of fascination, and it was only when she turned to run away that she bumped into Andy, standing right behind her.

She'd been so ashamed. They hadn't talked about it, but she'd imagined each time she saw a group of snickering boys with Andy among them that he was telling them about Solange. She'd avoided him after that, and he hadn't really tried very hard to pierce the wall she put up. He was the first and last real boyfriend she'd ever had.

Not that she'd been so traumatized that she had a major psychological thing about sex or about men. Oh, at first, certainly, with all the passionate conviction of an insecure, shy and angry teenager, she'd vowed that she'd never be like Solange. But as time passed, Miranda found the men who might have initiated her unappealing. In college they were often drunk or drugged or desperately immature, or, she suspected, using her to get over some other girl. And suddenly the years had gone by, and it was more and more humiliating to admit to anyone that she really didn't know how to do it. She felt foolish, as if she'd grown up in every way but this one.

It wasn't her mother's fault that she was like this, Miranda concluded. Her mother's wantonness was probably genetic, handed down from Jacques Desjardins and his French ancestors; Miranda just hadn't inherited the gene.

The fire was dying, and as she got up to put another log on the flames, Gram snorted, startled and sat up, fumbling for her glasses. She hooked them over her ears and peered at the clock.

"Oh, fudge. I went and slept right through midnight, didn't I. Well, Happy New Year, darling. And because it's the final year before the millennium, we have to make it a special one." Gram yawned and then added, "If I were going to make a resolution, it would be to find some way to keep Bethel Farm in the family."

Miranda smothered a sigh and forced a smile. They both knew the only way to do that was for Miranda to have a baby before the year 2000, a circumstance about as likely as Solange heading for a nunnery.

Miranda considered telling Pearl about Solange's engagement and the damage to her new Jeep, then decided to leave such bad news until morning.

"I think I'll head up to bed." Gram yawned again, and, with her cane and Miranda's help, struggled out of the blankets and got to her feet. She made her way slowly over to the stairs, where she stopped to look at the old photos Miranda had enlarged, framed and hung there.

One was of Pearl and a small group of other young women, all wearing boilersuits, standing beside an Oxford twin-engined plane. The photo was taken in 1939, but Pearl had learned to fly twenty years earlier.

When she was nineteen, she'd met a twenty-three-year-old First World War hero who made his living giving aerobatic exhibitions at fairs. He'd taken her up, and she'd fallen in love, not with him but with flying. She'd learned to pilot a plane, and when the Second World War came, she heard about a select group of female pilots, the Air Transport Auxiliary. The women ferried planes for the Royal Air Force from the factories where they were made to the airfields.

Pearl made her way to England and enlisted, and from late 1939 until 1942, just scant months before Solange was born, Pearl had picked up and delivered planes all over Britain.

There were several pictures of Solange as a curly-headed beautiful infant. There was a photo of Jacques Desjardins, Solange's father. The dashing French bomber pilot had made an emergency landing in a field at Bethel Farm when Pearl was there on leave, late in the summer of 1941, and they'd fallen in love. He was killed before he even knew he was about to become a father.

There was also a beautiful yellowed blowup of

the stone farmhouse and the front garden at Bethel Farm.

"I look at that and I can almost smell the roses," Pearl said now. "Funny, how Solange inherited that gardening streak from my mother. It skipped me completely."

"You have other talents, Gram." Miranda kissed her, and Gram's arms closed around her in a ferocious hug.

"I've been so blessed, having you, Miranda. Are you coming up to bed soon?"

"In a few minutes. I'll just sit here until the fire burns down a little, maybe have a look at the book you gave me. Thank you again."

"I'd give you your heart's desire if I could, my dear—you deserve it. But I guess nobody can give us that except ourselves. 'Night, Miranda."

"'Night, Gram. I love you."

"I love you, too, pumpkin."

The use of the old nickname once again brought tears to Miranda's eyes. Was it simple weariness making her weepy tonight, or was it the undeniable fact that her life was passing by with so many of her dreams unfulfilled?

As the clock on the mantel edged toward one, then two, the first log burned down and then the second. Miranda stared blindly into the flames, thinking of the things she'd dreamed of when she was a little girl: the babies she'd wanted; the perfect man, very much like her father, whom she'd meet and someday marry.

Where exactly had she taken the first wrong turn that had led her away from her heart's desire?

Of course it was all mixed up with this stupid virginity issue, a humiliating situation that had now assumed monumental proportions. What had started as a teenage rebellion against her promiscuous mother had become an albatross around her neck.

She sometimes had mortifying fantasies that began with her in the arms of a man she wanted desperately to make love with. When he found out she was a virgin, however, he laughed so hard his equipment wouldn't work, or he stared at her as if she were a freak, grappled for his clothes and backed out of some dingy motel room.

It had dawned on her, certainly, that she didn't have to make an announcement, but there was the awful conviction that when the moment came, she'd do something awkward and he'd know anyway. She'd always been clumsy at games; she'd never figured out even the basic rules of basketball.

As Gram had said, now was the time of year for resolutions. Miranda added a prayer to hers just to cover all bases. Screwing her eyes shut, she said out loud, "Please, please, help me with this. If the doomsday people are right and the world is going to end at 2000, I only have 364 days left to make sure I don't go to my grave a virgin. And even if they're wrong, which I'm sure they are, this virginity thing seems like such a *waste*."

Gram had always insisted the universe abhorred waste, so maybe that particular plea would do the trick.

Miranda could only hope.

CHAPTER FOUR

VIRGINITY HADN'T BEEN an issue for Joe Wallace since two months after his fifteenth birthday, and he was now 37. But the riotous New Year's party he'd attended the previous night in Chelsea had left him with a monstrous headache. He'd already swallowed three aspirins, two vitamin tablets and a large glass of water, to no avail.

The plate of eggs and sausage Larry, his manservant, had just set in front of him convinced Joe really should move from his father's house and get a flat of his own. That would at least get him out of things like this New Year's breakfast. The reason he hadn't long ago was twofold: Joe worried about his father, although he hated to admit it; and Larry's presence usually made being a bachelor easy.

This morning, however, was a painful exception.

The thing was, Gabriel had also been out the night before, and Joe knew by his father's bloodshot eyes and the stiff way he turned his head that Gabriel, too, had had more than a few drinks and probably felt as wretched as Joe.

But the older man wasn't letting on. He was sitting directly across the meticulously laid table, shaven, pressed and perfectly groomed, pretending to relish every morsel of the disgusting mess Larry had just heaped on his plate.

For the sake of his pride and his position as his father's only child, Joe knew he had to pretend the same nonchalance, so he cut into a fried egg, and tried not to notice when the yolk erupted and mingled in a disgusting fashion with the tomato sauce. Courageously, he speared a sausage and forked up a mouthful of egg, using every ounce of Wallace fortitude in an effort not to gag before he swallowed.

"More sausage, sir? Or perhaps some kippers?" Larry proffered a plate on which the grease was congealing.

"No thanks, Larry." Larry Pelcher had been a member of their male household since Joe was seventeen. Joe's mother, Anna, had died earlier that year, and Gabriel had hired Larry in a desperate attempt to bring some order to the increasing household muddle.

Larry was an expert at order. He was also a stickler for formality, but over the years he'd proven himself to be a good friend, despite still calling both Wallaces "sir" on occasion. He was a teetotaler and a vegetarian, and because of these two irritating habits, he could be thoroughly aggravating and more than a little smug. He also managed to look forty, when Joe knew for a fact that he was sixty-two, just two years younger than Gabriel.

Joe knew, too, that at this moment Larry was thoroughly enjoying his discomfort and probably Gabriel's, as well. Larry had undoubtedly spent New Year's Eve in front of the television with bottled water and carrot sticks, and gone to bed at a reasonable hour—disgusting behavior in a grown man.

"More coffee would be nice, Larry. Please." The coffeepot was empty, and because Larry painstakingly ground the beans and turned coffee making into a sacred ritual, Joe would have at least ten minutes during which he didn't have to confront Larry's disgustingly clear eyes, faint smirk and general annoying air of superior health and well-being.

"Well, Joseph, have you made any resolutions for 1999 that you intend to keep?"

Gabriel's tone was light, but Joe was instantly on guard. His father could use any casual remark as a prologue to THE LECTURE, whose topic was how he should perform his familial duty by marrying someone suitable as soon as possible and producing an heir immediately thereafter.

Because Joe was the only son of an only son, the Wallace name was in danger of vanishing unless he took action. And because law was the family business, he had the added responsibility of producing a child who would become a solicitor and carry on the tradition.

Gabriel had fond hopes of changing the name of the firm from Wallace and Houmes to Wallace and Wallace. The elderly Monkford Houmes had passed on five years earlier, and if Joe had toed the party line and not gone walkabout after his acceptance to the Bar, the change would already have been made. As it was, he was still very much on probation in Gabriel's view.

Gabriel claimed he could retire when he turned

sixty-five next year, but that was highly unlikely; the firm was Gabriel's life.

"Resolutions, Dad?" Joe shook his head and instantly regretted it. The motion made him seasick. "I gave up on resolutions long ago. How about you?"

"Oh, the usual. Play more golf, be less involved in the firm. Find the time to travel."

"I didn't realize you wanted to travel. Where would you go?"

"Oh, places you've already been, undoubtedly. India, Australia, the South Seas." Gabriel's voice took on a martyred tone. "Unlike you, I didn't have the opportunity as a young man to gallivant around the globe. My father was a stickler for responsibility. He would have disowned me had I gone adventuring the way you did."

Hell's bells. Too late, Joe realized where this was heading. "Well, I think travel's made me a better lawyer than I would have been otherwise. Broadened my outlook on life, given me a wider view of the human condition." His pathetic attempt to throw Gabriel off course didn't succeed. Joe hadn't expected it would. His father was, after all, a solicitor renowned for sticking to the issue at hand.

"A better lawyer? That remains to be seen. Certainly, it doesn't seem to have settled you into a responsible path. By the way, who *was* that young woman who came by to pick you up early last evening in that reprehensible car?"

Joe was starting to enjoy this a little. "Oh, that was Kitty Fleming. She's a receptionist at my dentist's office. The car's a vintage Porsche, just a bit worse for wear.''

''I daresay the muffler seems to be missing. And is it now customary for young ladies to collect their dates instead of the other way 'round?''

''Kitty's very liberated. She enjoys being in control.''

Gabriel's expression of disgust and his *humph* did more for Joe's hangover than the aspirins had. ''And you don't, I suppose—feel any desire to be in control?''

''Not particularly. It takes far too much energy. Certainly not control of Kitty. She's rather like a force of nature. Trying to control her would drive a man bonkers. She's great fun, though.''

And she was in bed at this moment with Joe's best friend, Tony Patterson, where she belonged. She was Tony's girl, not Joe's. She didn't drink, and she'd volunteered to drive last night in the likely event that Joe and Tony might just succumb to one too many whiskeys at the party. Tony, an obstetrician, had been called to deliver a baby at the last moment, so Kitty had come alone to pick up Joe.

He wasn't about to explain all that to Gabriel, however. His father always assumed the worst, and Joe enjoyed teasing the old boy a little. It kept Gabriel's blood pulsing through his veins in a healthy fashion. It also evened the playing field when it came to THE LECTURE and the ever-increasing stack of nuisance files that Gabriel kept piling on Joe's desk at the office.

''Of course I'm no expert on women, but it would

seem to me that this, um, *Kitty* would be unsuited to the mundane life a solicitor leads. She'd likely find it boring.''

"I'm sure she would.'' Joe chose to misunderstand. "Fortunately, she doesn't want to be a lawyer, and she certainly doesn't want to marry one.''

Kitty wanted Tony, and although Patterson was resisting as well as he was able, Joe's money was on Kitty. "She's told me she wants to have children, and I don't think she's concerned about marriage. A great many women in my age group are opting for single parenthood these days.''

Baiting the old man this way was probably unfair, and it was certainly misleading, but Joe couldn't resist.

Larry appeared with the coffee just then, so Gabriel's heated comments about lack of responsibility, what the world was coming to and what had happened to the young women of today were interrupted by the ceremony of serving fresh coffee with cream and two lumps of sugar and more toast.

Joe took pity on his father and changed the subject. "How was your New Year's Eve, Dad?''

"Very nice. Quiet. I was in bed by two.''

Joe noted with private glee that Gabriel didn't specify *home* and in bed. He knew that his father had had a mistress for many years, a cheerful attractive woman named Dierdre Payne. She was Gabriel's personal secretary at the office, and Joe considered her his friend.

Neither she nor his father ever hinted of their relationship, and of course Gabriel had never discussed it with Joe. He had found out years before quite by accident; he'd come home unexpectedly early from a golfing trip to Scotland and caught Dierdre in a diaphanous white nightdress in the up-stairs hall.

Joe had brought up Gabriel's mistress only once, during a particularly tiresome lecture about respon-sibility, honor and the family name. He'd asked point-blank why Gabriel himself was still single; certainly he'd had ample opportunity over the years to remarry and produce a spare to take the pressure off the heir. Dierdre was only in her early forties, Joe had remarked boldly. It wasn't inconceivable— no pun intended—that she have a child.

Gabriel hadn't lost his temper as Joe had expected he would. He'd simply said in a quiet resigned tone, "Marriage doesn't suit me, Joseph. I'm not good at it. I don't know how much you remember, but your mother and I were not happy. Not at all. I wouldn't want to repeat the experience."

Joe did remember from his growing-up years the bitter quarrels, tears and silences. Those memories, and watching several of his friends marry, then quickly and painfully divorce had convinced him that marriage wouldn't suit him any more than it had suited Gabriel. Plus, there were his files at the office; he'd taken on the family law portion of the business, and it seemed at times as if every couple in the world was involved in litigation.

Joe had fallen in love twice, and both times the expectations of the women had made him fall out of love and end the relationship. The women had wanted him to make them happy, and he was clear about not wanting to be responsible for anyone's happiness but his own. Romantic love seemed to bring with it a ton of emotional baggage.

So he'd grown older and wiser and had decided to wait until he met someone different, someone as realistic as he was about the entire love myth. He thought he'd prefer a business arrangement to a romantic liaison in which one or both parties ended up arguing over the china and the silverware.

The trouble was, he'd never met a woman who'd agree to a business contract instead of a romantic fairy tale. From his own experience and conversations with his male friends, he was fairly certain he never would, which posed a very real problem when it came to the matter of the Wallace heir.

He'd discussed it at length with Tony, and they had concluded the best path to follow would be surrogate motherhood: Joe would find a suitable woman who, for a specified sum, would bear him a child and disappear from his life forever. He'd then give the sprout to Gabriel and Larry to raise, he decided vindictively. Serve smug old Larry right to have to deal with nappies and croup.

The problem was finding a woman to be the surrogate. She'd have to have good genes, be intelligent, reliable, honest and circumspect. And attractive enough to take to bed in the first place, of course. There didn't seem to be many women like that around, although Joe suspected he probably wasn't looking in the proper places.

''If you've nothing planned for the next few

hours, Joseph, I thought we could take a stroll in the park. Nothing like a good brisk walk to blow the cobwebs away,'' Gabriel was saying as he finished the last of his eggs. ''There's a particular file I'd like to discuss with you as we go.''

Joe's heart sank. He'd wanted to crawl back into bed and sleep away the afternoon. It was drizzling, the kind of dreary London drizzle that soaked through even the finest Burberry raincoat. And his father's idea of a stroll was a four-mile hike at breakneck speed.

Well, he was a grown man; he'd simply look his father in the eye and say no. He opened his mouth to do so, really *looked* at Gabriel, and abruptly changed his mind.

JOE SAW THAT his father looked old this morning, the lines on his face silent markers of a life spent laboring at the difficult task of doing what was expected of him.

Joe had always sensed that part of Gabriel's resentment of his own streak of irresponsibility was actually envy. He knew that even THE LECTURE was rooted in fear, an awful dread that everything Gabriel had worked so hard to maintain would be lost if there was no one at the end of his life to carry the torch.

Gabriel wanted an heir, but even more he wanted a son like himself: steadfast and loyal and rooted in tradition.

At this moment the old man looked lonely and rather sad. Joe set down his fork. ''A walk sounds fine. I'll just change my shoes and find my umbrella.''

Fifteen minutes later, he regretted his decision. It was cold as well as wet, and his head throbbed with every step. In a spirit of rebellion, Joe set the pace, a faster march than even Gabriel usually demanded. Yet his father's breathing increased only slightly as they climbed the incline that led to the park. The old man was tough, Joe admitted with grudging admiration.

''That file I mentioned,'' Gabriel began as they crested the hill. ''It's one I turned over to you before Christmas, the Irving trust.''

Joe did remember it. It was a moth-eaten piece of legalese concerning a twenty-acre property, Bethel Farm, situated in the Cotswolds near Cheltenham.

''That file is something of a tradition at the firm, Joseph. It was placed in my hands by my father, who inherited it from his uncle.''

Just what he needed, Joe thought despondently, an heirloom file. ''And you're entrusting it to me?''

Gabriel either missed or ignored the sarcasm. ''It's only fitting that a younger Wallace carry the thing through to completion. And I have that Doyle case, which is taking all my time and energy at the moment. Have you had an opportunity to read the Irving file in its entirety, Joseph?''

Joe admitted he hadn't. The thing was at least a foot thick. But he'd identified the concern, which was the impending sale of Bethel Farm in January of 2000. ''I sent a letter off to the Irving heir, explaining that International Harvester was interested in purchasing the property.''

''The Rural Development Authority,'' Gabriel stated, ''is trying to attract manufacturing groups into the area by offering tax holidays, low-interest rates and industrial grants, which makes the purchase very attractive to commercial buyers. That particular company is interested in establishing a forklift manufacturing division, producing small farm tractors for the European market.

''Did you know, Joseph, that the Irving trust was originally set up by your great-great-uncle Harold Wallace, one of the founding partners of Wallace and Houmes? He established the trust back at the turn of the century.''

Joe didn't know. At this moment, neither did he care. He was wet through, and his headache was getting worse instead of better.

Gabriel, of course, didn't notice. He trudged on, outlining in excruciating detail the terms and conditions of the trust, stressing that since there was only one female Irving in the present generation and she was a spinster of 28 years without progeny, the trust would be ending.

Joe had to smother a grin at his father's antiquated terminology. Kitty would verbally castrate the old man for using the term *spinster* to describe a woman of twenty-eight.

Through some peculiar twist of fate, Gabriel went on, all the Irving women had remained unmarried, although they had each produced a child, except for this Ms. Miranda Jane Irving.

"All of them had sprouts without the benefit of marriage vows?" This bit of trivia captured Joe's attention, mostly because he'd heard Kitty going on about emancipated women who chose to have babies instead of husbands. She'd love to hear about this lot, who had done it as a matter of course long before it had become fashionable.

"Except for this youngest Ms. Irving, yes." They were obviously an eccentric lot, Gabriel commented with more than a hint of disapproval.

"Have you ever met any of them?"

"Ms. Pearl Irving. She visited several times after the war. She's quite elderly now, and her granddaughter has taken over the family's business affairs."

"What about the tenants at Bethel Farm? A number of people are living there. Do you know them?"

"Not all of them. I met Natalie Makepeace and her father, Elijah, when they signed the lease on the property six years ago," Gabriel said. "Miss Makepeace is a midwife, and at first she planned to use Bethel Farm as a maternity home, but apparently she ran into problems with licensing. Her sister, Elizabeth Scott, moved in when her husband died, along with the two Scott children, and the women began to operate the farm as a bed-and-breakfast. A year ago, an Irish doctor, Ronan O'Donnell, came as a guest and stayed. He opened a practice in the village, and apparently he and Natalie are planning to marry."

"Have you met him?"

"I spoke to him on the telephone concerning repairs to the stable roof. He seemed a gentlemanly sort.''

In spite of being Irish, Gabriel's tone implied, and again Joe smothered a grin. His father's prejudices were amusing.

''I must confess I haven't been conscientious about visiting the farm recently,'' Gabriel acknowledged. ''I authorized renovations to some of the outbuildings two years ago, and I drove out myself and checked that the work was done, but I haven't actually been out since.'' He stopped and did an abrupt about-face. ''We should start back, Joseph. This rain is getting worse.''

They walked along in silence for several minutes, then Gabriel said, ''It's probably time someone went out to the property again, just to make certain everything's in order.''

Joe allowed a few moments to pass before he replied in a suitably laconic tone, ''I suppose I could drive out this week. I'd have to check, but I think my calendar is clear.''

There were times when a file became interesting, when the personalities behind the stilted legal phrases took on life. Those were the times Joe felt a passion for his career.

Slogging along beside his father through the rain, he wondered if this Irving trust might be one of those times. Certainly the opportunity to get out of the office for a day was appealing. But first he'd do his homework; he'd learn everything there was to know about the Irving trust and Bethel Farm.

At nine the following morning, Joe began reading

the unwieldy stack of papers. By lunchtime he was so intrigued he ordered in a sandwich and went on reading. By two o'clock, he had not only a good grasp of the legal issues involved but also a revealing glimpse into the life of his long-dead relative, Harold Wallace.

Numerous letters were in the file, letters to and from Cordelia Irving. They all concerned business, but often there was a reference in them to other letters, private letters the two must also have exchanged, which weren't included in the file. That old Harold had been in love with his client wasn't hard to guess.

There was an allusion to a trip he'd made to visit Cordelia in 1909, and Joe felt a stab of sympathy for the geezer when he came upon the letter from Cordelia's daughter, Geneva, dated August 23, 1918, saying that Cordelia had died suddenly of influenza.

Harold had gone on managing the trust until 1932, at which point he wrote out a formal letter turning over responsibility for the Irving trust to his nephew, William Wallace.

In America, meanwhile, management of the Irving affairs had in time gone from Geneva to her daughter, Pearl, and then, skipping a generation, to her granddaughter, Miranda Jane Irving. Apparently Pearl's daughter, Solange, had been a hippie in her twenties and had refused to have anything to do with the trust.

It seemed a shame that Bethel Farm would be sold when the millennium arrived, Joe mused. He knew that the Cotswolds had gained a reputation in recent years as a rural retreat for the rich, and it was reassuring to know that many small holdings like Bethel Farm still belonged to ordinary people.

He wondered why this Miranda Jane didn't just follow family tradition and produce a baby, thus ensuring that Bethel Farm remained in the family.

What did Miranda Jane look like? Considering her ancestry, she was no shrinking violet. He came up with a mental image of Ms. Irving that resembled a cross between an amazon and Golda Meir.

CHAPTER FIVE

LATE IN THE AFTERNOON on New Year's Day, Miranda stared through rain-streaked glasses at the ugly scrape and large dent on the fender of her Jeep, and thought of slow and painful ways to kill Leon Baillie.

He and Solange had just come home, hours later than they'd promised. Miranda hadn't waited to hear the string of excuses Baillie began mouthing the moment he walked through the front door and saw the look on her face. Instead, she'd thrown on her coat and boots and stomped up the hill to see for herself what had happened.

It had begun to rain heavily that morning, and the snow was giving way to dirty slush. The world seemed dark and wet and dismal, and rage filled her when she surveyed the damage. Her new Jeep no longer looked new, and the worst part was that short of murder, she could do nothing about it. She'd just have to call the insurance people after the holidays and see about repairs.

Damn Leon Baillie. Damn Solange for bringing him into their lives. Miranda turned and started reluctantly down the hill, hating the thought of even being in the same room as Baillie.

"It was unavoidable, my dear," he blustered as she stormed back in the house and glared at him. "The truck slid into us. There was no way to dodge it."

"I don't want to hear about it. The damage is done. Don't ever ask to use my vehicle again." Miranda tore off her coat and boots and stamped up the stairs to her room. She slammed the door, and the sound reverberated through the house. She was instantly sorry, because she'd forgotten Gram was napping.

Fortunately, Baillie didn't stay long. Miranda watched from her window as he slipped and slid up the driveway in his van, sending mud and stones flying and digging deep ruts that would have to be filled with gravel.

From across the hall, Miranda heard Gram moving around, and a moment later a tap sounded on her door.

"Is he gone?" Pearl came in and Miranda nodded.

"Solange is downstairs waiting to show us her ring."

Pearl rolled her eyes and said a four-letter word Miranda had never heard pass her grandmother's lips before. It made her giggle, and the tension inside her eased. Gram laughed, too, but it was obvious she was troubled.

"What're we going to do about this mess, Miranda?"

Miranda sank onto her bed and shook her head. "Darned if I know."

"Too bad she doesn't just meet somebody else. That's what's always happened before."

"She's talking about getting married at Easter. That doesn't leave much time."

On the desk by her computer was the letter from Wallace and Houmes. Miranda had read it over again this morning, and as she stared at it the far-fetched idea that had niggled at her early this morning returned in vivid detail.

She tapped her trousered thigh absently with her fingers and thought it over for a moment, then concluded it might be workable.

"Spring break, Gram," she announced excitedly in a voice that made Gram jump. "It's late this year. We'll all go to England and visit Bethel Farm at spring break. Remember that poem you always quote, 'Oh, to be in England now that April's there'? Well, we're gonna be."

It suddenly seemed like the ideal solution.

MIRANDA GREW more convinced about her plan as she thought it through.

"It'll get Solange away from Baillie long enough for her to maybe come to her senses or even meet somebody else!" she exclaimed, holding up fingers as she listed advantages. "You'll get a chance to see the farm again, and it'll give me something to talk about in the staff room when everybody's going on about their Caribbean cruises. We can legitimately write the whole thing off as a business trip, so we'll get a break on our taxes. Gram, it's perfect."

Gram was shaking her head before Miranda even

stopped speaking. "Oh, I don't think so. Not me, at any rate. You and Solange go. I'm too old now to fly off to England."

"Your birthday is in April. This will be your birthday gift, so don't argue." Miranda got a calendar and penciled in dates. Then she picked up the phone and called Alma for the name of a reliable travel agent. As Miranda's enthusiasm became contagious, Gram stopped protesting and got involved in speculating about the clothing they'd need for England in springtime.

Gram was in the middle of a rambling reminiscence of what they'd worn during the war years, when Solange came in.

"What's going on up here?" Solange sounded suspicious and put out. "It seems to me you could have at least come down and congratulated Leon and me on our engagement, Mother. And you know, Miranda, you're overreacting about that silly accident. It's only a little bump. Given the size of that truck, you should have been relieved neither of us was hurt."

That was true, and Miranda felt embarrassed because it hadn't even crossed her mind. There was tension for a moment, then Pearl held out a placating hand. "Nobody was hurt. No sense dwelling on what never happened. Now, let me see your ring." Pearl examined it, and it was obvious she was making a real effort not to say anything nasty. "It looks very nice on your finger, Solange. You're quite sure you really want to get married?"

Solange snatched her hand away. "I wouldn't

have said yes if I didn't, would I? I know neither of you care much for Leon, but I love him. And I'm the one who has to live with him, so that's all that matters.''

Unless you decide to live here. Miranda carefully avoided Gram's eyes. ''You're getting married at Easter?''

Solange shook her head. ''We changed it to May. We thought Easter at first, but the weather can still be nasty then, and I don't want everyone to have to wear coats.''

''Well, then, that fits perfectly with what Gram and I were talking about a minute ago.'' Miranda knew she had to be careful here. She pointed at the lawyer's letter. ''You know the trust is ending at the millennium. We thought what fun it would be for the three of us to go to England in April, Gram wants to visit the farm again before it's sold.'' With a burst of inspiration, Miranda added, ''And you could shop for your wedding dress and trousseau in London. What do you think, Solange?''

''Buy my trousseau in London?'' The mention of shopping did it. Solange clapped her hands. ''Oh, that would be fun. And we've never really traveled together, just the three of us, except for that one trip to California. Let's do it!''

By bedtime that night, the plans were made. There was a sense of rightness to the trip, almost inevitability, Miranda concluded.

She thought excitement would keep her awake, but instead she slept deeply. As soon as the travel office opened Saturday morning, she made reserva-

tions for her, Pearl and Solange to fly out of Seattle
on the 3rd of April. The prospect was exhilarating.
Then, acting purely on impulse, she dialed the phone
number that appeared on the Wallace and Houmes
letterhead. What time would it be in London? Eight,
nine hours later than Seattle, she calculated. Certainly stodgy Joseph Wallace wouldn't be in the office late on a Saturday evening, but she'd leave a
message for him, telling him that the Irving women
were about to invade England.

She was taken aback when, after only two rings,
someone picked up the phone. A rich baritone voice
wished her good evening.

"Um, I'm just calling to leave a message for Joseph Wallace."

"Speaking. How may I help you?"

The call suddenly seemed ridiculous. Why should
he care whether some clients from Seattle were coming to see England? She swallowed and considered
hanging up, then quickly said, instead, "This is Miranda Irving, Mr. Wallace. From Seattle. You wrote
me a letter concerning Bethel Farm."

"Oh, yes, Ms. Irving, of course."

He sounded terribly English—big surprise there,
idiot, she told herself. And he didn't sound old at
all, but then, how could you tell on the telephone
after one sentence? And why would she care?

Rattled, Miranda swallowed. "I didn't mean to
bother you, Mr. Wallace. You see, I thought no one
would be in the office on a Saturday, and I was just
going to leave you a message. I didn't really want

to talk to you." She realized she was babbling. She could feel herself starting to blush.

"I see. So you'd prefer talking to a machine, Ms. Irving. How refreshing." There was humor in his voice. "Most people feel exactly the opposite." He chuckled, a deep rumble, and she felt her face burn.

"Actually," he went on companionably, "I just dropped by to pick up some documents I'd forgotten, so if you hang up and wait ten minutes, you'll be able to leave me a message after all and we can pretend this entire phone call never happened."

"That won't be necessary." Annoyed with him for his teasing and feeling a total fool, she blurted out that she and her mother and grandmother would be coming to London. "Perhaps we could arrange a meeting at that time," she said stiffly, "to discuss the trust and the sale of Bethel Farm. We're planning to visit the farm, of course, if it's convenient for the tenants, but we'll be staying in London, and I thought..."

"Absolutely." The teasing note was absent now; he sounded sincere and accommodating. "I'm delighted you're coming over, Ms. Irving, and I look forward to meeting you. In the meantime, if I can be of service in any way—perhaps in arranging a hotel?"

The man had an intoxicating voice, smooth and deep and intimate. "Thank you." Miranda realized she hadn't thought about accommodation yet. "That...that would be very kind. If it's not too much trouble."

"Not at all. It would be my pleasure. Is there any particular area in which you'd like to stay?"

"Piccadilly." She'd heard Gram speak of it often enough. "Something not too...elaborate?" They weren't broke, but they weren't wealthy, either.

"The Hotel Atheneum," he said instantly. "Moderately priced and gracious."

"Oh, yes, please. Three single rooms." She gave him the date of their arrival and, when he requested it, the number of their flight.

"Well, a pleasant journey to you, Ms. Irving. As I said before, I'm looking forward to meeting you. Your mother and grandmother, too, of course."

"Thank you, Mr. Wallace." She hung up the phone and realized she was trembling. Now, why on earth should a conversation with a stranger have that effect?

It must be the sunshine-warm voice and the suave English accent, she decided. He was undoubtedly barely five feet tall, paunchy and pushing fifty.

But during the next ten weeks, at odd moments, she found herself remembering that conversation with Joseph Wallace, and wondering what sort of man he really was.

ON APRIL 3, Joe stood at the meeting point at Gatwick Airport, watching the passengers from Flight 679 trickling out of Customs and wondering what on earth had possessed him to drive out here on a Saturday afternoon to meet the Irving women and escort them to their hotel. They could just as easily have taken a cab, or had the hotel send a car for them. They were going to meet with him at the office on Monday anyway, so there was no real necessity to see them today. They weren't among the firm's more lucrative clients, after all, and he had a date in—he glanced at his watch—a scant two hours with a titian-haired flight attendant named Betsy whom he'd met at a party last Friday. The drive back to London would take at least an hour, and Betsy lived in Holland Park, another twenty-minute drive, so practically, it would have made sense to stay home. But the simple truth was, he was curious. The trip out to Bethel Farm had aroused his interest in the trust, and he wanted a look at these Irving women.

Which could prove difficult, because he had no idea what they looked like, he mused.

When three women moved toward him a few moments later, of course he recognized them instantly. He smiled, then angled his way through the crowd.

The younger woman, no doubt Miranda Jane, was only a few inches shorter than his own six feet, Joe noted as he reached them. She wore tan trousers and a tailored brown jacket exactly the shade of her tumbled curly hair, and she had round glasses that emphasized very blue eyes that were a trifle glassy and tired looking after the long flight. She was pushing a cart stacked high with luggage, and she looked harassed and weary.

In contrast, the stunning middle-aged female at her side appeared wide-awake and vivacious. She was meticulously made up, and wore a stylish black pants ensemble and heels so high they had to be causing her extreme discomfort, although she gave no indication of it.

The very old, very tiny woman was all in purple, sparse silver hair gleaming and step firm in spite of the exhaustion all too apparent on her deeply lined face.

"The Irvings, I presume. Hello, I'm Joe Wallace. Welcome to England." He held out a hand to Miranda.

She took it, gazing into his eyes through her glasses for a long moment before a tentative smile spread across her features. "Hello, Mr. Wallace. I'm Miranda."

"Delighted to meet you. I trust you had a pleasant flight, Ms. Irving."

"'Miranda,' please. We're all 'Ms. Irving', and it gets confusing. The flight was fine, but it was longer than anyone should have to sit. It's good to be here at last," she said in the pleasant, husky voice he remembered from their telephone conversation. "It's very kind of you to meet us."

He noted that she had freckles on her nose and cheeks, and that when she smiled her intensely blue eyes crinkled at the corners behind her glasses. She took his hand, and her long-fingered ringless grip was strong and warm. She held the contact for only an instant, letting go to shove a thick strand of unruly hair behind one ear before she gestured with an open palm at her companions.

"This is my mother, Solange, and my grandmother, Pearl."

He extended his hand first to the old woman.

From behind her glasses, penetrating hazel eyes took his measure.

"How do you do, Mr. Wallace?" Her hand was trembling slightly, fragile, as if the flesh were retreating from the bone. "You resemble your father, young man."

Joe felt disconcerted to suddenly realize that this ancient lady was the baby referred to in many of the letters in the Irving file. He knew Pearl Irving was almost a hundred years old, but she wasn't decrepit and she didn't seem as infirm as her years might suggest.

"Please, call me 'Joe.'" He gave her a courtly bow and then turned to Solange. "How do you do?"

"Hello, Joe." Her manner was openly flirtatious, and he was amused. She had to be the age his mother would have been. "How sweet you are to come and meet us this way." Her beringed fingers slid like silk into his, and she held on a fraction longer than necessary. He noted that she wore a large diamond on the engagement finger of her left hand. Her smile was that of a woman entirely confident of her appeal to the opposite sex.

"I'm parked nearby. Let me manage that for you." Joe took over the luggage cart from Miranda and wheeled it smoothly toward the exit doors. In a few moments he had the cases in the boot and his passengers settled in the Bentley he'd borrowed from his father; his sports car wouldn't have held this many people, to say nothing of their luggage.

Solange claimed the front seat next to him, murmuring something about motion sickness, while Miranda and Pearl sat in back.

Miranda sat directly behind the driver's seat, and gazed curiously out the window. Once he was away from the airport and making his way at top speed down the M4, Joe was able to glance at her through the rearview. She wasn't superficially pretty, in the obvious way her mother was, he concluded. Instead, she had an understated attractiveness that could easily be overlooked. She was definitely too thin, but in spite of her spareness he rather liked the way she looked, he concluded.

He chatted politely to Solange, asking what the weather was like at this time of year in Seattle and whether this was her first trip to England. She reminded him that she'd been born at Bethel Farm, and he mentioned that he'd recently spent a day there.

"The surrounding countryside is beautiful, and the farm buildings must look very much as they did when you were born."

"What are the tenants like?" The question came not from Solange but from Miranda. "I wrote them a note to say we were hoping to drive out one day next week, but I didn't receive an answer."

"I found them very friendly." He caught her eye in the mirror, and she nodded.

"I know they run a bed-and-breakfast. I thought we'd stay in London part of the time and then maybe spend the weekend at the farm as guests. Gram's really excited about seeing the place again, aren't you, Gram?"

A distinct snore sounded, and Miranda giggled. Pearl had fallen asleep, and Joe noted how gently Miranda cushioned her grandmother's head on her own shoulder, one arm protectively around the old woman. There was obviously a deep bond between Pearl and Miranda, and for a moment Joe felt nostalgic; he'd been close to his grandmother, his father's mother, but she'd died about the same time his mother had, while he was still a teenager.

For the rest of the trip, Pearl snored and Miranda was silent. Solange asked a number of questions about shopping in London, then wanted to know what shops there were in Beechford, the village near the farm. When Joe explained the village was tiny and the amenities few and simple she was alarmed.

"I'm not sure I'll want to spend much time out there. We have only ten days, and I have reams of shopping to do."

"Your hotel is very near the best shops," Joe told her.

Next, she asked whether he had a wife and children, and he explained that he was single. She asked, too, what part of London he lived in, and he told her about sharing a town house with Gabriel and Larry. "I've thought of getting my own flat, but the town house is very comfortable, and I'm afraid I have a lazy streak. My mother died when I was seventeen, and my father's never remarried, so we've settled into a bachelor existence that suits us."

"I know what you mean," Solange said. "Mother and Miranda and I all live in the old house my great-grandmother built when she emigrated from England. I'm a firm believer in families living together. I've always worked, and after Miranda's father died, it was good to know there was always someone around when she got home from school.''

He glanced in the mirror and caught the dumb-founded expression on Miranda's face. She saw him watching her and looked away immediately.

''What sort of work do you do, Solange?''

''I'm a florist. I have my own little shop in down-town Seattle. It's called Bloomers.''

He raised his voice slightly. ''And you, Miranda? What do you do?''

''I'm a schoolteacher, first grade.''

Conversation lapsed after that. Traffic was mer-cifully light, and they arrived at the hotel in good time. Joe made certain the women were well taken care of and confirmed Monday's appointment, tell-ing Miranda that the offices of Wallace and Houmes were only six blocks away, at No. 84 Curzon Street. He explained the route if they cared to walk, then added, ''My father and I would like to take you to lunch on Monday, if you have no other plans.''

''None at all. Lunch sounds great, thank you.''

''Good.''

He noted she didn't consult the other two about the invitation, and they seemed to accept that she made the decisions for the three of them. Miranda thanked Joe again for collecting them at the airport, then he made his way outside and sprinted for his car.

Checking his watch, he realized he'd have to hurry to be on time for his date. He stepped hard on the gas and maneuvered his way with adroit efficiency through backstreets to avoid the worst of the weekend traffic.

Making this opportunity to meet the Irving women had been worth it, he concluded. Luncheon should be interesting; it might be entertaining to watch his father's reaction to the ravishing Solange, he decided with a wicked grin, narrowly missing a lorry backing out of an alley.

He wondered who had given her the ostentatious ring on the third finger of her left hand. He wondered, also, if Miranda had a man in her life, and if so, what type of person he might be. She seemed intelligent and sensible, and she had a rather engaging smile, if not a high degree of sex appeal.

His thoughts turned to Betsy, whose smile was nothing remarkable and whose intelligence probably matched. Ah, but Betsy had other attributes, and she'd given him every indication she was more than willing to share them with him. His tires squealed around a corner and he shot into a narrow alley and out again, eager to get on with his evening now that duty was done.

CHAPTER SIX

MIRANDA PULLED BACK the heavy damask floral curtain on the hotel window and looked across Piccadilly Circus to a treed boulevard. Who would have thought London would be so colorful. Candy-apple-red buses, green trees, yellow daffodils in big straw baskets, women wearing all the colors of spring. Why had she expected soot and black overcoats?

Across the hall, she'd tucked Gram under the comforter, and before she even left the room, Pearl was fast asleep. Solange's room was next door, and she, too, was having a nap.

Instead of being sleepy, Miranda felt as if every nerve in her body was electrified. Jet lag of some crazy sort, she told herself, with a dose of Joe Wallace thrown in for good measure.

Heavens, he was handsome. She'd done her best to imagine him as a portly middle-aged man, balding, with a mustache, a pretty wife and three children in boarding schools. The reality had been both pleasing and disconcerting. She'd watched the dynamic broad-shouldered man with the thatch of thick, wheat-colored hair approach them, and somehow she'd known it was Joe.

She'd felt flustered and embarrassed, as though

he might actually be able to guess that she'd been fascinated by the deep timbre of his voice on the telephone, that she'd spent more time than she cared to admit fantasizing about his appearance.

Amazingly, his looks were exactly the kind that should go with that voice. He didn't look at all like an English solicitor, although what such a person might look like she couldn't say.

Joe Wallace was not much taller than her own five-ten, with well-developed muscles and long strong legs. He'd been dressed casually, in jeans and a tan windbreaker, with a white golf shirt underneath. His face was attractive without being classically handsome, and his dark brown eyes held mischief in their depths. There was a deep cleft in the center of his square stubborn-looking chin. Alma would have called him edible—she described men the way Miranda did food.

Judging by his take-charge manner, Miranda imagined that he was a man who liked having his own way and would go to some lengths to make certain he got it. Both his smile and his actions were confident and easy.

He drove his expensive, conservative car at terrifying speed. It had been all she could do not to ask him to slow down, until she realized he was excellent at cutting in and out of traffic. Slowly, she'd relaxed. For some obscure reason, she'd felt safe with him.

She found him attractive, she admitted, which was ridiculous, because she didn't really know the man at all.

She let the curtain fall back in place and smiled at her foolishness. As if the faintest chance existed that Joe Wallace would be interested romantically in someone like her. He was the kind of man who'd have an address book filled with the numbers of beautiful women. He was unavailable in every sense.

So stop mooning over Joe Wallace. She was jet-lagged she told herself again, which probably accounted for the way her mind was working. She also felt grubby after the long flight, so she'd relax in the tub and then she'd sleep.

But as she soaked in steaming hot water, Miranda speculated about him, letting her imagination run rampant.

What if she chose Joe Wallace to resolve her virginity issue, for instance?

How would she go about it? He was so exquisitely polite and so gentlemanly it would be almost impossible to bring up something so intimate.

But there was also that wicked humor lurking just beneath the polished surface, which was reassuring. From everything she'd read about having sex, a sense of humor would certainly be a welcome addition.

So how would she ask him? Something along the lines of "There's a small technical problem I'd like you to take care of for me, Joe." Or should she say, "Joe, I need a personal favor"? Or maybe, "I have this annoying longstanding condition, and I wonder if you'd be willing to help." Or there was always blatant honesty: "Joe, I find you attractive. I'd like you to make love to me, if it's convenient. Oh, by the way, I've never done it before, so excuse my clumsiness, will you?''

Giddy, she started to giggle, then couldn't stop as she imagined the ridiculous conversation unfolding.

''By all means, Ms. Irving—Miranda—I'm happy to be of service. Lie down, won't you? Are you comfortable?''

She needed to sleep. She was getting hysterical.

Miranda climbed out of the tub and donned the thick robe the hotel provided, deciding that before she went to bed she'd check again on Gram. If the flight had been hard on her, it had been much worse for the old woman. Pearl had been shaky and far too pale when Miranda helped her out of her dress and into bed.

At Pearl's request, the desk had given Miranda a spare card that would allow her entry to her grandmother's room. Drawing the robe close around her, she looked up and down the deserted corridor before she slipped across the hall and quietly opened Pearl's door.

All remnants of her lightheartedness faded abruptly as she caught sight of Pearl lying flat on her back on the bed, just the way Miranda had left her. Gram's wrinkled skin was parchment pale even against the gleaming white of the bed linen. She looked ancient, her face sunken, the arm resting on top of the blanket skeletal. For one awful moment, Miranda wondered whether she was even breathing.

Then her grandmother gave a little snort and moved her arm slightly. A hot wave of relief went through Miranda, along with the acknowledgment of how tenuous Pearl's life was, simply because of her age. It was inevitably coming to a close. Despite the arduous airplane trip, this journey to Bethel Farm was necessary and symbolic, Miranda assured herself, a chance for Gram to relive the happiest and the most tragic moments of her long life and to say goodbye to the place she loved.

Back in her own room, Miranda doffed the robe and slid under the sheets. In the moments before sleep claimed her, she contemplated her own life.

Her father's death had been tragic, but it was long ago. Since then, the word she would have used to describe her life was *mediocre,* without many highs or lows. Unlike Gram, she'd never grieved a lover's death. Unlike Solange, she'd never fallen in and out of lust or borne a child. She'd led a cautious life, Miranda decided, too cautious.

As she tumbled into sleep, she knew she wanted more. The years were slipping past uneventfully, and she wanted something to happen to her soon, something monumental, something that she'd remember when she was old.

THE RAIN that had begun on Saturday intensified on Sunday, a chilly London downpour that promised to make the sight-seeing Miranda had planned difficult.

Gram seemed rested and filled with energy, but Solange declared that she was too tired to move out of bed, adding that Leon had called her earlier that morning and because she'd been too sleepy to talk to him, she'd promised to call him back.

"You two go on without me. I'll see you at dinnertime." She yawned.

"Gonna run up a fortune in phone bills," Gram complained as she and Miranda left the hotel. "Probably would have been cheaper in the long run just to bring that idiot along the way she wanted."

At the last minute, Solange had begged Leon to come with them. Fortunately, he'd had his television broadcasts to do, so he'd reluctantly refused.

Even though both she and Gram were hoping distance would make Solange rethink her attraction to Baillie, Miranda was beginning to believe there wasn't much chance of it happening. The guy must have some hidden attributes for Solange to feel the way she did about him.

With the assistance of the desk clerk, Miranda had booked a tour on a double-decker bus, and she and Pearl climbed to the top level and peered out through the rain as they were driven past Buckingham Palace, the Tower of London, Westminster Abbey and the Tower Bridge. In spite of the downpour, Gram greatly enjoyed the trip.

Solange was in a better mood when they returned. Leon missed her desperately, she confided, adding with a grin that it was "good for him." He'd appreciate her all the more when she got home. Miranda marveled at her mother's confidence with men. Why couldn't she have inherited it?

MONDAY, THE WEATHER cleared. The sun came out and by midmorning the temperature had gone from pleasantly warm to out-and-out hot. Helping Pearl

out of the cab in front of the Edwardian building
that housed Wallace and Houmes, Miranda could
feel perspiration beading on her forehead.

Inside, the old building was comfortably air-
conditioned. The receptionist, a young man with a
severe case of acne, asked them to take a seat in an
empty waiting area, which was paneled in oak and
furnished with comfortably worn antiques.

In a few moments, Joe appeared. Today, Miranda
noted, he was wearing an elegant three-piece char-
coal suit, tailored to perfection. Today, he looked
every bit an English solicitor.

Miranda was glad she herself had put on a suit, a
dark blue tailored silk she'd bought to wear to a
colleague's wedding the previous spring. The skirt
was shorter than she would normally have worn, but
apart from that, she felt good in it.

Joe smiled into her eyes when he greeted her, but
she reminded herself that he undoubtedly did that
with Solange and Pearl and the cleaning person and
the mailman. The natural ease and intimacy in his
manner would be easy to misinterpret, she warned
herself.

"Dad's just finishing a conference call. He'll be
done in a few minutes," Joe said, after asking how
they'd spent their Sunday and listening attentively
to Pearl's comments on how the city had changed
since the war years.

"Perhaps you'd like to tour the building. Apart
from new wiring to accommodate faxes and com-
puters, and the addition of air-conditioning and
modern plumbing, it hasn't changed a whole lot

since the day the trust was drawn up back in 1900. May I, Ms. Irving?'' He offered Pearl his arm, and Solange and Miranda followed as he guided them through the maze of small offices on the main floor, introducing them to clerks and secretaries and other solicitors and then leading the way up the stairs.

''This is my office.''

Much to Miranda's surprise, it was small and windowless, the desk piled high with file folders, books overflowing from an oak bookcase. A framed poster of an Australian cowboy hung on one wall, and beside it was a photo of Joe and another young man, bearded and weather-beaten, grinning ear to ear, wearing climbing gear and struggling up the steep side of a snowy mountain.

''Where were you climbing?'' Miranda studied the photo, thinking that Joe looked even more attractive in the rough garb and beard than he did wearing the suit he had on today.

''Mont Blanc, in the French Alps. They're the most interesting and exciting group of mountains if you're a climber, magnificent and challenging. Mont Blanc is the highest summit in western Europe.''

''That's your hobby?'' Miranda was still studying the photo, thinking that whoever had shot it had done a fine job with the light and shadows.

''It was then. I haven't done any climbing recently.''

''When was this taken?''

''Five years ago. During my rebellious stage.''

She wanted to ask who'd taken it, but he was leading Pearl along the hallway, and Miranda followed. He stopped at an outer office filled with plants, baskets of dried flowers, a wide bowl of hyacinth and several vases of daffodils. The room looked and smelled cheerful and the plump, pretty woman working at the computer had a smile that matched the flowers.

"This is Dierdre Payne," Joe introduced. "Dierdre's Dad's personal secretary, but she's also the real reason this place operates like a well-oiled clock. She keeps us all in order."

"How do you do?" Dierdre smiled at them, getting up to shake hands. She was short and rounded, with heavy graying blond hair drawn back in a thick knot on her neck. Her features were even, her clothes tasteful and conservative. She was probably in her late forties, Miranda guessed. She had a creamy English-porcelain complexion and lovely wide gray eyes that sparkled with intelligence and good humor.

"I'm so pleased to meet you," she said in her precise English voice. "I hope you enjoy your stay, and if I can be of any assistance, please ask."

The intercom on Dierdre's desk buzzed, and she said, "Mr. Wallace would like you to come in now." She gestured at a door directly across the hall, and Joe ushered them into a large office, carpeted in old plush area rugs and outfitted with leather chairs, framed lithographs of horses and dogs and an immense oak desk.

Gabriel Wallace was an imposing figure of a man, Miranda thought as he came from behind the desk. Lean and handsome, with luxurious white hair, a

Grecian profile and penetrating dark eyes, he was several inches taller than Joe, and much more formal than his son without being pompous.

"Delighted to meet you again, Ms. Irving. It must be what, fourteen years?" He bowed over Pearl's hand, then nodded cordially to Solange and Miranda as they were introduced. "Sorry to have kept you waiting. Joseph, if you'll bring my car around front, we can be on our way. We'll have lunch at the Grosvener."

With a nod and a mock salute, Joe went to do his father's bidding, and Gabriel escorted the women downstairs and out to the car. This time, Miranda found herself seated beside Joe in the front of the same huge black Bentley that Joe had driven to the airport. Gabriel sat in back, Solange on one side of him and Pearl on the other.

Gabriel asked questions about Seattle, and in an animated tone, Solange began to recite some of the city's history. Pearl interjected comments about changes she'd observed during her lifetime, pointedly adding that she was almost a hundred years old, so she'd seen plenty of change in her time.

Gabriel obligingly commented on how wonderful it was that she'd made this trip back to her homeland, and that he'd never have guessed her to be as old as she was; she'd hardly aged a day since they'd last met. Miranda had to smile at his gallantry.

"So you're a teacher, Miranda." Joe turned to her and Miranda nodded, trying to ignore the warmth of awareness that rose in her throat now that he was only inches away.

"Primary school, didn't you say?" He was still looking at her instead of the road, as she grabbed for the dash and barely kept from screaming when the car ahead of them stopped suddenly, while the Bentley kept on going.

They were about to have an accident.

CHAPTER SEVEN

—

JOE MUST HAVE HAD some sixth sense, because he suddenly stepped on the brakes, bringing the Bentley to an abrupt halt only inches behind the other vehicle's back bumper.

"Joseph, we really don't need such excitement," Gabriel reproved.

Miranda swallowed and tried to remember what they were talking about. "I, um, enjoy kids who are just starting their education. They're spontaneous and they haven't learned yet to dislike school, so teaching them is easy." She added, "Did you hate school, Joe, or did you enjoy learning?"

She wanted to know so much about him. She wanted to know *everything* about him—besides the fact that he drove like a maniac.

Traffic was moving again, and he darted from one lane to the other, nonchalantly cutting off other drivers and ignoring their horns. "I was packed off early to boarding school, of course. That's the custom over here. And the process you describe was reversed for me, because at first I despised school, then came to like it more and more the older I grew." He pulled in front of a taxi and waved a hand at the rude finger sign the driver directed his way.

In spite of the very real chance of a car crash any instant, Miranda was listening to his words and the cadence of his voice. She was also watching his strong hands on the wheel of the car. They were competent hands. The nails were cut short and there were several scars across the back of the right. Miranda wondered if he'd gotten them mountain climbing or in a car accident.

"So you enjoyed your own education, Miranda, or you wouldn't have chosen to teach."

It was much more complex than that, and his assumption irked her. "That's too obvious a conclusion, and not accurate." Her tone was challenging. "Did you become a lawyer because you enjoyed the law?"

"Not at all." He glanced at her appreciatively and grinned. "So the lady has .teeth," he commented under his breath, adding, "I wasn't a scholar, you see. And I had no stomach for medicine, no talent for acting, not enough intestinal stamina to become a professor. Law was the family business, so I simply yielded to expectation." His smile was roguish, his dark eyes dancing. "Actually, I've always felt I was born into the wrong century." He leaned across, still driving at maximal speed, and in a stage whisper added, "I would have made an exceptional pirate, don't you think?" They came within a centimeter of broadsiding a bus, and Joe had to slam on his brakes to avoid hitting a pedestrian.

She braced her hand against the dash to keep from

being hurtled against her seat belt, but she had to laugh, because she could see him in that role.

"Joseph." Gabriel's voice held a warning note. "Do you think you could pay a little more attention to your driving, or should I take over?"

"Sorry, sir." Joe winked at Miranda and stepped on the accelerator. "And what about you, Miranda? If you hadn't chosen to be a teacher, what would you have become?"

A mother? A wife? "Oh, a photographer, I guess."

His eyebrows went up. "You're interested in photography?" He suddenly braked and pulled the car smoothly into a parking spot that seemed much too small, maneuvered into it with ease and turned off the motor.

Miranda nodded in response to his question, feeling her body relax now that the car had stopped. "Solange bought me a camera for my fourteenth birthday, and I've been hooked ever since."

"I see." He opened his car door and came around to open hers, then took her arm and smoothly handed her out the way his father was doing for first Pearl and then Solange.

Miranda was clumsy getting out, conscious of her short skirt riding high up her thigh, but Joe didn't seem to notice, which was either very gallant or very disappointing, an indication that her legs weren't as appealing as she'd hoped. She'd always considered them one of her best attributes.

Gabriel moved ahead of them, Solange on one

arm and Pearl on the other. Joe fell into step beside Miranda.

"What sort of photos do you like to take?"

"People. Children, mostly, lots of pictures of the kids in my classroom—I give them each a photo of themselves for birthdays and Christmas. Families in the park. Ethnic groups having picnics. Street people. Interesting faces. I'm not very interested in scenery." And it didn't take a psychology degree to figure out that she immortalized in her snapshots many of the scenes she longed to be a part of. She'd figured that out a long time ago.

The maître d' greeted both Gabriel and Joe by name, then escorted them all to a table by the window, which looked out on Park Lane and, across the street, Hyde Park. Again, Miranda found herself seated beside Joe. Gabriel nodded at a waiter, and menus appeared.

It wasn't until the ordering was done that she noticed Solange had temporarily forgotten the reverend; she was using every ounce of her considerable charm on Gabriel.

Miranda watched Solange touch him lightly on the arm and twinkle at him when he poured her wine. Gabriel was responding in the bemused way men usually did to Solange.

Miranda glanced at Pearl, and her grandmother gave her an almost imperceptible nod and a wink. Just maybe their plot was beginning to work after all. Baillie out of sight, out of mind? Miranda could only hope.

Joe seemed unaware of the interaction between

Solange and Gabriel. He turned to Pearl and said, "I couldn't help overhearing you confessing your age in the car. Tell me, Ms. Irving, what's the secret of such a long healthy life?"

Miranda noted that he'd guessed that Pearl was losing her hearing. When he spoke to her, he raised his voice so she could hear him without straining.

Miranda had heard Pearl answer that question numerous times. Gram loved to talk about her longevity.

"Oh, I suppose there's always been something more I wanted to do," she replied now, head tilted thoughtfully to one side. "When I was a girl, I wanted to fly planes, and I learned how. Then the war came along. I enlisted in the RAF in 1939. I'd been ferrying planes for two years when I met Solange's father. After she was born I gave up flying, and when she was four months old, I went home with her to Seattle and took a course in accounting. My mother was a wonderful doctor, but she had no head for business, although my grandmother Cordelia did."

Joe nodded. "She certainly did. She set up the Irving trust, didn't she?"

"With your great-uncle's help," Pearl acknowledged. "But then Geneva, my mother, lost most of the family money in the crash of '29. I worked as an office manager for the same company for years, didn't retire until I was long past seventy. And of course there was my granddaughter to enjoy." Her eyes rested lovingly on Miranda. "She's the finest gift Solange ever gave me. When Miranda started university, I decided to enroll in a few courses myself. I took cooking. All my life I couldn't boil water without burning it. Now I almost can.''

Everyone laughed. Pearl beamed. "So in answer to your question, I'd just say, keep busy, young man. As far as health goes, I never followed any diets or paid much attention to fads. I smoked for years. Gave it up when I turned eighty-one and some fool doctor told me I had a spot on my lung. The spot disappeared, but I was too scared to start smoking again, more's the pity. I still miss a cigarette after a meal. And I always did enjoy a drink.'' She lifted the wine Gabriel had poured her. "Still do. In moderation, of course.'' In one long draft, she finished what was in her glass and held it out for a refill, amid clapping and laughter.

"You have no idea how comforting all this is.'' Joe finished his wine and refilled his glass and Miranda's, his face reflecting both amusement and respect. He held up his glass in a toast.

"To Ms. Irving and her philosophy. Father's always insisted that if I want to live a long life, I'll have to give up all the things I enjoy. You've just assured me I needn't.''

They laughed again, although Miranda thought Gabriel didn't look that amused. Obviously, there were differences between father and son.

Over dessert, the conversation turned to the trip to Bethel Farm.

"I spoke to Dr. O'Donnell last night," Miranda explained, "and he said we should come out as soon as possible. He was very kind and friendly.'' She added that he'd suggested the train could drop them at the village, and he'd be happy to pick them up, but she felt the most convenient thing would be rent a car early the following morning and drive to the Cotswolds, then return in the evening.

"Could you give me directions, Joe? I have a map, but I'm afraid I'm not much good at following one."

"Why don't I drive you. There's nothing on my calendar that can't be put off a day or so, and I need to check out some details concerning the property. We can borrow Father's car again, right, Dad?"

"Of course." Gabriel might have been less than pleased, but he was far too much a gentleman to show it. "That's a fine idea."

Miranda hesitated. "Thank you, that would be wonderful. But I feel as if we're taking up an awful lot of your time, Joe."

"There'll be time enough to worry about that when you receive my billing," Joe said with not a trace of a smile.

Again, Miranda caught the reproving glance Gabriel sent his son's way. Joe grinned at his father, clearly teasing him.

They left the restaurant, and Joe drove them to the hotel. The traffic was heavy, and there was no opportunity for speed, which doubtlessly frustrated him.

"I'll pick you up at eight tomorrow morning, if that's convenient," he said to Miranda as he and Gabriel escorted them into the lobby. "That will give us a good long day at Bethel Farm."

Miranda agreed. "Thank you for a lovely lunch," she said, smiling at both men.

"Our pleasure," Joe said with a wide smile, giving her a little salute as he and his father left.

"Now, don't they have wonderful manners?" Pearl remarked as they rode up in the elevator. "They're perfect gentlemen. Gabriel always was, and he's taught his son well, except for the boy's driving. That could stand improvement."

"They're sexy and handsome and single," Solange purred, fussing with her hair in the mirror that covered one wall of the elevator. "I can't believe Gabriel's been alone since his wife died all those years ago. These Englishwomen must be blind."

This was one of the few times in her entire life that Miranda felt in total agreement with her mother, except that of course it was Gabriel's son she was picturing in her mind's eye.

When she got to her room, Miranda actually found herself worrying over what she'd wear the following morning, a situation so rare it brought her to her senses with a jolt.

You're being a fool. You're mistaking good manners for personal interest. Where's your old common sense?

It seemed to have gone on sabbatical.

"WELL, THAT WAS PLEASANT," Gabriel commented as Joe drove the few blocks to the office. "They're very agreeable women."

"For Yanks they certainly are," Joe said, enjoying Gabriel's chastising *humph.* "Pearl's amazing for her age, and that Solange is a bit of a knockout, isn't she?''

He wondered if his father would rise to the bait. He'd watched from the corner of his eye as Gabriel paid more than adequate attention to Solange during luncheon.

''Attractive woman, very attractive, certainly,'' Gabriel said offhandedly. ''Engaged to some televangelist, she confided.''

''Televangelist?'' Joe found it nearly impossible to imagine Solange as a minister's wife. ''Now, that's an unlikely pairing if ever there was one.''

''What's your impression of the daughter, Joseph?''

''Miranda?'' To give himself time to think, Joe cut in front of a bus. The driver shook his fist and leaned on his horn. Gabriel braced himself, knuckles white, and made a choked, cautionary sound in his throat. Joe waved a breezy apology over his shoulder to the bus driver. ''Oh, she seems quite intelligent and sensible. I like that in a woman.''

''Really? I'd never have guessed intelligence and good sense were attributes you valued in any female.'' Gabriel's tone was sardonic. ''They've certainly been missing in any of the women you've introduced.''

Joe suppressed a grin as he parked the car and followed Gabriel into the law firm and up the stairs. Dierdre met them at the door to Gabriel's office. She smiled at them and gave Gabriel several yellow message sheets.

''Mr. Stanhope just rang. He asked if you'd call

back as soon as you arrived.'' As always, her voice and manner were totally impersonal and professional, as was Gabriel's when he thanked her and requested that she dig out a file for him.

Watching them, Joe couldn't help but wonder what their private moments were like. Was his father a considerate lover, or was Gabriel as unimaginative in that area as he was in so many others? And how in blazes could one make love in an undemonstrative fashion?

"Come in for a moment, Joseph." Gabriel interrupted Joe's reverie, leading the way into his office and closing the door, gesturing at a chair.

"I'm concerned about this sale of Bethel Farm. As the trust stipulates, Miranda Irving will decide whom to sell to, but it's our responsibility to best advise and protect the interests of our clients. Ms. Pearl Irving made it plain to me today that she's very upset at the idea of Bethel Farm becoming a factory. Obviously, she and Miranda are close, so I suspect the grandmother's feelings will influence Miranda's decision. In my opinion, selling to International Harvester is the smartest move they could make financially, and it will also benefit the community. A factory will provide jobs and growth for the entire area. Agriculture is no longer a profitable undertaking in the English countryside. But unless the Irvings make a commitment to the company by September, Harvester will naturally look for an alternative location."

"I pointed all that out in the letter I sent them. And financially, you're absolutely right, Dad. The factory will realize the best profit. But after visiting the farm, I have to sympathize with Ms. Pearl.''

When he'd left Bethel Farm the other evening, it was already growing dark, and during the long drive back to London, Joe had realized that the motor that usually raced inside him had slowed down to a lazy purr. He felt mellow, relaxed, filled with optimism, and the feeling had lasted for several days. If that was a result of spending time in the English countryside, he was all for leaving the farm exactly as it was.

''Sympathize or not, I trust you'll stress to the Irvings the points I've just mentioned. They need to know that if they turn down the factory opportunity, they could sit for some time waiting for another offer as generous. And selling is mandatory, according to the terms of the trust.''

''I'll talk to them on the way to the farm tomorrow.''

''When you were out there, did the tenants mention anything about the termination of their lease December next?''

''Dr. O'Donnell asked if there was any way of extending it, and I explained that it was impossible, of course without mentioning details.''

''As long as they know they'll have to move, so there'll be no problems when the time comes.''

''They have a letter of notification, I sent it to them weeks ago.''

Back in his cubbyhole of an office a few moments later, Joe slumped into his chair and locked his hands behind his head.

Offering to drive the Irving women out to the Cotswolds the following day had been impetuous, but on reflection, he realized that he didn't regret the offer at all. He wanted to go back to Bethel Farm, just to see if that peculiar sense of peace and happiness he'd experienced could possibly be replicated.

And, he admitted, he wanted to continue his conversation with Miranda. She was bright, and, unlike the women he was accustomed to, she seemed interested in something besides sex. He didn't have the feeling, as he so often did, that she was mentally undressing him and judging what she saw against the last bloke she'd been with.

He'd be sure to maneuver the seating in the car so that she sat beside him again.

JUST PAST ELEVEN the following morning, Joe steered the car into the tree-lined driveway that led to Bethel Farm. He felt like giving a huge sigh of relief. In her seat beside him, Pearl was concluding a long involved story of a mission she'd volunteered for in 1941, and how icy cold the winter had been that year. She'd been relating similar tales ever since they'd left the hotel that morning, and although Joe found her narrative interesting enough, he was annoyed at not having Miranda as a seatmate. It had further annoyed him when Pearl admonished him several times about his driving and ordered him to slow down.

"You have a heavy foot, Joseph," she'd said disapprovingly. "I piloted airplanes, young man, and I understand the desire to fly. An automobile is not equipped for flight, and I have no intention of dying at the age of ninety-nine in a speeding car on an English motorway.''

In the rearview mirror, Joe had caught Miranda's wide grin.

He'd tried to bring up the subject of the factory, but Pearl wouldn't listen. ''It's too fine a day to talk of depressing things. Besides, it's early days yet, and who knows what might happen between now and next December. If I've learned anything, it's that nothing in life is a certainty.''

There were death and taxes, but Joe decided not to mention them lest Pearl verbally slap him down again. It was a real relief to have the journey end. He braked with a flourish in front of the arbored garden gate that led to the rambling old stone farmhouse.

CHAPTER EIGHT

"LOOK AT THOSE DAFFODILS." Solange stood admiring the neat flower beds and tall, flowering lilac bushes in the neatly squared-off garden. A cobblestone path bordered with a profusion of snowdrops and bluebells led the way to the front door. "Can you imagine what this must look like in the summer?"

"It's breathtaking," Pearl said. "There are probably flowers still growing here that your grandmother planted."

Before any of them could use the ornate knocker, the door was thrown wide by a tall, broadshouldered man with a strong-featured Irish face that could have belonged to either a rogue or a priest.

"Welcome, welcome, Irvings. Hello again, Joe. Come in, everyone. We've been expecting you."

Joe smiled a greeting at Ronan O'Donnell. He liked this man with the thick iron-gray curls and comfortable round belly. But Ronan was a man it would be hard not to like. His ruddy face and his girth telegraphed his love for good food and Irish whiskey. He had a ready wit, a hearty laugh, an easy facility with words and a charming manner.

Natalie Makepeace and her sister, Elizabeth Scott,

were waiting inside, and Joe introduced everyone. Natalie was a warm and smiling dark-haired woman in her late thirties, heavyset, with a quiet air of competence about her.

Elizabeth Scott was probably only a few years younger than her sister. She was taller and slighter, with blond hair blunt-cut at shoulder length.

After Ronan ushered them all into the sitting room and made sure everyone was comfortable, the women hurried off to bring tea, and Ronan turned to Pearl.

"And do you find things much changed, Ms. Irving?" he asked. "I understand it's many years since you last visited the farm."

"The village is different, a few more shops than I remember, but this house seems very much the same as it always was." It was obvious Pearl was deeply affected by being at Bethel Farm. Her voice trembled, and she lifted her glasses to wipe away tears as she gazed around at the thick stone walls, the immense fireplace, the worn furniture. "That rocking chair brings back such memories. I used to sit there and nurse you, Solange."

Natalie appeared just then with an enormous wooden tray filled with plates of cakes, cookies and sandwiches. Behind her came Elizabeth with a second tray, laden with teapot and cups.

The atmosphere was exactly as Joe remembered it—easy, warm and welcoming. "Where's Elijah?" He'd hoped the old man would be present. Elijah Makepeace had impressed him with his knowledge of farming and his homespun sayings.

"He's out with the sheep. It's lambing time. He'll be in a little later. The girls are with him," Natalie said.

Miranda turned to Elizabeth. "How old are your kids?"

"Daisy's six and Lydia's just turned four."

"I can't wait to meet them." Miranda was sitting beside Natalie, and Solange sat next to Ronan on the low sofa, crossing her curvaceous silky legs and allowing her short tweed skirt to ride high on her thighs.

Joe glanced over at Miranda. She was wearing jeans today, and they hugged her narrow hips and thighs. Her legs weren't on show the way her mother's were, Joe thought, but they were impressive all the same, long and slender and elegant.

Talk ranged from the weather, which was wonderfully warm for April, to the preparations being made to seed the fields and plant the kitchen garden behind the house.

"I'd like to think it won't be our last spring here on the farm." Ronan dropped the comment smoothly into the conversation. "I understand it's to be sold, and I'd like to speak with you about making an offer to purchase, Ms. Irving." He was looking at Pearl, and Joe felt a flash of annoyance.

Ronan knew that Wallace and Houmes managed the business affairs for the farm. Any offer should properly come in writing, through them. Ronan hadn't said a word about an offer when Joe was here last.

There was an uncomfortable silence for a moment.

"Perhaps we could discuss this a bit later, Ronan," Joe suggested.

"That would be grand. Could we have a few words before you return to London today?"

"Of course."

Ronan smiled at him, a charming open grin that for some reason irritated Joe.

Pearl changed the subject. "You were born in the large bedroom just at the top of those stairs, Solange." She turned to Natalie. "It was the birthing room, the same room I was born in, and probably my mother before me."

"That must have been a fortunate room for birthing." Natalie smiled her wide warm smile. "Would you like to come and get reacquainted with it and the rest of the house, Ms. Irving?"

"Oh, I'd like that." Pearl reached for her cane, and Ronan sprang to his feet to help her.

"Thank you, Doctor. Come along, Solange. Come see where you drew your first breath. You, too, Miranda." Pearl followed Natalie out of the room, the others trailing after her, and Joe found himself alone with Ronan.

"About the offer to purchase the farm, Ronan. Perhaps you'd make it in writing and send it to our offices."

"Sure, and I should have thought of that myself. Doctors are not good businessmen, unfortunately. I apologize if I spoke out of turn. My mouth's ahead of my brain more often than not."

Joe's earlier irritation vanished. "No harm done. It's just that the senior Ms. Irving becomes upset at any mention of selling the farm."

"I can see why. It's a beautiful place. I'm most fond of it, and Natalie and I would like to make it our home after we're wed."

"Have you set a date for the wedding, Ronan?"

"Not yet, not yet. There's a bit of bother with my divorce papers. You'll understand how that goes."

"Your former wife's in Ireland?"

"No, no. That would present even more problems, wouldn't it, now?" Ronan glanced at his watch and leaped to his feet. "Look at the time. I wonder, would you excuse me, Joe? I'm late for office hours in the village."

"Of course. I'll just sit here and have another cup of tea and one of these scones, if that's okay."

"Sure. That's what they're for." Ronan took a jacket from the coat tree by the door. "I'll be back by teatime."

He hurried out, and Joe relaxed, enjoying the warmth and homey atmosphere of the large plain room, smiling at the women's lilting voices upstairs. The group sounded as if they were singing, he mused as he drank tea and wolfed down another scone.

Miranda was the first to come down, and she smiled at him. "You look very comfortable. Where did the doctor go?"

"Clinic, in the village." He got to his feet. "I'm full of food and almost asleep. I need some fresh air or I'll soon be snoring. How about coming out for a walk. Maybe we can find Elijah. I'd like you to meet him.''

"I'd like that, but I didn't bring any boots, and these shoes aren't made for strolling around barnyards.''

"How about these? They look about the right size, and no one's going to mind if you borrow them.'' He extracted a pair of gum boots from the row beside the door. She took off her plain black flats, and Joe knelt and helped her on with the boots. She was blushing when he glanced up at her, and he liked it. Women hardly ever blushed.

"How about you, Joe? Those loafers aren't designed for barnyards, either.''

"I'll borrow a pair, as well.'' He kicked off his shoes and stuck his feet into a worn pair of boots, then tucked his trousers into the tops.

Children's laughter sounded from the direction of the old stable.

"Let's go and find the little girls, Joe. Just let me get my camera from the car.'' She did, and with it slung on her shoulder, she strolled along beside him.

It was dark inside the old building, and they had to stand a moment as their eyes adjusted to the gloom. Joe located the girls, who were kneeling by a box in one of the stalls while a patient mother cat allowed her blind kittens to be lifted and stroked.

"Hi,'' Miranda greeted the children. "My name's Miranda, and you've met Joe before, haven't you? Oh, aren't your kittens adorable.''

She dropped to her knees in the straw, reached out a finger and stroked one of the tiny creatures as two pairs of round blue eyes flitted from her to Joe and back again.

"Have you named them yet?" Miranda smiled at the older girl. She had straight red braids and a faceful of freckles. The younger girl also had red hair, but hers was wildly curly.

The child shook her head. "They don't have names yet, miss. They're too little."

Miranda persisted. "What's the mommy's name?"

"Mittens," the girl volunteered. "Because of her white paws."

"Of course. What a good name for her. How old are the kittens?"

"Four days." The younger girl took charge. "Their eyes should open soon. It usually takes a week, Grampa says."

"I know one of you is Daisy and the other Lydia, but I don't know which is which," Miranda teased.

The smaller girl pointed an accusing finger at Joe. "He knows our names. He was here before."

Joe pulled an apologetic face. "I'm so sorry. I don't remember which is which, either. I'm so ashamed of myself. It's old age setting in." He dug in his pocket and pulled out a package of mints. "Would these help you to forgive me?"

They giggled, and Joe doled out the sweets, giving Miranda one, as well. She and the children popped them into their mouths, and the younger girl took over the introductions. "She's Daisy and I'm Lydia. Our father's name was Michael, but he got cancer and died. He's in heaven. Then we came to stay here. Our grampa lives behind the farmhouse in Lilac Cottage. He lets us stay with him sometimes. His name's 'Lijah.''

"Aren't you lucky to live in such a wonderful place. Where do you go to school?"

"In the village. Mummy drives us."

Miranda looked up at Joe, hair tousled, smile revealing her white even teeth, a tiny gray-and-white striped kitten cuddled against her coat.

"Oh, Joe, isn't it sweet?"

"It is indeed. I've been told they grow into cats, however, with a definite mind of their own."

She laughed, putting the kitten gently back beside its watchful mother.

He took Miranda's hand to help her to her feet, holding on for a moment longer than necessary. He was more and more curious about her, strangely attracted to her.

"Come and see Grampa's doves, miss. They're in the loft. The ladder's right over here." The girls ran to a corner and scrambled up a wooden ladder into the loft.

"You go first, Joe." Miranda waited until he'd pulled himself up and through the opening. He reached a hand to her when her head and shoulders appeared, and he held on to her hand instead of releasing it after she was standing beside him.

She gave him a puzzled look, but she didn't pull away, allowing him to lead her over to the dovecote, where the children had taken several birds out of their cages and were caressing them.

Joe and Miranda admired the birds, and when the

girls climbed up to a rafter and began to leap down into the hay, Miranda pulled out her camera and began snapping photos, moving from one vantage point to another, making practiced and rapid adjustments with light and focus. She talked constantly to the children, asking them questions, responding to their comments. She was obviously very comfortable with them, more relaxed than Joe had yet seen her. She laughed several times at things they said, and he liked the husky, free sound of it.

He watched and listened, spreading his jacket on a bale and sitting down. After ten minutes or so she joined him, applauding as the girls jumped and tumbled in the straw.

"Tell me, Miranda Jane Irving, what were you like as a little girl?" Joe turned from the children and looked at her. He was very conscious of her long body and her lemony scent. She had straw in her hair, and he reached over and removed it, noting the flush that came and went on her cheeks whenever he touched her. He hadn't thought so at first, but he realized now she was sensual.

She didn't reply for a moment, then she said softly, "I was a wild child, a tomboy, much less civilized than these little ones."

Her answer surprised him. He'd have guessed her to have been a quiet, rather sedate child, an echo of what she was now. "Did you grow up like this, in the country?"

She nodded. "Until I was twelve we lived on a commune my father founded in rural New Mexico."

Again, he was surprised and intrigued. "And what was that like?"

"Wonderful," she said. "Carefree, joyful. The best life a child could hope for."

He tried to imagine Solange living on a commune and failed. He'd gathered that Miranda and her mother weren't at all in synch. "You were close to your father?"

"I adored my father. Everyone did. He was the unacknowledged leader of the clan. There were thirty-seven adults and eleven kids in the group. We didn't go to a formal school. He and one of the women, Angela, taught us. It was nothing at all like formal schooling. We were encouraged to learn about anything that intrigued us."

"Didn't that system leave huge gaps in your education?"

She shook her head, and her curly hair flared, before settling again into a tousled mass. "What happened was that whenever I got interested in one thing, I found I had to have knowledge of another for the first to make sense. So quite naturally I acquired a grounding in all the basics."

"Give me an example." He was fascinated.

"Well, music. There was an old piano, and I wanted to play it. In the course of learning to play I found I needed to know about mathematics so I could understand tempo and rhythm. And wanting to learn about the composers and where they lived led to history and geography."

"Did you have regular school hours or were they fairly haphazard?" He remembered the rigidity of bells and the rules about lateness, things he'd hated about his own schooling.

"We couldn't wait for our lesson times. And, of course, so much of our learning was incorporated into the regular work of the commune." Her voice was animated, her eyes sparkling behind her glasses. "We learned a lot about science from planting and watching things grow. My father knew about crop rotation and organic gardening. We were vegetarian because he insisted that anyone who ate meat or poultry had to kill the animals themselves."

"That's astounding. Your father must have been a brilliant man to teach you in that way."

"I think he was, and so was Angela. As much as possible, I use their methods with my students. They instilled a natural curiosity in us, a sense that learning was a privilege."

Daisy came running over. "We have to go now, miss. We're hungry. We missed our dinner. Will we see one another later?"

"I think so. But if we don't, it's been a great pleasure to meet you, Daisy. You, as well, Lydia." Miranda smiled at the girls and held out her hand. Each of them put a grubby paw in hers and they shook. "I'll send you these photos when I develop them."

"Oh, thank you, miss."

They waved goodbye, ran to the ladder and scurried down.

"Nice kids." Miranda's eyes were soft.

"Very." Joe was still thinking about the commune. "You said you lived there until you were twelve. What happened then?'' There were so many questions he wanted to ask her.

Miranda's voice was suddenly bleak, and the light went out of her eyes. ''My father died in an accident, and Solange took me back to Seattle to live with Gram.''

CHAPTER NINE

JOE THOUGHT of the three women living together so many years. "Didn't your grandmother ever consider getting married? Weren't there men in her life?"

He couldn't imagine Solange having a celibate life, but envisioning Pearl as a younger woman was more difficult.

Miranda paused and then shook her head. "Gram had male friends, but there was never any suggestion of romance. She fell in love with my grandfather, Jacques Desjardins, here at Bethel Farm. He was a French bomber pilot who'd escaped out of France after Dunkirk and joined the French squadron of the RAF. He and his crew made an emergency landing in a field near here one afternoon, when Gram was home on leave. He was killed in a raid three months later. Gram never loved anyone else."

"What about your mother?"

Miranda hesitated, and he had the feeling she was choosing her words carefully. "Solange was different. She's always had a number of relationships. She never stayed with any one man for very long. Until now. She seems certain she wants to marry Leon Baillie." Miranda's mouth curled into a parody of a smile. "Solange and her romances caused a lot of heated arguments with Gram over the years."

He nodded. He could understand perfectly how that would occur, just from the short while he'd known Miranda's mother.

"You call her 'Solange.'" It had shocked him. He couldn't imagine ever calling his father "Gabriel."

"She insisted on it. I never did call her 'Mother.'"

Again he understood without need of further explanation. Solange wouldn't want to advertise her age.

"So you had to begin attending a regular school when you were twelve. How was that?"

Miranda grimaced. "Awful. I looked weird. I'd never given clothes a second thought. None of the kids at the commune did. We wore hand-me-downs and stuff the mothers made. I soon learned that what a person wore to school was a big issue. Fortunately, Solange was good about that. She took me shopping and got me dressed right." Miranda grinned. "She's been trying to dress me right ever since, actually. But I still didn't belong. See, the other kids viewed school as a punishment and learning as a chore. In most academic areas I was light-years ahead, but in social situations and sports I was the same distance behind. There were no competitive sports at the commune. Father thought competition was detrimental, that it negated cooperation. And of course I'd never watched television, so it sounded as if the students were talking a foreign language to me when they discussed sitcoms and cartoons.''

''How long did it take you to fit in?''

She gave him a wry look. ''You're kind, Joe. What makes you think I ever did? I simply resigned myself to being an outcast. Our house is isolated, quite a distance outside Seattle. Inviting friends home for the weekend wasn't a good idea. My home life was eccentric, to say the least. Gram worked Saturdays and Solange...'' She paused and seemed to change her mind about what she'd been about to say. ''Well, it just didn't work.''

''So you were lonely.''

She shrugged. ''At first. I was used to being surrounded by people at the commune, and it took a while to adjust to spending time alone. I started taking pictures. That helped a lot. After a while I fixed up a darkroom in the basement and enrolled in a couple of courses in photography, and I got to like being alone. I chose to attend college in Seattle, so I've never really lived on my own.''

''I did. I went traveling, but I moved in again when I got back.'' He wanted to know still more about her. ''It seems peculiar that you decided to become a teacher, in spite of intensely disliking public school.''

Miranda shrugged. ''I guess I felt I owed it to my dad to show kids that learning can be fun instead of drudgery.'' She looked straight at him. ''But it wasn't as if I was saying, ''Tis a far, far better thing I do,' or anything like that. I'm really interested in how kids are taught. And the curriculum isn't as rigid as it was. Educators are becoming aware that there has to be more flexibility. Mostly, I love my job. I adore working with little kids.''

"Ever considered having some of your own?" The words were out before he realized it wasn't a kind question, that of course she must have thought about it. She was a woman who loved children.

Hell's bells, he was thick sometimes. He had no right to pry into her intimate affairs.

But Miranda didn't seem to take offense. "Sure I have. Often," she replied. "Goodness knows Gram's been nagging me for years to have a baby and keep Bethel Farm in the family. Her nagging has gotten lots worse these past few months, with the deadline approaching. You know, I really figured when I was a girl that I'd get married and have half a dozen kids. But the right, the right…circumstances…just haven't occurred."

He was relieved that she wasn't insulted, was eager to share what they had in common. "God, Miranda, this is uncanny. I know exactly what you mean. Dad constantly reminds me that I'm personally responsible, as his only son, to produce a sprout who'll carry on the family name. But finding someone to have children with is not exactly like picking out a breakfast cereal in a market, is it?".

"Nope, it's really not." She shook her head. "You'd think it would be easy. People get together and have babies all the time."

She was a bright, discriminating, most engaging woman. She stirred his curiosity. She touched him with her honesty. The beginning of a preposterous idea was niggling at his brain, but he needed to know a great deal more about her. He'd gone this far; he might as well go on asking questions until she stopped answering or clouted him on the ear.

"Are you seeing someone at the moment who might qualify?"

"Qualify?" She gave him a quizzical look.

"As a husband. Or a genetic donor. I don't know about the U.S., but in England a number of women are going about having a family quite on their own, exactly the way your female relatives all seem to have done."

"I've thought about it." She'd done more than just think. She paused and then added, "I actually made an appointment at a clinic last fall, because of Gram and this whole millennium thing with Bethel Farm, but I couldn't go through with it. At the last minute, I canceled the appointment." Single parenthood would have been the answer to so many problems, but for her it wasn't right. She wanted a baby, but she wanted it to be the outcome of a relationship, an extension of the feelings between two people, instead of a decision made by her alone simply for practical and convenient reasons. And, most important of all, there were the feelings of the child to consider.

She stared down at the hay beneath their feet. "You see, even though Solange didn't marry him, I did have a father, a wonderful father. And I'd want any child of mine to have one, as well. It's tough to explain a test tube to a kid. But I don't date much, so the other way seemed a good idea at the time."

She gave him a look from under her eyebrows. "Hopeless, huh?"

He raised his eyebrows. "You don't date?" He couldn't keep the scandalized note out of his voice.

She shook her head and avoided his gaze. "Hardly ever."

"Are you gay?" *Wallace, belt up. Now you've really gone too far.*

Her head came up and she gaped at him, blue eyes opened wide behind her glasses. Then to his relief she laughed, a hearty, deep chortle that made him want to laugh, too.

"I never even considered that. I certainly don't think so." She gave him a teasing glance and turned the tables. "Are you?"

"Absolutely, unequivocally not. I find women enchanting and endlessly desirable." He waited, but she didn't say anything more, and he decided he'd gone quite far enough. After all, he didn't want her to feel this was an inquisition. *Or an interview?*

"That's settled all the details, then, Ms. Miranda Jane Irving. So we can get on with getting to know each other better." In light of the intimacies they'd just shared, he figured she'd laugh at that, but she didn't.

"Is that what you want, Joe? For us to get to know each other better?"

She was serious. And she was blushing, of all things. Again he found it charming. It had been far too long since a woman had blushed in his presence, although why she would was beyond him.

"Are *you* dating someone, um, someone special, Joe?"

"Not at the moment." Betsy had shown him that he was getting on in years, because in spite of intensely pleasurable episodes in bed, the absence of humor or even a snippet of intelligent conversation between them had proven more than he could bear.

Miranda swallowed hard. He could hear it because it was more of a gulp than a swallow. "I, um, there's something, that is, I wondered if…"

She got to her feet and stood, her back to him. He got up, too, moving so that he could see her face.

The blush had become a magenta flush. He studied her, curious about what was upsetting her to this degree. She was clutching her camera so hard her knuckles were white. He wondered how much pressure the case could bear before it cracked open.

Acting totally on impulse, he took her hands and moved the camera out of the way. He drew her into his arms and held her a moment, breathing in the sweet scent of her faint perfume, getting a sense of her tall slender body and how it fitted, amazingly well, against his own.

"What is it, Miranda?" He stroked a finger down her cheekbone, feeling the warmth of her skin, the classic sculpted bones of her face, and when she didn't answer or move away, he dipped his head a little and found her lips.

They were full and soft. She tasted of the peppermint he'd given her earlier, warm and sweet and minty. She was willing but clumsy. It required coaxing to get her to open her lips even a little.

He took his time, touching her mouth gently with his tongue, making encouraging sounds in his throat, and with a tiny sigh, she gave in. Her arms slid up and circled his neck and he pulled her close, then closer still; she felt delicate and very womanly against him.

His hands cupped her waist and then slipped lower. In spite of her slenderness, her hips were subtly rounded, and as the kiss deepened he drew her even closer to him. His body reacted pleasurably, and she made a tiny sound against his mouth that could have indicated either apprehension or desire.

A hayloft was just too predictable for seduction, although for a mad moment he considered it. With a depth of regret that surprised him, he ended the kiss and eased away from her.

Behind her glasses, her eyes were luminous, the pupils enormous.

"That was very nice," he whispered, delighted by the soft wash of color that slid up her cheeks, thrilled by her shy nod of affirmation.

"Now, what was it you wanted to ask me?"

She opened her mouth to reply, but Solange's voice from the stable below interrupted.

"Miranda? Joe? Are you up there?"

Miranda sprang away from him like a teenager caught with her beau. "What is it, Solange?" She hurried over to the ladder and scrambled down. Joe had no choice but to follow.

"Good grief, it's freezing in here." Solange was shivering, arms wrapped across her breasts. She sounded petulant. "The kids said you were up there.

I hope I'm not interrupting anything interesting.'' She gave Joe a knowing glance. ''Listen, Miranda, I've absolutely had enough of traipsing around this place and listening to Mother go on and on about old times. Now she's talking about all of us staying out here for God only knows how long, and I can't do that, sweetie. You know I have to get my shopping done, and besides—'' she lowered her voice to a whisper ''—that doctor gives me the creeps. Don't you think we could start back to London right away?''

''Gram wants to stay out here? For how long?'' Miranda was frowning.

''I don't know. A few days, a week. Who knows.'' Solange shrugged. ''Natalie invited her, and Elizabeth, who does some writing for the local papers, told Mother she wants to take down those tiresome stories about the war. But I'm absolutely not staying. You're not, either, are you, sweetie?''

''I don't think so.'' In silence they walked out of the barn, blinking at the sunshine, into the farmhouse, where Pearl was relating a story about piloting a plane with a faulty rudder, as Elizabeth, sitting cross-legged on the sofa, scribbled away in a notebook.

Pearl broke off her narrative when she saw them. ''These kind women have invited us to stay here at the farm for a few days,'' she announced. It was obvious she was delighted. ''Natalie's even offered me the bedroom I used to have, the blue one at the end of the hallway. I told her nothing could please me more.''

"But you don't have any clothes, Gram."

Pearl dismissed the objection. "Elizabeth has some pajamas we can borrow, and she says there's a trunkful of odds and ends—something should fit us."

Joe caught the look of consternation on Miranda's face and came to her rescue. "Ms. Irving, I'd like to take Miranda to dinner this evening in town, and I have tickets for a show." He'd actually been planning it just before Solange interrupted them. "I do hope you won't mind if I kidnap Miranda and take her back to London?"

Miranda gave him a look, but Gram waved a hand at them. "Of course not. You young people go off and enjoy yourselves. Solange and I will relax and soak up this good country air, and then we'll take the train down to London."

"I'm going back today, Mother." Solange, by her tone, didn't brook any argument. "I have to start looking for a wedding dress tomorrow. I don't have much time."

"Oh, fudge. I guess I'll have to come with you." Pearl was crestfallen. "I'm not sure I could manage the train alone."

"I'll rent a car and come back for you whenever you want, Gram," Miranda offered, and Natalie urged, "Oh, do stay, Ms. Irving. If you want to take the train, I'll ride back to London with you. I'd love a day in the city. I haven't been for ever so long."

So it was settled. Pearl would stay.

After another cup of tea, Joe suggested they start the journey back.

"Ronan will be sorry to have missed you," Natalie said. "I called the clinic a moment ago, but he's either on his way home or he's stopped to see a patient."

It was Elijah rather than Ronan that Joe had hoped to see, but the old man was still off somewhere with his sheep.

Amid a flurry of goodbyes and good wishes, Joe handed Solange firmly into the back seat, then put Miranda beside him.

"I gather you don't mind my getting carsick all over these leather seats," Solange griped.

"Just give me fair warning and I'll stop for you." Joe wasn't about to give in to her bullying.

She made a disgusted noise, tucked a car blanket under her head and announced she was going to take a nap, as Joe steered the Bentley down the narrow road that would eventually lead to the motorway.

Miranda was quiet beside him, and finally Joe slipped a CD into the car's player, realizing too late that it was one Betsy had left. Backed by heavy acoustic guitars, two brothers from Edinburgh insisted they'd be the ones to wake up next to the bird they fancied.

"What kind of music do you like to listen to, Miranda?"

"All sorts. Classical, rock-and-roll, some western, some blues."

Basically the same eclectic mixture he enjoyed.

She picked up the CD case and studied it. "I've never heard of the Proclaimers."

He hadn't, either, before Betsy, but he couldn't

very well admit it. "Apparently this lead song was the theme for a movie." Betsy had told him which one, but he couldn't remember. "Do you enjoy the cinema, Miranda?"

"I don't go very often. Gram and I rent tons of movies. She's fond of action thrillers, the gorier the better."

For the next half hour, they argued over movies that one had liked and the other hadn't, hotly defending their points of view. Miranda was adept at remembering particular scenes, even scraps of dialogue, and he could do accents, which made her laugh.

In the back seat, Solange was silent, either sleeping or pouting. Neither Joe nor Miranda bothered to check.

From movies they progressed to books. He was a mystery fan, while she preferred biographies, but they'd read some of the same bestsellers.

Next they talked about food. Joe told her about Larry being vegetarian and the way he managed to either under- or overcook the meat. When Joe was all done being sarcastic and condescending about vegetarians, she sweetly said that she was one, and again they laughed.

It seemed to Joe that they arrived at the hotel far too soon. He parked and escorted Miranda and Solange into the lobby.

"Dinner at seven, Miranda?" It was already five-thirty.

"Sounds great." She gave him a wide smile.

"I think I'll order room service, but maybe I

could just tag along with you two to this play,"
Solange suggested. "You wouldn't mind, would
you, Miranda?"

Joe certainly did, and he saw that Miranda looked
stricken.

Solange didn't notice. "Surely it wouldn't be hard
to get a spare ticket, would it?"

Before Joe could answer, she added, as if the idea
had just surfaced, "Maybe your father would like to
join us, Joe. Three is such an awkward number. Call
him, why don't you."

Joe wasn't a lawyer for nothing and he wasn't
about to be shanghaied this way. "I'm sorry, Solange. I know Father has a board meeting tonight,
and unfortunately the show is sold out. My apologies."

"Well, I guess I'll have an early, boring night,
then." Solange sounded snippy, and Joe felt a moment's sympathy for the televangelist whose ring
she wore.

Solange wasn't done. "Miranda, do you think you
could spare the time to come shopping with me in
the morning? I do need to get a trousseau. And shopping alone isn't fun."

"Sure, Solange." Miranda smiled at her mother,
and finally Solange strolled off to the elevators.

Miranda watched her go, then turned to Joe.
"Thank you for rescuing me," she said fervently.

"You're most welcome." He took her hand and
pressed a kiss in the palm. "See you at seven."

CHAPTER TEN

MIRANDA FUMBLED with the entry card to her room, then stumbled inside when she finally got the door open. She sank onto her bed and tried to assimilate what had happened to her in the space of one short day.

Joe Wallace had kissed her, and she'd come within a sentence of blurting out what she wanted from him. She was amazed and more than a little impressed at her own audacity—and furious with Solange for interrupting. It could all have been settled now, one way or the other. As it was, she'd have to find another opportunity in the next few hours.

Joe Wallace. She flopped back on the bed and imagined his face. She'd talked to him, really talked, about things that mattered, and he'd listened. He'd asked her questions about herself. He'd *wanted* to be alone with her; he'd been firm and less than honest with Solange, just so they'd be able to spend the evening by themselves. Now he was taking her out for dinner, and then...

What would happen tonight? When she asked him to make love to her, would he do it immediately? A shiver of anticipation and sheer nervousness went through her. She'd simply have to find a way to bring up the subject of lovemaking. She had to, because her time in London was limited.

And what would she wear tonight?

Heart hammering, she leaped up and went to the closet, where she'd hung the minimal wardrobe she'd packed. Apart from the silk suit that she'd worn to lunch, only two dresses were possible—one a short basic-black knit and the other a longer, more tailored style, navy blue with buttons up the front.

Probably more important than the top layer was the bottom, just in case. She pulled open the drawer where she'd put her lingerie and began to pick and choose.

Makeup. She should do more than the usual mascara and lipstick, but how much was right?

For an instant, she considered asking Solange's advice, but she came to her senses quickly. She didn't need Solange; she could do this herself. Goodness knows, she'd watched often enough as her mother prepared herself for one man or another. Surely she'd memorized the ritual. It always began with a bubble bath.

She turned on the taps, pinned up her hair and let hot water run into the tub.

SEVENTY MINUTES LATER, the phone buzzed, and Miranda answered, still struggling with a pearl stud.

"Hello, Miranda. I'm in the lobby."

The deep timbre of his voice reminded her of the fantasies she'd spun about him before they'd even met, fantasies that involved the meeting of minds, shared laughter, an instinctive understanding of all the wounded parts of herself that love might heal.

"Shall I come up and fetch you, or do you prefer to meet me here?"

"I'll come down." Miranda glanced around at the disastrous mess she'd made. She'd become progressively more nervous as the minutes passed, and she'd spilled and dropped and discarded things everywhere. Makeup littered the countertop in the bathroom. The bed held the hotel's terry robe, still soaked from her bath; the clothing she'd worn to the farm; a silky assortment of underwear she'd tried on and rejected; and the dress she'd tossed aside before deciding on the basic-black knit. Two pairs of panty hose she'd managed to ruin were flung on the carpet, and the entire contents of her handbag had spilled on the seat of the armchair. She'd been looking for a coral lip pencil she was sure she'd tucked into the bag somewhere.

"Be there in a moment." She hung up and grabbed her black raincoat. Should she put it on or carry it over her arm until she reached the lobby? Would she need her handbag? Better take it. A scarf. She should drape a scarf around the coat collar. She dug a long filmy one with roses on it out of the drawer, stuffed everything back in her bag, glanced around one last time—

A horrible thought struck her. What if Joe agreed to her request? What if he came up with her afterward to…?

She snatched up her discarded clothing, then crouched and thrust everything under the bed.

A final desperate glance in the mirror told her she looked exactly the way she had five minutes earlier.

"Get a grip, Miranda Jane," she muttered. "Probably every minute of every twenty-four hours, some woman somewhere is having sex. It can't be that difficult."

But she'd reached a state of near panic. Taking a deep breath that did nothing to stop her knees from trembling, she shoved her glasses up her nose and went down to meet Joe.

She stepped off the elevator and there he was, resplendent in a navy three-piece suit and white-on-white striped shirt with a silky tie that resembled a muted rainbow.

"You are ravishing," he murmured, taking her coat and holding it as she slipped her arms in the sleeves. He held the ends of the long narrow scarf in each hand and slid it around her neck like a lasso, and when she smiled at him in thanks, the warmth and open admiration in his eyes made her suddenly *feel* ravishing.

It had begun to rain. The porter held the door for them and shielded them with an immense umbrella as they walked to the curb. The vehicle parked there wasn't the stately Bentley but a sleek, white two-seater sports car.

She'd thought she was growing more accustomed to the way he drove, but her stomach lurched and her throat tightened as the powerful motor purred to life and Joe accelerated into heavy London traffic, nonchalantly darting like a hummingbird this way and that, changing lanes at top speed and sliding into spaces not there a second before he occupied them.

The large heavy Bentley had provided some sense of security. This space-age machine felt vulnerable and perilous to Miranda. She was grateful for the seat belt.

"Did you ever dream of being a race-car driver?" She had to force herself not to grab for the dashboard as they rounded a corner and narrowly avoided a delivery truck illegally parked by the curb.

"You must be psychic." Joe flashed her his wicked grin and whipped around the truck, cutting off a small car driven by a timid-looking man in a bowler hat. "One of my earliest dreams was competing at Indianapolis."

"Was that before or after climbing mountains? Because if you do that with this same reckless abandon, it's a miracle you're still alive."

He laughed. "You sound like my father. Actually, I read a book when I was about fourteen by George Mallory, whom many believe to be the finest climber of the nineteenth century. He died on Everest in 1924. Climbing fascinated me, so during my teens I convinced a friend, Tony Patterson, to come climbing in Wales. He got hooked, and we went on to the Peaks, the Lake District, Scotland. And of course we dreamed of the Alps."

"You did more than dream. You climbed Mont Blanc." She remembered the photo in his office and repeated word for word what he'd told her: "'Mont Blanc, in the French Alps. The most interesting and exciting group if you're a climber.'"

"You're amazing to remember that."

She laughed. "I admired the photo. Who took it?"

"Tony did, and it was sheer luck it turned out. He's no photographer."

"Who was the other man?"

"An Australian friend, Chris Greenlaw. The three of us knocked about together a few years back."

"During your 'rebellious stage.'"

He shot her a puzzled glance. "Do you memorize every word I say?"

"Don't flatter yourself. I remember just the memorable ones. Tell me about this rebellious stage of yours."

"My friend Tony Patterson graduated from medical school the same year I finished law, and we agreed that we'd work for two years, save our money, then go to France and climb the Alps. We did, and we met Chris there. Coincidentally, he was also a lawyer, and the three of us got along famously. We joined forces and headed for India."

He'd taken a shortcut through a series of alleyways so narrow it felt as though the sides of the car were brushing the walls. She couldn't imagine what would happen if another car came toward them.

"You climbed Everest?"

He laughed. "Hardly. We weren't anywhere near accomplished enough to take on Everest, but we climbed a lot in the Hindu Kush region. We met a Yank there who offered us a job crewing on his yacht in the South Seas."

"Nice work if you can get it."

"Very. We took him up on it. We were more than half-frozen by that stage, and we ended up in Indonesia, where we spent a few months helping some villagers build a temple in the jungle. From there we made our way to Australia and Chris's dad's sheep station."

He pulled the car up in front of a restaurant with a striped awning and idled the motor, waiting for the parking valet. "I worked there for four months, then came home. I've been back two years now."

"You like Australia?"

"I love Australia. I've seriously considered emigrating. Chris has set up practice there, and he keeps offering me a partnership."

Why should that bother her? "What keeps you from going?"

He frowned and tapped the wheel impatiently with his fingers. "Oh, my father, the firm. Familial responsibility. Where *is* that attendant?"

"You like to travel." It wasn't something they shared. Before this trip, she'd never had any desire to go farther than California.

"Love it. I strongly suspect I'm simply not designed to stay in one place for long."

For a mad moment, she fantasized about his coming to Seattle instead of going to Australia.

"Sorry to keep you waiting, sir." The valet opened Joe's door, and Joe came around and helped Miranda out.

Dinner was extravagantly delicious, but there was little opportunity for intimate conversation. Joe seemed to know half the customers and all the serving staff. Every few moments someone came over to greet him, and although he politely introduced Miranda, he didn't invite anyone to join them.

There was a small dance floor and a string quartet playing waltzes, and between courses he asked her to dance. She'd never been good at it, and if she hadn't had several glasses of champagne, she would have refused. But the bubbly wine gave her courage, and she found that after a few preliminary disasters in which she stepped all over his feet and he apologized, she was finally able to relax and enjoy being in his arms. It helped that he was confident and that his style was not too flamboyant.

By the third dance and after a fourth glass of champagne, she closed her eyes and floated, aware of the warmth of his hand on the small of her back, the intimate woodsy scent of his aftershave, the heady sensation of his strong body close to hers.

The theater he took her to was comfortably shabby, and the play hilarious. Miranda laughed until her stomach ached. It wasn't until they were in the car again, zipping along the still-busy London streets that she remembered what she needed to ask him. She started planning the conversation in her head, but he interrupted.

"Do you like Indian tea, Miranda? There's a small place I often go to after the theater. It's quiet and not too busy."

The café was just as Joe described—nearly deserted and quiet except for soft recorded music. They were served by a tall Hindu gentleman, who placed a platter of honey cakes and cups of milky *chai* in front of them, then disappeared into the back.

Miranda sipped the beverage, worrying over how to begin with Joe, trying out openers in her mind.

Joe sat in silence for a few moments. Then he blew out a breath and said in a tentative voice, "There's something I'd like to discuss with you, Miranda. It's very unorthodox, and I hope you won't get angry. It's been on my mind all day, ever since we talked up in the hayloft."

She looked across at him, puzzled by his uncharacteristic nervousness.

"Yes, Joe?"

"We get on amazingly well, and I find you one of the most levelheaded and reasonable women I've ever met." He paused and stirred his tea, frowning into it as if it might show the future in its depths, if only he could decipher it.

"Thank you, Joe." She wondered if that was a compliment a man paid to someone he might be willing to sleep with.

"The incredible thing is, we have a problem in common, and I can't help but think we could solve it in a rational and adult fashion."

For one insane moment, she thought he was going to confess that he, too, was a virgin.

"You see, Miranda, just as we discussed today, finding suitable…companionship…is terribly difficult, and my father will *never* let up on me until I produce an heir, damn it." Joe smashed a fist on the table, making the spoons and Miranda both jump.

"Sorry, sorry. I get a bit daft over this whole

thing. See, he's bloody well fixated on preserving the Wallace name and heritage. And because I'm the only son of an only son, the matter becomes more urgent to him with every year that passes. And I feel responsible, even though I've done my damnedest not to worry about it—it's not as if I'm in my dotage, after all." He was becoming more distraught with every sentence.

She struggled to understand, but she didn't get it, so again she waited.

"And the most amazing coincidence, the thing that made me even consider asking you this in the first place, is that you're in an identical situation. I mean, I don't know if there's enough time left for my idea to solve your dilemma, but one never knows. What is this—April?" He held up his fingers and his lips moved silently as he counted.

His voice was filled with elation when he finished. "Nine months. By God, with some luck, we could manage it. Wouldn't it just be super all-round if we could do it, Miranda?"

"Do what?" She was beginning to suspect, but it was so insane she couldn't bring herself to acknowledge it.

"Miranda, I think we should attempt to have a baby together."

CHAPTER ELEVEN

SHOCK RIPPLED through Miranda, and along with it came a hysterical and overwhelming urge to laugh. She struggled against it, and she could feel her face turning red with the effort. Joe misinterpreted her reaction.

"I've insulted you. I know you have every right to haul off and belt me, but don't be angry, Miranda, please don't," he begged. "I know it's an outrageous thing to suggest, but at least take a moment to think it over, to discuss it with me. Our having a child makes a great deal of rational sense, you know. Good families, good genes, strong motivation." He reached across and took her right hand, which was clenched around a spoon on the tabletop. He undid her fingers and held them.

"One of the things I so admire about you is your intelligence, your reasonable approach to life," he went on in a pleading tone. "You haven't fallen for this whole ridiculous romantic charade that society perpetrates on us."

She felt her brain wasn't functioning properly. She heard what he was saying, but she couldn't make much sense of it. "What charade is that?" Her voice seemed to rattle around inside her head.

"Oh, you know, fall in love, try to get the other person to act the way you want them to act. Make that person responsible for your happiness, marry them, then make life living hell if they don't manage the impossible, which is to make you totally happy. Each partner spews out piles of guilt and blame and disappointment, until divorce becomes inevitable." He shuddered. "I see it every day in my practice. Now, the sensible approach to me is to treat the matter entirely as a business proposition. People still do that in certain parts of the world, and statistics prove that it works better than our haphazard system. The two parties lay out their terms clearly and make certain each understands exactly what his or her role is."

"You're talking about marriage?" She knew she sounded stunned. Heaven knows she felt stunned. She was still trying to digest his version of love and happily-ever-after.

"Not right away—only if we succeed in getting pregnant. We'd have to marry. The child would be the Wallace heir—and the Irving heir, too, of course—so we'd have to make it legal. But afterward, we'd divorce. We'd have joint custody. I'd want to be involved in the child's upbringing to some extent." He looked uncertain for a moment. "Not with nappies and bottles and that sort of thing. I wouldn't expect you to be involved in that, either, unless you wanted to. We could hire a nanny for all that. But certainly, once it reached a reasonable age, I'd be part of its life."

"But Joe, I live and work in Seattle."

"Yes, that is a slight problem." He thought it over, frowning. "You wouldn't consider immigrating temporarily, I suppose?" He didn't wait for her answer. "No, no, unfair of me even to ask that. Not that it's necessary. We could always work around it. It's only a matter of geography. As a teacher, you get generous holidays. England is lovely in the summer. I could fly over at regular intervals. There's always Larry to baby-sit, if need be. And Dad, for that matter. Baby-sit, fly over to America. He keeps insisting he wants to travel." This time he picked up on her dazed expression.

"Sorry, I'm thinking out loud. Dad would want to see a lot of the nipper, you know. Basically, I'm doing this for him. But I'm getting much too far ahead here, when at the moment all that you need decide is whether you even want to attempt it."

Another thought struck him, and he leaned toward her, consternation on his face. "Bloody hell, of course you're concerned about disease, blood tests and all that, and rightly so. Not that I'm promiscuous or in any sort of high-risk category. I did have a blood test some years back. Negative, of course. And since then I've been meticulous about protection. But of course you can't just take my word for that." He sank back in his seat and looked totally crestfallen. "Well, that settles it, I suppose. The damn results can take weeks to come back."

She could see herself dying a virgin. "I…I'd take your word."

"You would?" He scowled across at her. "You

shouldn't. Not as a rule, you know. Blokes tend to lie about such things.''

"But you aren't, are you? Lying.''

He shook his head. ''No. Definitely not.'' He looked across at her, his eyes on hers. ''Will you at least think it over, Miranda?''

She swallowed hard. ''I already have. I accept.''

"Hell's bells.'' It was his turn to look dumbfounded. And then a grin appeared. ''That's excellent. Why, that's bloody wonderful.'' He gazed at her, and the grin grew wider. ''I didn't get around to physical attraction, but it did dawn on me a few minutes ago that you might find me too repulsive even for a business arrangement.'' His eyes were twinkling. ''I take it this means you don't.''

She tried for a smile and almost made it. ''No. I, um, don't at all.''

"I'm so relieved. That could have been a major stumbling block.'' He reached across and touched her cheek gently with one finger, his voice suddenly husky. ''I also neglected to mention that I find you most desirable.''

His words touched her heart, even if they weren't true. He was so unfailingly polite. ''I guess it's my turn to be relieved,'' she managed to murmur.

He was suddenly all action. ''We don't have a lot of time. We'd best get started straight away.'' He flung money on the table and sprang to his feet. ''Will there be any problem with you not returning to the hotel until morning?''

Miranda shook her head and stood. She couldn't remember the last time her legs had felt this shaky.

"Solange is probably asleep by this time, and I'm not exactly a teenager. I've never known her to check on me."

She'd never had reason.

"Good. Then shall we be off?"

FORTY MINUTES LATER, in a hotel suite larger and much more lavish than her own at the Atheneum, she stared into an ornate bathroom mirror and thought, *So this is how you look when you're terrified, Miranda Jane.*

Joe was waiting in the other room. He'd ordered champagne from room service, doffed his suit jacket, helped her off with her coat and then tried to kiss her, before she'd mumbled something about the bathroom and fled. She'd been locked in here for eighteen minutes now, and there was no way out except the way she'd come in. She'd heard the room-service waiter bring the champagne quite some time ago, and she knew Joe must be wondering what was wrong with her.

Her stomach churned, and she wondered if the Indian tea was about to make a curtain call.

Get a grip, idiot. You're not sixteen. You've watched enough movies to have some idea what's about to happen.

The difference was that it was about to happen to *her,* and she'd waited far too long, and she was scared spitless. Why did people have to learn about sexuality in the privacy of their own lives? There was saturation when it came to sex in modern culture, on television, in movies, on billboards, on everyone's lips, and she'd missed the natural time for exploring it.

She wished fervently that she *was* sixteen again. She wet a washcloth and patted her face and neck. Then she rubbed some hotel lotion on her hands and was considering a long hot bath, when Joe tapped on the door.

"Are you all right, Miranda?"

"Fine." Her voice was bright and high and breezy. "I'm fine. I'll be right out." Should she leave her glasses on or take them off?

He was a stranger, for heaven's sake. How did one go about getting naked and intimate with a stranger? And he didn't know she hadn't done this before. Could she get away with not telling him? She'd already decided she was going to try.

She'd leave her glasses off. That way, everything would be blurred.

Slowly she opened the door. Joe had turned most of the lights off in the room, and music was coming from somewhere. He was sitting on the sofa in his shirtsleeves, shoes off, tie loosened, one muscular leg propped across the other, the unopened bottle of wine on a low table in front of him.

He smiled at her and patted the seat beside him. "Come sit here, have a glass of wine, talk to me."

She sat, aware of his leg almost touching hers, aware of the arm he wound loosely and casually around her shoulders, aware of the smell of him. He smelled so...masculine.

She gulped the first glass he poured her, and he

refilled it, commenting as he handed it to her, "First times are difficult, aren't they?"

For a paralyzed instant she wondered how he'd guessed, and then it dawned on her that he meant first times with *new* partners.

"Really difficult," she agreed, more fervently than she'd intended. At least she was managing to sip her wine this time. And conversation was happening. Maybe if they talked about this enough, she'd be able to relax. There were things she'd wondered about most of her adult life, questions that books didn't answer. She really had nothing to lose by asking him.

"What goes through a man's head the first time he's with a woman?" Was it permissible to inquire about things like that? "I mean, not the first time ever." She swallowed hard, and the wine went down the wrong way. She coughed and gasped, and he rubbed her back until she caught her breath. "I meant—the first time with a new person."

"I know. Good question." Joe tipped his head back against the pillows, his hand still tracing idle patterns on her shoulders. "Let's see. Well, above all else he wants to please her. That's paramount. And he doesn't want to offend her in any way, so he worries about halitosis that his best friend hasn't been able to tell him about, and whether the garlic he ate at noon is coming out of his pores. And he wants her to think he's the best lover she's ever had." He reflected a moment and added in an exasperated voice, "And he tries not to think about the inescapable fact that first nights are the same as they are at the theater—something inevitably goes wrong.''

Surprised, she giggled. "Always?"

"Always. There's some sort of law." He sipped his drink. "What about women? What do they think about?"

"Oh, the same sort of things." She racked her brain for comments she'd heard Alma and other women make.

"Whether he'll think her hips are too big or...or her breasts are too small." She had thought about that a lot this past hour. "Women worry about how their bodies look."

"Men do, too. They want their woman to find them irresistible. Men are often self-conscious about their bodies."

"Not you, surely." The wine was making her bold. "You have a wonderful physique."

His arm encircled her shoulders and tightened as he hugged her. "Thank you, Miranda. And you have fantastic legs." His hand dropped easily to her knee, cupping it, caressing it. She heard the whispering sound his fingers made on her panty hose, the warmth and tingles of pleasure as his lazy fingers stroked the inside of her knee, moving just a little higher, touching her inner thigh, so that she shivered. He stopped; bent forward; slid her high-heeled shoes from her feet one at a time, rubbing each foot slowly and soothingly as he freed it. His touch was soothing, comforting, reassuring.

"Come here." He turned her to him then, his lips

barely touching her skin as he kissed her temple, her cheekbone, the outer corner of her lips.

She held her breath, anticipating the moment when his mouth would meet hers, but he teased her, nibbling at her chin, trailing tiny kisses along her jawbone and making her gasp as his tongue delicately outlined the hollow of her throat.

Then, only then, did he kiss her, using his mouth in persuasive ways until she welcomed his tongue, needed it. And at last, she used her own to answer whatever urgent thing it was he was asking of her. Her arms crept up and encircled his neck, and she wanted to press herself against him.

She remembered these feelings, this growing sense of urgency, from when she was a teenager necking in the back of a boy's car. She'd always called a halt right about the time the feelings threatened to escalate out of control. Right about now.

No stopping, Miranda. Just jump in and do your best not to drown.

His warm palm stroked her breast, touching her nipple through layers of cloth. He went on kissing her, his lips teasing and pulling, his mouth certain and hungry. He undid the zipper at the back of her dress and slid the dress off her shoulders, her arms. She tensed, anticipating the moment when he'd undo her bra and look at her breasts.

Instead, he lowered his head to the black lace covering her nipple and suckled there, and unexpected waves of pleasure rolled over her, through her.

She made a noise in her throat, and he repeated the caress on her other breast. She was lying back on the sofa, and he stripped her dress down and off. She was conscious of being in her underwear, while he was fully dressed, but he remedied that. Rapidly, he undid shirt buttons, stripped off trousers, got rid of socks. He was wearing boxer shorts, blue ones patterned with white dots, and he had a mat of hair on his chest and legs. He also had an erection, and her eyes lingered there.

This was the furthest she'd ever come from feeling safe. She'd always known that intimacy involved danger, and she could feel herself racing down that path now, into darkness, with no desire to turn back.

He took her hands and pulled her to her feet. "Let's move over to the bed, before you get a crick in your neck." He was so natural and easygoing.

She stood, still in panty hose and bra, now more fully clothed than he, but only for a moment.

When they reached the wide bed, he hooked his thumbs under the elastic at her waist and smoothly slid the hose over her hips and down her legs, leaving her black panties in place. He slid his shorts off, as well, then pulled the bedspread and blankets back, making a nest for them on the snowy white sheets.

She was trembling as he eased her down, grabbing pillows and arranged them under her head so she was comfortable, then propped himself beside her.

"Are you cold, my dear?" He stroked her arm, her bare shoulders, curving his body around her.

She shook her head, trying without success to stop

the shaking. It rippled through her body in waves. It wasn't fear but something else, an anticipation so extreme it was beyond control. Before, she'd thought only of the burden of virginity, of getting rid of it, not just with anyone but certainly not with someone specific. Now she couldn't imagine this happening with anyone but Joe.

"Easy, sweetheart." He bent his head and kissed her again, unhooked her bra, peeled it back. "Delicate, so delicate, deliciously long and slim, so beautiful, Miranda. I love this part of you..." Slow kisses, urgency increasing, her hips beginning to move. "And here, right here, this wonderful hollow..." His mouth, his tongue, exploring her; her panties gone now. "And touching you, ah, dearest one, so wet and hot here...so tight..."

Slowly, fingers were replaced by another part of him, and her body, separate from her mind in a way it never had been before, rose of its own accord to welcome him, a primeval instinct dictating what to do.

But the intensity of pleasure lasted only an instant, and then she was being torn apart. She held her breath and endured and endured, and then she couldn't stop herself. She cried out and struggled frantically against him, against the pain.

"What? Miranda, what is it?" He drew back, separated their bodies, and she knew she was a dismal failure, just as she'd always suspected.

"You're bleeding." Shock and puzzlement mingled in his tone. "Lie still. I'll get a towel."

She wished she could bolt while he was in the

bathroom, but it wasn't possible. All too soon he was back. She lay with one arm across her eyes, shielding herself from what was inevitable.

With the gentlest of strokes, he ministered to her with the towel. She waited, but for the longest time there was only silence.

Then she heard him mutter, "It's preposterous. It simply can't be." He was quiet again, and she felt paralyzed, unable to move. "Miranda, this is an idiotic question, but...have you ever done this before?"

Caught. She was caught. Miserable, she shook her head.

"Why didn't you say something, for heaven's sweet sake?"

And then there was impatience in his tone. "Miranda, will you at least look at me?"

She withdrew her hand and glanced up. He was kneeling beside her on the bed, naked and scowling.

"Why in bloody blue hell didn't you tell me you were a virgin, Miranda Jane Irving?"

CHAPTER TWELVE

SHOCK AND AMAZEMENT overwhelmed Joe, and when he finally was able to get beyond them, he realized he was furious with her.

She'd tricked him.

Miranda Irving, whom he'd thought to be the most honest and straightforward of women, had led him straight down the garden path. She'd let him make assumptions, she'd *encouraged* him to make assumptions, that were far from accurate.

"Damn it all, I feel a proper fool. I've gone along believing that we were both knowledgeable adults, with a certain degree of experience upon which to base decisions. And now I find that you haven't had any experience at all?" His voice was rising.

"Nope." She moved her head back and forth on the pillow. "I haven't. I tried to find a way to tell you, to *ask* you...but one thing just led to another, and then I didn't have the courage."

"Ask me? Ask me what?"

She sat up and tucked the towel more securely underneath her, reached for the sheet and tugged it up over her breasts, clutching it to her chest.

"I wanted to ask you to make love to me," she said in a tiny voice. "I'd almost gotten around to it, when you suggested this baby thing. And I guess I just thought that maybe…that there was a chance…'' She swallowed hard. ''That you might not have to know.''

''Not have to *know?*''

She flinched.

He realized he was shouting at her, and he took several deep breaths, trying to regain his composure. ''Sorry. Sorry, I don't mean to yell. But what did you think—that I wouldn't notice you were in extreme pain, wouldn't notice that I'd hurt you? That you were bleeding?''

''From everything I've read, those things don't always happen. I mean, at my age, I didn't expect anything like that to happen. It's so pathetic.'' She paused, then added, ''Does it, every time? In your experience?''

He gaped at her. What did she think—that he was a professional at deflowering virgins? Didn't she know that she was the first one he'd ever bedded? It had given him a profound shock. And the humiliating part, the part that was making him squirm and rage at himself, was knowing that he'd bollixed it. But on second thought, how could she know it was his first time, too?

''I've never been with a virgin before,'' he admitted in the quietest voice he could manage. ''It's not exactly an everyday occurrence for a man. At least not in my experience.''

''Oh.'' She nodded. ''Sorry, I didn't realize.''

She moved her legs into a more comfortable position under the sheet. He was very conscious that she was naked, and her extreme slenderness made her seem fragile, all long arms and willowy throat and neck. And legs—she had the longest, most splendid legs.

He tried not to admit to himself that he hadn't been particularly gentle or considerate. And now *she* was apologizing.

"I'm really, really sorry, Joe. I never intended to trick you. See, this—this stupid situation has gone on so long, and it's awfully embarrassing for me to talk about. I know I should have told you, but the fact is, I haven't ever told anyone."

"Nobody knew? Not your best friend or your grandmother?" Now that was a truly idiotic thing to say. Who would go around telling their grandmother the details of their sex life?

But apparently it didn't seem idiotic to Miranda.

"Gram was the only person I ever considered telling, because she'd have understood. I think she was probably a virgin herself until she met Solange's father, Jacques Desjardins. But she was so eager for me to have a baby I just couldn't talk to her about it."

Which brought them neatly back to the reason for this full-scale catastrophe.

"You *do* want a child? Or was this whole thing just a ploy to…to…" He didn't finish because he couldn't figure out how to word what he wanted to say.

"Both." She heaved a sigh.

She had small, perfect breasts, exquisitely rounded,

their nipples prominent, and they were clearly visible under the sheet. He tried not to look.

"When you said that about having a baby together, it just seemed such a perfect solution to everything." Her chin quivered, and he saw tears trickling down her cheeks onto the sheet. "I so much want a baby."

"Well, it was a perfect solution. It *is*." What was wrong with him, making her feel bad because he'd spoiled things? He reached out and pushed her hair back, used his fingers to wipe her cheeks. They were wet and burning, and the freckles stood out like ripe kernels of wheat. He leaned across and kissed them, one after the other.

"I'm a beast. Please don't cry. I'm not angry with you half as much as I am with myself. Your first time should have been special, and I botched it."

"Not...your...fault."

She was sobbing in earnest now, and he snatched a handful of tissues from the box on the night table and clumsily dabbed at her eyes.

"Shhhh, please don't cry. Crying makes me suicidal." He wrapped his arms around her and turned her so that she was resting against him, her head snuggled under his chin, and he rocked her. The sheet slid away and her hot bare back was pressed against his front. She had the most remarkable skin, golden and silky. She smelled a bit like lilies, an elusive scent that made him want to find the exact spot where it had been applied and put his nose there, breathing it in until he was sated.

Damn, he was aroused again. He edged away so

it wouldn't be evident. No point scaring her any more than he already had. But he couldn't help himself; he had to kiss her. So he parted her hair and kissed her ear, then her nape. The vertebrae stood out, and he kissed them one by one, gradually easing her down on her side.

To his vast relief, the sobbing stopped, and she reached for the tissues and blew her nose. Then she sighed, and he trailed his palm down her arms, barely touching her skin. She sighed again and turned on her back, and he nestled beside her, murmuring to her, telling her she was beautiful, because she was.

He put his lips on the hollow at her throat and felt her heartbeat, rapid and light. He kissed her neck, nibbled her chin, found her lips and explored the corners of her mouth.

Her hands stroked his arms, slid to his back, touched him lightly, and then not so lightly as he began to kiss her in earnest, her mouth for a timeless time and then her breasts, licking and teasing before he allowed himself to suckle.

Slow, go slow, Joe. Half speed. Don't rush her—

And she started to come alive for him, hips undulating, breathing urgent, little shy half words and phrases whispered into the heated spaces between them. With only hands and mouth he encouraged her, wanting to rush but ruthlessly curbing himself. His reward was her drawn-out cry as she reached for and found climax. Then, before her body had time to recover, he slid inside her, gentle, cautious, clenching his jaw and exerting control over every uncontrollable urge.

He looked down into her face, watching for signs of alarm, of pain. Her eyes were wide and astounded. Her full lips were swollen and slightly parted, the skin on her high cheekbones moist.

She looked up at him as if she were dreaming, and then she smiled, a tender grateful smile that clutched at his heart. With each controlled movement her breath caught and sighed out, and at last he could feel the tension rising in her, tension not of pain this time but renewed pleasure. He felt a hero, so powerful and virile that he was caught unawares when an instant later he could no longer control his body.

"Miranda. Sorry. Can't wait..."

He groaned and moved, helpless, and to his absolute delight she erupted beneath him. Her back arched and her arms clenched, her tight inner muscles tugging at him in blinding, agonizing, ecstatic rapture.

Afterward, he did his best not to crush her, but he couldn't roll away. He murmured senseless words of praise and admiration and wonder, and she made soft little sounds of appreciation and astonishment.

At last, he cuddled her to him and closed his eyes. Just before sleep claimed him, she said, "Joe?"

"Mmm-hmm?"

"What you said about something always going wrong."

"Umm."

"You're a genius at damage control."

He was smiling as he slid into sleep.

IT WAS AFTER FOUR in the morning, and Solange was wide-awake again. She'd napped twice, but she couldn't seem to fall into a really deep sleep. She pulled on her housecoat, went into the corridor and tapped at Miranda's door. She needed company; being awake and alone in the middle of the night was awful.

There was no answer.

Miranda was obviously still out with Joe.

Solange thought that over. It meant that Miranda was having a romance, which was nice, but it annoyed Solange that her daughter wasn't there when she needed her.

Finally, she returned to her room, picked up the phone and went through the complicated process of calling Leon in Seattle.

After an interminable wait, the overseas operator informed her that she was having trouble getting through and would call back when she succeeded.

Seething with impatience, Solange wished she hadn't given up cigarettes. Miranda had no business staying out this way and worrying her, she told herself. It was inconsiderate of her not to let Solange know what she was doing. What if there'd been a car crash? The way that man drove it wouldn't be surprising.

And how would she ever find out? Miranda's ID would all be from Seattle. There was only one way to set her mind at rest, she decided. She found the awful reading glasses she'd secretly bought, and opened the phone directory.

Wallace, Wallace.

Who'd think there'd be so many? Pages, practically.

She persevered until she finally located Wallace, Gabriel, Solicitor. She dialed the number. It rang five times before a groggy male voice answered.

"Gabriel?" Solange managed a tremor. "Oh, Gabriel, it's Solange. I'm so sorry to call at this ungodly hour, but I'm out of my mind with worry. You see, Miranda went out with Joe for dinner hours and hours ago, and she hasn't come back." She gave a brave little laugh. "I know it's silly to get in a state, but this just isn't like Miranda."

That was absolutely true; Miranda was always totally reliable. She *was* concerned about her daughter, Solange assured herself—maybe just not as concerned as she was pretending to be.

"I see." Gabriel cleared his throat and Solange could almost hear him waking up. "If you'll hang on a moment, I'll just go and see if Joseph is home."

She waited, studying her manicure. She'd chipped two nails; she'd find out in the morning if the hotel had a decent manicurist on staff.

"Solange?" He was definitely awake now. "Joseph isn't home. I can only assume he's with Miranda. I didn't see him this evening. I was at a meeting."

So maybe Joe had told the truth after all when she'd suggested phoning Gabriel. "You...you haven't had a call from any hospital, have you? You don't think there's been an accident?''

"No, absolutely not. Of course I would have notified you at once.''

"Oh, how silly of me. Of course you would have. And now I've gone and woken you, and there's probably no reason whatsoever to be upset. After all, they're young and healthy and both over the age of consent.'' She did her best to sound embarrassed and contrite. "I feel such a fool, Gabriel. But you know what it's like to be a parent without a partner. The mind plays tricks, especially in the middle of the night, no matter what age children are.'' She gave an audible sigh. "And I'm here alone in a strange hotel, in a strange city.''

"No need to say sorry, my dear. Of course I understand.'' There was much more warmth now. "I should apologize for my son, Solange.'' His voice hardened. "I'll certainly have a word with him. I assure you of that.''

"Oh, please don't. I'd be devastated if Miranda found out I called you. She does get so annoyed with me. She is a grown woman, although to me she'll always be my little girl.'' She gulped and sniffed. "Oh, Gabriel, forgive me. I feel so ridiculous.'' Crying and appealing to a man's protective instincts had always worked well for her.

"Now, now, my dear. Not to worry.''

She rolled her eyes. She could practically hear him thinking. These Englishmen really weren't quick on the uptake.

"Solange, how would it be if I drove over there? We could go out for an early breakfast."

She made sure she didn't sound too eager. "Oh, I couldn't possibly ask that of you. I feel just terrible for waking you at all."

"Really, my dear, it would be my pleasure. And I know of a café that's open. They serve quite decent meals."

"If you're certain."

"Absolutely. I'll be there in, shall we say, forty-five minutes?"

Solange hung up, feeling partly vindicated for the lonely evening and the sleepless night she'd spent. Now, the big question was, what should she wear? She went to the closet and began flipping through her choices.

The buzz of the telephone took her by surprise. She'd totally forgotten about placing the call to Leon, and she didn't really want to talk to him at the moment. She wanted to have a quick bath and put a mask on her face to get rid of the lines.

She snatched up the receiver.

"That you, honey bun?" Leon's voice was filled with warmth. "I just got back from a prayer meeting when the operator phoned. I'm sorry I missed your call. How you doin', Solange?"

"Oh, Leon, I'm exhausted." She did her best to sound plaintive. "It's almost morning here and I haven't slept at all. Can I phone you back later on?"

"What's got you upset, sweetheart?"

She was in a rush, but the temptation to unburden herself to Leon was irresistible. "Oh, the trip out to

Bethel Farm was a nightmare. I don't like it out there, and I don't like that Dr. O'Donnell one bit. And now he's making noises that he wants to buy the farm. And Mother will want to sell to him, even if his offer is way less than the other one. She stayed out there, and Miranda didn't come home last night, so I'm here all alone and my nerves are a wreck.''

"Listen, honey, I was going to just surprise you, but it sounds like you need good news now." His mellifluous voice was charged with excitement. "I'm coming over. I called one of those places where people sell tickets they can't use, and I got on a flight that leaves late tonight. With the time change, I'll be there sometime tomorrow evening. What do you think of that, honey?"

She wasn't exactly sure *what* she thought. A few days ago she would have begged him to come over, but with Gabriel on the scene, things had changed.

Well, she couldn't exactly explain that to Leon, could she?

CHAPTER THIRTEEN

"YOU'RE COMING to England?" Solange wasn't sure how she felt about his arriving. On the one hand, she wouldn't have to be alone anymore, but on the other, she'd been hoping to have a little fling with Gabriel.

"Now, don't worry about meeting me at the airport," Leon said, as if she'd thought of it. "I'll just catch a cab. I know the name of your hotel." His voice softened. "I can't wait to see you, babe."

"I'd better try to get some sleep so I'll be rested by the time you get here." She was watching the clock. She now had barely half an hour to get ready for Gabriel; she simply *had* to get off the phone.

"You do that, honey, because I plan to keep you awake all night once I get there." Leon growled suggestively.

Solange smiled. He was always making promises like that, but she'd learned they were mostly that. He was good enough in bed, though. She wondered what Gabriel would be like. More refined, probably, although you couldn't always tell about the reserved ones; sometimes they turned into wild men.

"'Bye, Leon. I'll be waiting for you." She made

kissing sounds into the receiver and quickly hung up.

She'd wear her gray flannel pants, with the petal-pink silk sweater under the matching jacket. She'd have to use more concealer than usual on the circles under her eyes.

Why did Leon have to decide to come now, just when things were getting interesting?

"I WON'T BE A MINUTE. Come in and see where I live," Joe urged Miranda. "Dad's been gone for a good hour. He's a stickler about getting to the office before the staff."

Miranda was naturally curious. She allowed Joe to lead her up to the massive front door, and then she felt like running when he opened it, ushered her into a spacious hall and nonchalantly introduced a formal little man with a totally impassive face and cool gray eyes, who was dressed in jeans and a spot-less white sweatshirt. He was dragging a vacuum along the rug, obviously about to plug it in.

"Larry Pelcher, Miranda Irving. Larry, take Miranda on a quick tour of the place and give her a cup of your famous brew while I change, would you, please?"

"Certainly, Joseph. Your father has called several times. He asked that you ring him as soon as you arrived."

Joe grunted and hurried up the stairs.

Larry watched him go, his expression unreadable.

Was he a butler? Miranda wondered. Did butlers vacuum?

Certainly he was an expert at not revealing the slightest flicker of surprise at her appearance here at 7:50 in the morning, hair still damp from a shower, wearing a dress and strappy sandals suitable for evening. She even had a conspicuous run that traveled right up the front of the right leg of her panty hose.

"Would you like to come along and see the kitchen, Ms. Irving?"

"Please, call me 'Miranda.'" Could he tell by the way she walked that she was more than a little sore? Could he sense just by looking at her that she'd spent the night making love, four separate times? She'd always wondered if people actually did that, or if it was just an exaggeration of writers and film directors.

She'd never imagined herself brazen enough to wake a man up and institute lovemaking, but she had. She'd never imagined that the physical pleasure would be so overwhelming. She fully understood now what all the fuss was about. And she couldn't help but wonder if, on some deep instinctual level, she'd known there'd be someone as perfect as Joe, if only she waited for him.

She was glad she'd waited.

Larry led the way into the gleaming white kitchen. "Have a seat, Ms. Irving." He indicated a stool by a center island. He clearly had no desire to be on a first-name basis. Did that mean she should call him "Mr. Pelcher"?

"Do you take cream and sugar?" He was being excruciatingly polite, and distant. Was he accustomed to Joe bringing strange females home early in the morning?

That created a pang of awful jealousy.

"Black, please."

Larry poured coffee from a carafe into a white mug and set it on the counter.

"Do you care for a cinnamon bun?" He set a small plate, a fork and a white napkin in front of her and offered a platter of buns, dripping with glaze and still warm from the oven.

"Thanks." Miranda couldn't resist. She and Joe had made love instead of ordering breakfast, and she was famished.

"You baked these? They smell heavenly." She took a bite, then another, savoring the rich sweetness.

"Baking is my hobby. Do you like to cook, Ms. Irving?"

Her mouth was full of the delectable bun, and she shook her head, adding after she'd swallowed, "The only thing I make is broiled tofu. I'm vegetarian, and I'm the only one in my family who likes it."

"You're vegetarian?" His face split in a smile that made him look much more human. "Why, so am I. And I'm also the only member of *this* household who eats tofu. What do you use as a marinade?"

"Sesame oil, soy sauce and Tabasco."

When Joe appeared ten minutes later, Miranda and Larry were deeply involved in a discussion about the health benefits of being vegetarian and he was calling her Miranda.

Joe snagged a bun and devoured it in two bites. He reached for another.

"Coffee, sir?"

Joe shook his head. "I'd love one, but I'd better get to the office before Dad has a coronary."

The phone on the counter buzzed. Larry picked it up.

"If that's Dad, I'm—" Joe swore under his breath as Larry handed him the receiver.

"'Morning, Dad, I'm just..." Joe listened and then frowned. "Well, yes, actually, but—" He listened again, his eyes on Miranda. "She did?" He listened still again. "I see. Yes. Well, she's right here, I was about to drop her..."

Larry and Miranda watched and waited in silence until at last Joe replaced the receiver in its cradle.

"Shall we be off?" He tapped his foot impatiently while Miranda thanked Larry for the coffee and buns.

Once in the car, he started the motor and backed out of the drive, then explained. "It seems there's a bit of bother. Your mother called my father at four this morning."

"What? What's happened? Is it Gram?" Miranda felt panic rising in her. "What's happened to Gram?"

Joe put a hand on her arm. "No, no, nothing like that. Sorry, I shouldn't have put it to you that way. Apparently Solange phoned Dad because she was concerned about you not being in your room."

That took a moment to sink in. "What?" Miranda turned to stare at him. "She actually called your…?'' She shook her head, flabbergasted. ''But she's never bothered once about where I was or what I was doing. It was always me worrying where *she* was.'' She'd tried as a teenager to convince herself that she hated her mother, even, when she was mad enough at her, that she wished Solange dead, but nights when Solange didn't come home, weekends when she went off with men who talked too loud and laughed too much, Miranda had been unable to sleep or eat, agonizing over whether her mother was safe, whether she'd ever come home again.

She'd lashed out only once at Solange, raging on and on, accusing, finally starting to cry hysterically, stammering that she was scared Solange would leave and not return.

Solange had been angry at first, then defensive, and last of all astonished. She'd wrapped her arms around Miranda and patted her back. ''With me, men will always come and go. You've just gotta get used to it. But you and I are forever. Don't you know that, a smart kid like you?''

It was one of the few times Miranda had really felt that Solange understood something about her and cared.

''Dad ended up going over to the hotel early this morning and taking her to breakfast,'' Joe was saying.

''Is he furious with you?''

Joe looked puzzled and shook his head. ''I'd have expected him to be raving, but he wasn't. He didn't even mention that I'm late for work.'' Joe shook his head. "It's not like him, I can tell you that. He's probably saving up to blast me in person."

"Well, it's not like my mother, either." Miranda thought for a moment. "Or maybe it is."

"What do you mean?" Joe was doing his usual terrifying dance amid the congested morning traffic, driving at top speed on a roundabout and then accelerating instead of slowing as he took an off-ramp. Miranda hardly noticed.

"I think she'd like to, to…get to know your father better." That was the only polite way Miranda could think of to say it. "And I think she used this as an excuse."

"You think she wants to seduce the old man?" Joe grinned. "I'd say she has her work cut out for her."

"Not necessarily." He didn't realize her mother was an expert.

"If she succeeds, it'll certainly spice up the old man's life, particularly if Dierdre finds out."

"Dierdre? Dierdre Payne?" Miranda remembered the friendly secretary. "She and your dad are involved?" She'd never have guessed.

Joe nodded. "Have been for years. Everyone knows it, but they both keep up this pretense at the office."

Miranda thought that over. "Solange should be told. Dierdre seems like a nice woman. And my mother does have some rules." Solange had often claimed she didn't mess with married men. The question was, would she consider a long-standing affair the same as a marriage?

"Dierdre is a fine person. I'm very fond of her."
Joe pulled up in front of the Atheneum. The doorman came over to help Miranda out, but Joe caught
her arm, pulled her across to him and kissed her
thoroughly. "Dinner tonight, about seven?"

She could only murmur, because he was kissing
her again.

"You do understand that we'll need to work hard
at this project of ours. We only have a few more
days if you're going back next week. That means
every night. Work, work, work."

"Every night?" She'd tried to turn the question
into a martyred whine, but her smile got in the way.

"We must. Be brave. And I'll draw up an agreement that we can both sign, setting out exactly what
the terms are, for marriage and for divorce. I think
that's the wise thing to do, don't you?"

Her heart sank. "Yes. Yes, of course." It was a
business arrangement, she knew that, but the pleasure she'd been feeling disappeared.

The doorman was still discreetly waiting. She
reached for the handle, and he swung the door open.

"Until tonight, then, Miranda."

She got out and Joe pulled away with a screech
of rubber.

Slowly, Miranda walked into the hotel and over
to the elevators. She was tired. That was why she
suddenly felt so drained. She'd have a long hot bath
and then a nap.

She'd barely inserted the card in her door when
Solange's door burst open.

"So you've finally come back, sweetie," she said. "I was worried about you."

She didn't look worried, Miranda thought. She looked pleased and excited. Irritation turned to anger as Miranda thought how Solange had used her to manipulate Gabriel.

"I'm a grown woman, Solange." She kept her voice even, although the desire to holler at her mother was overwhelming. "You have no business checking up on where I am or who I'm with."

Solange seemed astonished, then hurt. "But I was here all alone," she said in a pathetic voice. "I couldn't sleep. I needed someone to talk to, and you weren't around. You should have told me you were going to stay out all night."

Miranda sighed. Reasoning with Solange was like reasoning with a two-year-old. "I didn't know I was going to. I probably should have called you. I'm sorry."

"That's okay. No harm done." Solange's good humor was instantly restored. "Now, let's go shopping as we planned. I'm meeting Gabriel again—for lunch—so we'd have to be back by one, but that gives us lots of time."

Miranda thought of what Joe had told her about Gabriel and Dierdre Payne. She had to talk to her mother about that, but not out here in the hallway.

Solange followed Miranda into her room. "And guess what? Leon's on his way over. He'll be getting here this evening sometime."

That was about the last thing Miranda wanted to

hear. Disgusted, she tossed her coat and handbag on the bed.

"I suppose you invited him."

"Not really, but I guess I mentioned that I was lonely when I spoke to him," Solange admitted. "Now I suppose you're mad at me because he's coming."

Damn right, Miranda wanted to say. "You knew this was supposed to be a special trip for just the three of us," she pointed out in a tense voice.

Solange put her hands on her hips. "Well, I know you and Mother don't like him, but I'm glad he's coming. Neither of you consider me at all. Mother's out at that farm. You're having a fling with Joe. Which means I'll be spending most of my time here in London all by myself. At least Leon's company."

"And what about Gabriel?"

"What about him? For heaven's sake, Miranda, I'm having lunch with the man, not spending the night."

As you did with Joe. Solange didn't say it, but the implication was clear.

"That's a good thing, because Dierdre Payne would be more than a little upset with you."

Solange was taken aback. "Dierdre Payne? The mousy little woman sitting outside his office?"

Miranda nodded. "I thought she was very attractive. They've been seeing each other for years."

"So that's why he didn't want me to come to his office today. Men, honestly. Well, that makes me doubly glad Leon is coming over."

"How long is he staying?"

"I didn't ask."

"If he's planning to share your room, you'd better speak to the desk clerk," Miranda said bluntly.

Solange ignored that. "Are you going to come shopping with me or not?"

Miranda didn't want to. She wanted to be alone, to go over, moment by moment, her night with Joe. She wanted to try to assimilate the profound changes that had occurred in her life in the past twelve hours. She wanted to try to understand why she felt elated one moment and uncertain and scared the next.

But she had promised Solange.

"All right. I'll be ready in half an hour." It would only take her ten minutes, but she needed just a little time alone.

"Okay, I'll wait here." Solange settled herself in an armchair. "My stars, Miranda, what's this on the floor?"

The foot of a pair of discarded panty hose peeked out from under the bed. Solange knelt and began pulling out all the clothing Miranda had shoved under there the night before.

"Really, sweetie, this is no way to treat good clothing. I thought I taught you to take better care of your wardrobe than this." She sounded scandalized, and all of a sudden Miranda felt like weeping.

Solange *had* taught her to take care of her clothing. It was one of the few practical things her mother had taught her; the other lessons, the unspoken ones, had all been negative.

Why couldn't she have the kind of mother she could confide in about intimate things, the kind who'd give her positive guidance over this whole confusing man–woman thing? For the space of a heartbeat, she actually considered asking Solange's advice, but then she came to her senses. The last thing she wanted Solange to know was how ignorant she herself had been until just last night.

Last night had taught Miranda many different things—about sex, about men, about herself—but it had raised as many questions as it had answered.

Joe had made it clear their relationship was only a business proposition. She'd agreed because it was her only choice. But her feelings for him had nothing to do with business. She was being dishonest all over again, letting him think she felt nothing for him.

Yet didn't a woman always think she was falling in love with the first man she slept with? Miranda remembered hearing that somewhere. So maybe after she'd been with him a bit longer, she'd realize it wasn't love she felt at all. Maybe it was only lust. She'd just have to wait and see.

And how did you tell the difference between the two?

CHAPTER FOURTEEN

"WERE YOU IN LOVE with my father, Solange?"

"Really, sweetie, what a question." She was carefully brushing off and hanging up the dress Miranda had tossed under the bed. "Of course I was. He was the first man I ever really loved."

"Would you have stayed with him if he hadn't been killed?" Miranda had never asked that before. She'd never dared.

Solange hesitated, and with a sinking heart Miranda knew the answer. She hadn't really had to ask: she could remember them quarreling.

"That's hard to say. I was so young when I met him. People change as they get older. We were planning to leave the commune. That might have helped." Solange shuddered. "I got so that I hated that place."

"So why did you stay?"

"Because your father took care of me. At that stage in my life I needed someone to take care of me."

The answer was so typically Solange. It would never even cross her mind to pretend it had anything to do with loving her daughter, or loving John, or wanting to keep her family together.

"Are you ready to go, Miranda? I think I'm going to try to find one of those long camel coats all the women are wearing over here. It would go over so many things. The right coat is really important to a wardrobe. You should consider getting one, too."

Solange chattered on about clothes while Miranda changed into jeans and a white shirt. The clock radio beside the bed displayed the time and the date. It was Wednesday. Their return flight was booked for the following Tuesday. Her heart sank. She had only five days left to spend with Joe.

JOE LOUNGED in the leather client's chair across the wide desk from Gabriel. He'd been summoned to his father's office fifteen minutes ago, before he'd had a chance even to sit down at his own desk, and a lecture was under way.

"I trust you aren't misleading this young woman in any way, Joseph. There are serious issues involved here. She is a client of this firm. It's highly irregular to pursue a, um, personal relationship with a client." Gabriel cleared his throat. "On the other hand, I quite understand the attraction. Miranda is a most appealing young woman."

Where was this cozy little chat headed? Joe wondered. Thus far, the lecture was so mild and affable he actually thought the old boy was going to reach across and give him a companionable nudge on the shoulder, followed by a wink.

"What happened this morning was unfortunate," Gabriel continued in the same unruffled voice. "Miranda's mother was justifiably upset, and, given the circumstances, I felt I had no choice but to go over there and support her. I assume you'll be more circumspect if you see Miranda again, and of course this entire fiasco will remain completely confidential.''

So that was it, then. Gabriel didn't want Dierdre to know he'd spent the dawn hours comforting Solange, Joe deduced. And the reason for that had to be that Gabriel planned to see Solange again; if it had been a one-time thing, why not tell Dierdre the truth?

Joe had once or twice played similar games with women, and he'd learned they never succeeded. Imagine the old man not knowing that at his age.

Well, it would be amusing to watch, if it didn't get too bloody.

The intercom buzzed. "Mr. Frankle wonders if you'd be free for lunch today,'' Dierdre said. "He wants to go over the tax figures concerning that property acquisition. Your appointment book is clear. Shall I tell him you'll meet him at one?''

Fascinated, Joe watched Gabriel's face slowly take on a deep crimson hue. He avoided looking at Joe, although his voice remained completely in control. "Make my apologies, please, Dierdre. I have a previous engagement. See if Frankle can meet me later in the week.''

There was a pregnant silence. When Gabriel didn't elaborate on his engagement, Dierdre said in a cool tone, "Yes, I'll do that.''

It didn't take a Sherlock to figure out Gabriel was taking Solange out to lunch, Joe concluded. And

Dierdre was much smarter than Holmes had ever been.

As he got up to leave, he couldn't resist leaning across the desk and whispering, "Do be careful, Dad. Hell hath no fury..."

It was one of the few times Joe had ever seen his father speechless. Whistling cheerfully, Joe made his way back to his office. He felt comforted to know that he and Miranda didn't have to engage in any similar silly games. Absolutely everything between them was now open and honest. Granted, she had deceived him about the virginity thing, but he could certainly follow her reasoning, after he'd thought about it. The subject was difficult to broach with a man.

A sense of awe came over him, and a profound feeling of responsibility. It was up to him to teach her everything. He felt he'd made a decent start, after that first disastrous hour or so, but there was still so much ground to cover, and not much time to do it in. She was an amazing pupil, responsive and eager, and touchingly trusting of him.

She was sweet and innocent and intelligent and funny, and above all rational—all the qualities he'd been searching for in a woman. He'd made the right decision asking her to have his child. *Their* child.

He tried to concentrate on a file concerning a couple in litigation over the family dog, but his mind kept returning to Miranda and the evening ahead.

At last, he reached for a pad of lined paper and began to list the salient points of the agreement between them. He'd have to type up the agreement himself, of course. He wanted it to be clear, comprehensive and all-inclusive. She'd have to have independent legal counsel; she could take it back to Seattle and have her own lawyers look it over. There was no rush; it was necessary only if their plan succeeded and she did get pregnant. If she didn't, then the whole thing was a nonevent.

He paused, thinking about that. The chances of pregnancy were probably pretty slim; there were technical details like ovulation to consider, which Joe really didn't understand.

He'd ask Tony. He wouldn't tell Tony about her being a virgin; that was a special secret between him and Miranda, and he wanted to keep it that way. But he could ask about the medical details. He would also confide in Tony about the agreement. They'd discussed the advantages of this sort of relationship often enough; he wouldn't have to go into any lengthy explanations about what he was doing. Tony would be delighted that Joe had found such a perfect solution to the problem of inheritance.

If this experiment didn't work, Miranda probably wouldn't want to try again at some later date; timing for her was of the essence because of the whole Bethel Farm thing. If she didn't get pregnant, he might well never see her again.

For some reason, that bothered him more than a little. He scowled and picked up the pen again. No point in being negative; they had youth and health and enthusiasm in their favor. And he, for one, was going to give this project everything he had to ensure its success.

He had to grin at that. *Not exactly a sacrifice on your part, Wallace.* In truth, it was the most fascinating and appealing project he'd ever tackled.

GABRIEL DROPPED Solange back at the hotel at two-thirty. The day had been disappointing. She and Miranda had wandered about, gazing into shops. They'd tried Harrods, but Solange hadn't found the exact coat she was looking for and everything was expensive. She'd only bought a hat, a flirty little black thing with a veil.

She'd been looking forward to lunch with Gabriel, and had dressed up in a short-skirted baby-blue suit, only to be bored half out of her skull; all Gabriel had talked about were legal issues and his golf game. She'd tried to appear interested, but by the time dessert arrived she'd begun to yawn and couldn't seem to stop. She'd quizzed him about places to shop, but he didn't have a clue.

He kissed her when she got out of the car, and even that was disappointing. He was far too polite about it; he didn't put as much energy or honest hunger into it as Leon did. And there was the matter of Dierdre Payne.

Well, she was welcome to him, Solange concluded. As a matter of fact, she'd have been better off getting to know Dierdre; at least a woman could give advice about where to go shopping and who was a good hairstylist.

She had a nap so she'd be fresh when Leon arrived, and when she woke up at three-thirty she was once again at loose ends. Miranda was out; she'd told Solange she was going off to take photographs. It was far too soon to get ready for Leon. He wouldn't be arriving until late that evening.

Solange was hungry. She wanted to dress up and go somewhere wonderful for a traditional English tea, but she sure didn't want to go by herself. She'd had it with Englishmen, and with five days left and Leon coming, it didn't seem worth the bother to begin a new flirtation, even if she could find a likely candidate. And she didn't know a living female soul in this entire damn city.

Except one. And it would serve Gabriel right.

On impulse, she dialed the Wallace and Houmes number and asked the clerk who answered for Dierdre Payne.

"It's Solange Irving calling," she said when Dierdre came on the line.

"Yes, Ms. Irving, how may I be of assistance?"

She had those impeccable English manners, and it was impossible to tell whether she knew that Solange had been out with Gabriel. Probably not; Gabriel sure as heck wouldn't have told her. And Solange really didn't care; she was through with that little adventure now. This was one of those rare times in her life when she actually craved female company. "I just wondered what time you got off work."

There was a tiny, puzzled pause. "At four-thirty, Ms. Irving."

"Good, then how about coming out with me somewhere for one of these fancy English teas?"

"Me? Now? Today?" Dierdre was obviously taken aback.

"Yeah, where would be nice to go? Where they serve sandwiches and those little tea cakes and clotted cream? And afterward we could do some shopping. I want to go somewhere to buy one of those long camel coats."

"Well, I don't believe…I mean, I'm terribly sorry, but I'm just not able…"

"Oh, c'mon, my treat. I'm here all by myself. I don't have a clue where to go. It would be fun for a couple of hours. You did say the other day that if we needed anything to call you. I'd have to be back by eight or nine—my fiancé's arriving tonight from Seattle—so it wouldn't be all evening. I mean, if you've got a date later or whatever." *With boring old Gabriel.*

Silence. Then, with obvious reluctance, "I suppose…well, all right, yes, I could meet you for tea. Fortnum and Mason is a good spot, not far from your hotel." She gave Solange directions. "Shall we say five-fifteen?"

It was five-twenty by the time Solange's cab dropped her in front of the impressive building. Fortnum and Mason was a classy food store with a tearoom. As she swept in, Solange was glad she'd worn her new hat; many of the women were in hats and gloves, and all the servers had on formal uniforms. Dierdre Payne was waiting at a small round table.

"Good afternoon, Ms. Irving." She was wearing a dark green jersey dress with a single string of pearls at the neckline. Her hair was pulled back in a chignon.

"Let's make it 'Solange' and 'Dierdre,' okay?"

Dierdre gave a tiny nod and a polite smile.

Good features, twenty pounds overweight, expensive but frumpy clothes, Solange assessed, smiling and taking a seat. Maybe the shopping thing wasn't going to work; Dierdre didn't look as if she knew much about fashionable boutiques.

Solange wasn't so sure this had been a good idea, but she was starving, and a glance around confirmed that the teas being served were generous and mouthwatering.

A waiter appeared and they ordered, and almost immediately a three-tiered plate came with an assortment of tiny sandwiches and luscious-looking iced cakes, accompanied by a large teapot.

They discussed the weather as Dierdre sipped her tea and nibbled at a scone and Solange ate her way through four little sandwiches, drank half a cup of tea generously diluted with cream, then sighed with satisfaction as she spooned clotted cream and strawberry preserves on a biscuit.

"I was famished. I'm not used to this idea of a full meal at noon and then just sandwiches later on. We do it the other way around at home."

"So I've heard. More tea?" Dierdre poured. "Tell me about Seattle, won't you? I've always dreamed of visiting the United States."

Solange did her best, describing the city, emphasizing the good malls and the boutiques where she loved to shop. "I work downtown, so it's easy to go shopping on my lunch hour," she explained.

"What do you do?"

"I'm a florist. I have my own little shop."

Dierdre's face lit up. "Oh, I so love flowers. If I didn't work for Wallace and Houmes, I'd love to be a florist. I dream of someday having a cottage somewhere where I can grow things." She looked wistful. "Do you like to garden?"

"It's my hobby," Solange said with enthusiasm. "Our house was built really close to the ocean, and the yard was originally rocky and sandy, but my grandmother was a good gardener and she began building up the soil. I've continued. I grow a few vegetables and lots of flowers. I learned a lot about gardening when I lived at the commune."

"Commune?"

"In New Mexico, with Miranda's father," Solange explained. "We lived there for twelve years, and grew most of our own food. Then John was killed, and I moved back to Seattle to live with my mother and grandmother. Miranda was only twelve, so moving home made sense." She hadn't wanted to stay at the commune because she absolutely hadn't wanted to be alone. Being alone was her worst nightmare.

"It must have been horrible, losing your husband like that."

"We weren't married. I've never been married. This'll be my first time." She held up her left hand so Dierdre could see her ring. "Better late than never."

"Quite." Dierdre nodded, then said, "How fortunate you were to have family to turn to when you needed them. My father died in the war. I never knew him. And my mother passed on just after I began working for Wallace and Houmes."

"When was that?" Solange was curious now. How many years had Dierdre been involved with Gabriel, anyhow?

"Fifteen years this August."

"And you've never been married, either?" Maybe, like Solange herself, Dierdre had never wanted to be.

"No." Dierdre shook her head. "I always dreamed of marrying and having children, but it didn't work out that way."

So she'd fallen for Gabriel and waited for him too long, Solange deduced. Some women just didn't know how to handle men. You couldn't ever let them feel you were sitting around waiting for them.

"Well, after Miranda I never wanted any more kids. And I've had plenty of relationships over the years, but I never wanted to marry until Leon came along," Solange commented.

"What was different about him?"

Solange hadn't really asked herself that. She'd only thought about what was different about *her,* how all of a sudden getting married felt like what she wanted to do. For some reason, Dierdre's question made her uncomfortable.

"Oh, Leon's fun. He makes me laugh," she said in an airy tone. "He's good-looking—I like a good-looking man. He's generous—so many guys are tight with money." She frowned, groping for reasons. "He's good in bed," she added, wanting to shock Dierdre, but the other woman simply nodded.

"That's important," Dierdre said matter-of-factly, taking a bite of a chocolate wafer. "One reads so many stories about men who are hopeless in that area."

For a moment, Solange felt a pang of regret over Gabriel. He must be fairly good at it if Dierdre considered it important. But then, maybe she didn't have anything to compare him with.

"Leon's also reliable," she went on. "I've never had to worry about him with other women. So many men…" Too late, she realized this wasn't something she ought to have brought up.

"Yes." Dierdre stared her straight in the eye. "Having the person you care for take someone else to lunch is very painful," she said quietly.

CHAPTER FIFTEEN

THE MUTED SOUND of voices and the clinking of teacups went on all around them, but at their table there was total silence. It lasted until Solange blew out the breath she'd been holding. "So you were aware all along."

Dierdre nodded. "I know Gabriel very well. It's not difficult to tell when he's trying to hide something."

"It didn't amount to anything." Solange hated feeling defensive. She cursed herself for calling Dierdre in the first place. Thankfully, the other woman didn't appear to be having hysterics.

"That doesn't really matter, does it?" Dierdre's gray eyes were sad instead of angry. "The fact is, he wanted you. I can understand, because you are quite beautiful." Her chin trembled, but she controlled it. "And exciting. I suppose I'm a fairly dull person."

"Don't say that." Solange was totally unaccustomed to feeling sorry for her actions, but she felt that way now. In spite of herself, she'd started to like Dierdre Payne. So she was a little dull; for sure, Gabriel was no ball of fire. "Has he done this before? Taken someone else out?"

"Once. Two years ago. He never mentioned it and neither did I."

"Well, you and I are different that way," Solange said. "I'd have had such a fit he'd never have dared try it again." She thought for a moment. "Actually, I wouldn't have stuck around."

"You'd have walked out on a long relationship? On the basis of a single mistake?" Dierdre was astounded.

Solange considered pointing out that the mistakes had now doubled but thought better of it. "Look, Dierdre, men are wired differently from women." She reflected a moment. Putting her philosophy into words was really hard because it was second nature to her, something she was born knowing and didn't even think about most of the time.

"Men want a challenge. They want to have to struggle to get the prize. That makes it worth something to them. If something comes too easily, they don't value it the same as they would if they had to really fight to get whatever it is they want."

Dierdre's forehead creased into a frown. "You're saying Gabriel takes me for granted."

Solange nodded. "You've never given him any reason to doubt that you'd always be there for him, right?"

"Of course not. I *do* love him very much." Her eyes filled with tears. "Much more than he loves me, I'm afraid. I simply could never hurt him this way. It's agony."

Solange felt terrible. She'd never deliberately played around with someone else's husband; the few times a man had two-timed her, she'd washed her hands of him and moved on, viewing him as the loser. She'd always seen a relationship with a man as a kind of game, but she could understand that this Gabriel thing was almost life and death to Dierdre. She racked her brain for a way to help; obviously raking Gabriel over the coals wasn't something Dierdre could do.

"Look, why don't you take a holiday? Give him a chance to miss you for a while." She considered the idea that had sprung to mind. She wasn't exactly dying to spend more time with Dierdre, but Gabriel deserved a lesson, and the thought of his shock and surprise gave Solange a wicked feeling of pleasure. What the heck. The house was big enough, and she wouldn't be around all that much—she never was. Miranda and Pearl probably wouldn't mind. Even if they did, it wouldn't be forever, would it?

"Why not come over and visit us. There's plenty of room, and you could help me with the garden."

"That's very kind. Thank you." Dierdre didn't sound as if it were something she was liable to do, though.

Well, it was up to her. Solange had done the best she could. "Let's go shopping." Buying something always made her feel better, and she was a little down. "Where's this place I read about, where Princess Di used to shop?"

"That would be King's Road, in Chelsea. Sloane Square."

"Let's go." Solange took the bill and headed for the cashier.

MIRANDA PROPPED her head on her arm, and in the dim light that seeped from the bathroom, she watched Joe sleeping, memorizing every detail of his face. His nose had a slight bump halfway down, and she wondered if it had been broken. His lashes were short and thick, his cheekbones well defined. He had a tiny scar near one eyelid. A damp lock of wheat-colored hair hung down over his forehead, and she resisted the urge to stroke it back.

One well-muscled arm was under the pillow, the other draped across the sheet that covered her waist. It also partially covered him, carelessly hooked across his hips. His chest, with its mat of golden curls, was bare, and she thought of how that rough mat felt, pressed against the softness of her breasts.

She remembered reading somewhere that the Inuit phrase for making love translated into "laughing together," and she smiled. It was a perfect description of how her body felt after Joe loved her, as though every cell was joyful.

Did a woman get pregnant more easily if her body came alive to her lover's slightest touch?

In some secret place inside her, was a sperm penetrating an egg at this very moment?

On the dresser were the sheets of paper Joe had brought along, spelling out the details of exactly what would occur between them should that happen.

They'd marry. And after the baby came, they'd divorce.

She felt a tightness in her chest, thinking of that.

The child would bear both their names, Irving-Wallace.

Joe would assume full financial responsibility for all its needs, and for Miranda's, as well, should she choose to be a full-time mother. Custody would be shared equally, but Joe had agreed that during the school term, the child would stay with Miranda, and come to him during long holidays and the summer months. Miranda was invited to come, also should she choose. During the first years of the child's life, it was preferable that she accompany it.

There was more, much more, covering every conceivable situation. Joe was a lawyer; he was thorough, and he was more than fair. She knew right now, in the beginning, exactly how it would be between them. They'd maintain a cordial friendship, united in their concern for their child, free to live their lives the way they wished.

She'd agreed to everything. There were four more nights to spend here in Joe's arms. She vowed to live entirely in the moment, not thinking beyond now.

I love you, Joseph Wallace. The words were silent, a cry from her heart to his, a total betrayal of their agreement. She knew that she could never say them aloud; she'd already learned to choke them back in that moment after orgasm when she looked into his eyes and recognized his soul.

He was taking Thursday and Friday off just to be with her. They were going to spend a lot of time making love, but he'd also promised to show her London, the tourist haunts as well as places only Londoners frequented. She'd photograph them all, she decided, and put them in an album, ostensibly for Gram but also, if she was lucky, for their child someday. She'd show them the way Gram had shown her the yellowed old photos of Bethel Farm and the two treasured snapshots of her and Jacques Desjardins. *This is where we met. This is what he looked like when we were young.*

Sunday, she and Joe would drive out to Bethel Farm and collect Gram, and Tuesday…oh, Tuesday would be hard, saying goodbye, boarding the plane, flying home.

Leaving Joe would be agony, but at least Pearl would be there. She'd be able to tell Gram everything, confess her love for Joe, confide the details of the agreement and the fact that she'd fallen in love with a man who didn't believe in love.

Gram would help her through, whatever happened. Miranda had phoned Pearl twice, but the conversations had been difficult because of Pearl's hearing loss. Gram had done most of the talking, sounding excited about the articles Elizabeth was writing about her.

"Penny for your thoughts." Joe's arm tightened around her, drawing her against him.

"I was thinking of Gram. And thinking about that restaurant where you took me to for dinner," she improvised. "That was the best vegetarian meal I've ever had."

"Leave it to Larry," Joe snorted. "He actually gave me a written list as long as my arm of places to take you, every single one vegetarian. I think old Larry's fallen in love with you."

Why Larry? Why not you, Joe?

But the words she dared not speak were slowly buried beneath sensation as he stroked a palm down her side, detouring to cup a breast and tease the nipple with his thumb. His lips touched her shoulder, and he turned her toward him.

"Come here, my lovely." His voice rumbled in her ear. "Enough of this lolling about dreaming about food. We have work to do."

"BUT SWEETIE, of course we want to come with you. Joe doesn't mind. He can borrow his father's big car. There's plenty of room for all of us."

Too late, Miranda realized she shouldn't have mentioned that she and Joe were driving out to pick up Gram the following morning. But ever since that first disastrous night, she'd made a point of telling her mother when she was going to be absent.

She'd hardly seen Solange since Leon had arrived, and Miranda had to admit that for the first time ever, she was grateful to Baillie. If he hadn't been on the scene, Miranda would have felt guilty leaving Solange so much on her own.

"Leon wants to see the farm, and he hasn't even met Joe yet. You do keep him all to yourself these days. And I thought we could stop in one of those quaint little villages for lunch. I want to see if they have any hand-knit sweaters for sale. A woman who was getting her nails done at the same time I was told me she found the sweater she was wearing at a farmer's market in some little village. For hardly any money."

Feeling miserable, Miranda related the conversation to Joe as they drove to dinner at yet another of Larry's choices.

"Of course they should come along," said Joe. "If I weren't so depleted, I'd have thought of it myself. I'll switch cars with Dad for the day. He quite likes to bomb around in this." Joe took a corner at top speed and then accelerated past a police car. Miranda watched and waited, but nothing happened.

"Don't you ever get a speeding ticket?"

"Quite often, yes. I'm rather famous in traffic court because I contest the tickets on a regular basis. All the bailiffs know me by name." He spotted a parking place on the opposite side of the street and disrupted two lanes of traffic by steering straight across. "I'm rather looking forward to meeting this Reverend Baillie of yours."

"He's definitely not 'mine.'" Miranda had told him how much she disliked Leon. "After a few hours trapped with him in a car, you'll wish you'd never said that."

Joe just laughed.

IT WAS AFTER THREE by the time they finally arrived at Bethel Farm, and Miranda could tell by the set of Joe's mouth that he'd had more than enough of both her mother and Leon Baillie.

Before they'd even left London, Leon had asked Joe's opinion on the forthcoming millennium, and then he'd preached what amounted to a fire-and-brimstone sermon on his version of the cataclysmic changes the world would undergo once 2000 arrived.

Even Solange grew weary at last of his rhetoric.

"For heaven's sake, Leon, enough with the doom and gloom," she'd snapped. "Nineteen hundred came and went without the world ending. The same thing will happen with 2000."

Baillie was quiet for all of six minutes, and then he'd started a long harangue about British politics that really got under Joe's skin.

They'd stopped, at Solange's urging, in several villages, only to find all the shops closed because it was Sunday. By the time they neared Bethel Farm, she was sulking, Joe's jaw was clenched, and Leon was relating vivid descriptions of car wrecks he claimed to have investigated when he was in "the force," in what Miranda assumed was an effort at making Joe slow down. It had the opposite effect, and she felt limp with gratitude when at last they stopped safely, if abruptly, in the drive at Bethel Farm.

"You go in. I'll join you soon," Joe said, obviously relieved to get away. "I'm going around to the cottage to say hello to Elijah."

Miranda knocked and Elizabeth met them at the door.

"Is that them, finally?" Pearl came hurrying over to wrap her arms around Miranda first for a hard hug. "I've been expecting you for hours."

"Oh, Gram, it's so good to see you. I've missed you."

Solange bent to kiss her mother. "Don't believe

her, Mother,'' she said archly. ''I've hardly seen her all week. She and Joe have been inseparable.''

''Isn't that grand.'' Gram beamed at Miranda, but nothing more was said because Natalie arrived with the children just then. She'd picked them up from school, and they were excited at having company.

Leon was introduced to everyone, and Miranda felt grudging admiration at his easy way with the kids.

''Ronan is at the clinic. He'll be back at five for tea,'' Natalie said. ''You will stay, won't you?''

''Oh, yes, miss. Please stay,'' Lydia begged. ''You must come see how big the kittens have grown.''

Miranda smiled at her. ''I'd like that, but we probably should start back soon. We'll ask Joe.'' She knelt beside Daisy. ''Look what I have for you.'' From their protective envelope, Miranda slid out the photos she'd taken of the children in the hayloft. She'd matted the best of them, and she gave the children each a picture of themselves.

''Pearl told us you were an excellent photographer,'' Elizabeth said, admiring the photos. ''We wondered if you'd mind sending over copies of some of the photos of Pearl in her flying costume. It would add so much to the article.''

''Sure,'' Miranda agreed. ''We'll do it as soon as we get home. You can choose which ones you want to use, Gram.''

Natalie and Elizabeth exchanged glances, then both looked expectantly at Pearl.

''I have to talk to you about that, darling.'' Pearl

took Miranda's hand in hers and held it, and Miranda was surprised to feel a slight tremor in her grandmother's fingers.

"Talk to me about what?" Miranda stared at Gram, and a sense of foreboding made her heart race.

"You see, Elizabeth is helping me with my memoirs. Writing is something I've never attempted and always wanted to try. She's an excellent teacher. And I'm not getting any younger, so now's the time to do it."

Pearl tried to smile, but Miranda could see that it was a struggle for her to continue.

"I'm so very happy here, Miranda." It sounded almost like an apology, and there were tears in both her eyes and her voice. "I feel as if after all these years I've finally come home." Gram drew in a breath and then said in a rush, "Natalie and Elizabeth have invited me to stay, and I've accepted. What I'm trying to say, pumpkin, is I'm not coming back with you and Solange tomorrow. I've decided to remain here at Bethel Farm."

CHAPTER SIXTEEN

THE AIRLINE STAFF had collected the dinner trays some time ago, and now the lights in the aircraft were dimmed so passengers could sleep through the long night flight.

Miranda, in the aisle seat, kept her eyes closed and tried to ignore the monotonous sound of Leon's voice. He and Solange were bickering over something. He was by the window; Solange was in the middle where Gram should have been.

Miranda swallowed the choking lump in her throat. She couldn't let herself think about Gram right now. She couldn't let herself imagine what life was going to be like without Pearl to greet her every night after work, always ready to joke or listen to whatever Miranda needed to talk about. Being alone with Solange would be bad enough, but the addition of Baillie was going to be almost intolerable.

Something Joe mentioned had given her an idea, however. He'd been talking about the increasing number of women who had called Wallace and Houmes looking for a reliable investigator to determine whether the men they claimed to be in love with were actually all they purported to be.

"It's the new, fashionable trend in romance,"

he'd said. "I think women are clever to go that route, rather than find out after the fact that they're mixed up with someone unsavory." Eyes dancing, twirling an invisible mustache, he'd leered, "If you want a report on me, my beauty, just say the word. I have a fictional account of my background ready and waiting."

There must be investigators in Seattle. The moment she got back, Miranda was determined to call one and have Baillie exposed as the charlatan Gram had known him to be all along. Surely when Solange realized he was a total fraud she'd come to her senses and dump him.

Speaking of coming to one's senses, she herself had work to do in that area, Miranda knew. For her own sanity, she'd have to find a way to put Joe out of her mind. It had been five hours now since he'd kissed her goodbye at the airport, and every moment of those hours he'd dominated her thoughts.

She hadn't cried when they'd said goodbye, as she'd been afraid she might. She'd cried in the night, though, and he'd held her, mopped her face with his handkerchief, brought her a glass of water, rubbed her back. And she'd let him believe it was all because Gram wasn't coming home.

"I'll call you and I'll write," he'd murmured into her ear at the airport, holding her close for one last, long, poignant moment. "You do the same, Miranda."

She'd nodded, promised, tried to ignore the sudden mad urge to refuse to board the plane. Instead, she'd even managed a small smile. "Give my love to Larry,'' she'd said before her throat closed up too much to talk.

She'd waved nonchalantly and walked away, then turned as she passed through the security check, searching for a last desperate glimpse of him, but he'd already disappeared in the crowd.

Now she cupped her hands over the seat belt that looped across her belly. Was his child growing inside?

There was nothing to do but wait. It was almost mid-April. The next few weeks would determine whether she and Joe Wallace had any sort of a future together.

And knowing would make it easier, she told herself, recognizing the irony of it all. At least she'd understand whether she had to give Joe up now, or do it later.

''TELEPHONE, SIR.'' Larry held out the receiver, and Joe grabbed it.

''Hello, Miranda?''

She'd been home for a day and a half by now; she'd have gotten the playful message he'd left on her machine in Seattle. He'd dialed her home number a few hours after he'd taken her to the airport. Welcoming her home was the polite thing to do, he'd told himself. He'd listened to her quiet voice on the tape and then said officiously, ''Telegram of utmost importance for Ms. Miranda Irving. Welcome home, stop. Hope you had a pleasant flight, stop. Hope our plans progress in the exact manner we anticipate, stop. Looking forward to hearing from you soonest, stop. Fondest regards, with no stop in sight. Your English connection.''

'''Hello, Miranda'? You answer all your calls that way, and you'll get yourself in trouble, my friend,'' Tony teased. ''Where have you been, sport? I've left messages at the office and with Larry.''

''Sorry.'' Joe felt a bit flat. He had expected Miranda on the line. ''How are you, Tony? How's Kitty?''

''Same as ever—driving me berserk. Look, Joe, that's why I've been calling. Kitty's cousin is here visiting. I know how you hate blind dates, but believe me, you'll like this one. Name is Beatrice, marvelous anatomical specimen, face to match. Blond hair, skin like a baby's bottom, smart and funny, in advertising. How about it? Dinner tomorrow night?''

Joe hesitated. He'd been feeling kind of low ever since Miranda had left, which probably had to do with physical exhaustion. He might need some vitamins. Was there an Olympic record for achievement when it came to sex? If so, he and she both probably qualified.

Maybe this was just what he needed. After all, he was as free as ever to see other people if he chose. And so was she. That thought made him uncomfortable for a moment, until he remembered that by her own admission she didn't date.

''Sounds good, Tony. Beatrice, you said? Beatrice who? Smith? Well, that's simple enough. Beatrice Smith.''

They confirmed time and place, and after a few moments of banter, Joe hung up.

"Pardon me for pointing this out, but you're a bloody fool, Joseph." Larry's face was a thundercloud, and he was smashing china dishes into the cupboard as if they were unbreakable.

Joe gaped at him. "What the hell brought this on?"

"Far be it from me to interfere in your affairs, but what about Miranda?"

"What about her?" And why in hell should he suddenly feel like a bigamist? "We're good friends. We had a good time together. She's gone back to Seattle."

"I assumed you had the sense to recognize quality when you found it, but obviously I was wrong." Larry slammed the cupboard shut. "You're going to come a-cropper one fine day, you mark my words." He turned on his heel and marched out.

Shocked, Joe stared after him. "Male menopause," he muttered. "Imbalance of testosterone." He ought to feel insulted. Larry had no business listening to his phone calls. He tried for righteous indignation, but that didn't happen, either. What he did feel was an emotion that some buried part of him knew well as guilt, but he refused to acknowledge it.

He really didn't feel well. Maybe he was more exhausted than he realized. He'd better have an early night.

IT WAS STILL LIGHT; each May day brought more and more daylight and sunshine. Miranda had been back at work three weeks, and coming home was something she dreaded more every day.

She stopped at the top of the drive and hopped out of the Jeep to get the mail, glancing at her watch. Half past seven.

She'd stayed at school long after the kids had left. She'd lingered over a veggie burger at a fast-food place. She'd wandered around downtown, planning to see a movie, but there was nothing on she could bear sitting through. At last she'd dashed into a pharmacy and then driven home.

Her heart sank when she saw Leon's van at the bottom of the drive, parked—as usual—in the spot she preferred. Although he hadn't formally moved in with Solange, he'd been here more days than not since the trip to England.

She just knew he'd be sitting in Gram's recliner right now as if he owned it, reading the newspaper, commenting on every event, scattering the pages around the chair without a thought to the fact that the paper was Miranda's and she liked to read it when she came home. Solange would be sprawled on the sofa, poring over some horticultural magazine, seemingly deaf to Baillie's voice.

He'd greet Miranda in that booming pastoral voice of his and make some stupid joke that she didn't find funny. The kitchen would be a disaster; as usual, Solange would have made something from an instant mix and burned six pots in the process.

Miranda would make a cup of tea, take it up to her room, shut the door and stay there until they either went out for the evening or went to bed, at which time she'd go down and turn on the television to avoid hearing the sounds that came from Solange's bedroom.

She had become a prisoner in her own home.

She flipped through the mail, looking for an envelope with an English postmark, feeling let down when it wasn't there. Gram had written three times, but Miranda had had only one letter from Joe, and it had been so cheerful and impersonal that she'd wanted to rip it up and send the pieces back to him.

Today there was a thick envelope, however, addressed to her and marked Private and Personal, and her heart skipped a beat. *Access Investigations*. She'd been waiting to hear from them. She tore the envelope open, rapidly skimming the contents of the three pages.

Her heart began to hammer and she flipped back to the beginning, unable to believe what she was reading. Beside a precise list of dates, the report said:

Mr. Baillie was a member in good standing of the Canadian RCMP Auxiliary for a period of four years…
Mr. Baillie received an honorary medal for assisting in the release of a hostage…
Mr. Baillie has been married only once, for fifteen years. His wife is deceased…
Mr. Baillie won two million dollars in the B.C. Lottery…
Mr. Baillie became a licensed layman preacher

for the Seattle Chapel of Happiness...

The only thing he'd lied about was his age. Leon Baillie was actually sixty-seven years old, not the sixty-one he'd claimed.

It had cost Miranda several thousand dollars to learn that Leon Baillie was pretty much an honest man, if an old one. With trembling fingers and a sick feeling in her stomach, she refolded the report and slid it back into the envelope. It marked the end of the faint hope she'd harbored.

Oh, Gram, you were wrong. Oh, Gram, what am I going to do now?

If Pearl had been here, the two of them might have laughed at themselves for being so suspicious. But Gram wasn't here, and the last thing Miranda felt like doing was laughing. Now there was no ammunition that might convince Solange not to marry Leon Baillie. There was no reason for her *not* to marry him. He was exactly what he claimed he was, and what Solange believed him to be. And she loved him.

Miranda sat in the Jeep, motor idling, stomach tense, and thought about her options. She didn't have many; she could live here with the two of them or she could move out.

She released the brake, put the Jeep in gear and drove slowly down the hill.

There really wasn't any choice. She'd begin looking for an apartment tomorrow. She glanced at the bag from the pharmacy. It contained a kit that would tell her whether she was pregnant, but there wasn't

any point using it; she'd felt all day that her period
was imminent. She was only about a week late. She
couldn't bring herself even to hope. Nothing else in
her life was working. Why should that?

IN THE BATHROOM three mornings later, Miranda
stared at the tiny stick and, for the fifth time, read
the kit's instructions. Blue, pregnant. Pink, not. She
read it again, this time taking her glasses off to make
sure she was seeing right. She was trembling.

Definitely blue.

"Miranda? Sweetie, I need to get in there." Solange's peevish voice was accompanied by urgent
knocking. "Leon's in the other one. Why can't we
have more than two bathrooms in this gigantic
house?"

Hastily Miranda shoved the empty box and the
other paraphernalia in the cabinet and, in a daze,
opened the door.

Solange, a smoky gray satin negligee clutched
around her, hurried in, and Miranda floated past her
and into her bedroom, impervious for once to the
muted sounds of Leon belting out a hymn in the
shower down the hall.

She sank onto the bed and drew her knees up to
her chest. *I, Miranda Jane Irving, am pregnant. I'm
going to have a baby, Joe's baby.* They'd get married. For a period of time, she'd be Mrs. Joseph
Wallace. Then...

She refused to let any dismal thoughts mar this
miracle. *April, May, June, July...*she counted on her

fingers. *December? January?* She couldn't figure it out. She'd have to go to a doctor. It would be close.

She crossed her hands on her chest, just above her heart. Oh, Gram. Oh, dearest Gram. If only this happens in time to keep Bethel Farm in the family for you. She picked up the telephone on her night table and set it down again. What time was it in England?

But it was too soon to tell Gram. If something should happen, if—she wouldn't think of that. She'd just wait a few weeks.

Joe. Would he be at work? She tried to figure it out and couldn't, and then all of a sudden made up her mind that she wasn't going to tell him, either, not just yet. She was going to carry the news around with her, her special, private, stupendous secret. She was going to savor it, treasure it, bask in it, get thoroughly used to the whole magnificent idea before she told a living soul.

"Miranda?" Solange didn't bother to knock. She barged right in, holding out the empty box from the pregnancy kit.

CHAPTER SEVENTEEN

"SWEETIE PIE, are you or aren't you?" Solange waved the box like a trophy.

Like boiling water on softest wool, all Miranda's pleasure and excitement shrank into a hard tight knot. Solange was the last person she'd have considered confiding in.

"I am, but it's very early," she managed. "I really didn't want anyone to know."

"Except me." Solange plunked herself down on the bed beside Miranda and put an arm around her shoulders.

"Now, are you happy about this or not?"

"I'm as happy as I've ever been in my life." And with that admission, talking about it came easier, even talking to Solange. Talking suddenly made it more real. "I'm thrilled. But I'm also scared."

"Of what?"

"Of…I guess I'm afraid it's too good to be true," she blurted. "That—that something'll happen."

"That you'll miscarry the way I did with your brothers?" Solange had never talked with Miranda about the other two pregnancies she'd had. "Don't give it another thought, sweetie. We're not built the same at all, and I've never heard that a thing like that's inherited.''

It was comforting to hear, whether or not it was accurate. The tension in her body eased a little.

''It's Joe's?''

Miranda nodded.

''Are you gonna tell him?''

''Yes.'' She should tell him right away, she decided. It was his child, too, and whatever happened, he had a right to know from the very beginning.

Typically, Solange didn't ask the logical question about marriage. ''My God, imagine me as a grandmother.'' Solange shuddered dramatically, but Miranda could tell she was teasing. ''I hope it's a girl. There're such cute outfits for girls.''

Miranda smiled, because Solange was Solange. She babbled on. ''Mother's going to be ecstatic at the thought of a great-grandchild.'' A new thought struck her. ''And if the baby decides to come in time, the trust goes on. Bethel Farm stays in the family.'' She sighed. ''Well, there goes my wedding cruise. I was hoping you'd splurge on one with some of the money from the sale.'' She laughed at the look on Miranda's face.

''Just kidding, sweetie.''

''Leon might not think it's so funny.'' Miranda found herself able to joke a little about him. She was too happy to feel resentful of anyone just now.

''Oh, damn, I forgot. That's what I wanted to tell you. The wedding's off.''

Was she dreaming? Miranda wondered. She must

have missed something, misunderstood. "The wedding's off?"

"Yup. We're not getting married."

"But—but I thought...I mean, he's here all the time. I thought you two were happy. You've got your dress. You've made plans..." Suddenly shame filled her. She should never have had Leon investigated. It was wrong to meddle in someone else's life.

"That's what did it, I guess." Solange sighed. "Having him here all the time. I'm not used to a man being around constantly. There's no time when I can just be *me*. I don't want to always have to think about shaving my legs or looking good in the morning. And he's always *wanting* something— food or attention or the bathroom. It's always something."

Miranda noted that the engagement ring was still on Solange's hand. "How did he take it?"

"Oh, he doesn't know yet. I'm waiting for the right time to tell him. It's sort of tricky. I want to go on seeing him. And I really want to keep the ring. In my own way, I do love him."

"But not enough to marry him?"

Solange laughed softly. "Oh, sweetie, that's got nothing to do with love. I just lost my head for a while there and thought that I'd better make sure there'd be somebody around to take care of me when I got old. But the price is too high. I figure some women are cut out for marriage and others aren't. Obviously, the Irving women aren't."

"I am." The words slipped out easily, just as if

she were in the habit of confiding in Solange. "I want to marry Joe."

"God, sweetie, you didn't tell him that, did you?"

Miranda shook her head. "It was his idea." It was, but there were other things about it she couldn't say, however open the channels suddenly were with Solange.

"Thank *goodness* for that. Well, make sure he thinks getting you is the greatest honor and privilege of his entire life, because it is." She rumpled Miranda's hair. "You're the best, kid. He's getting the best. You're my daughter, aren't you?"

The declaration, even with the last bit, was astounding. Miranda burst into tears.

"THERE'S A TRANSATLANTIC CALL for you, Joseph." Larry was just outside the shower stall.

"I'll be there directly." Joe shut off the water and reached for a towel. Thrusting his arms through the sleeves of his robe, he trotted into his bedroom and picked up the extension.

"...and a touch of balsamic vinegar in the lentils, Miranda," Larry was saying in a sappy voice. "Simmer for an hour."

"Hello, Miranda?" Joe waited until he heard the kitchen extension click. "I'm very glad you called. I've been thinking of you." It was the truth; since the Beatrice fiasco, he'd tried his damnedest to figure out why the thought of Miranda should utterly ruin his enjoyment of other women.

He'd been celibate since he had been with her,

which was really beginning to worry him. He'd ignored Beatrice's blatant signals, which resulted in Tony cross-examining him about his mental health.

"I'm well, thank you." He drew a deep breath. "And you? How are you, Miranda?"

He listened, and his heartbeat accelerated. "You did? It was? You *are?*" He suddenly felt it necessary to sit down. "That's amazing. That's phenomenal. I can hardly believe it." Perspiration burst out on his forehead and he swiped at it with the sleeve of the robe.

"Forgive me for being so tongue-tied, my dear. This is wonderful. I can't begin to tell you how happy I am." He was; it was just going to take some getting used to, this idea of being a prospective father.

His mind was racing ahead. "We'll get married as soon as possible, of course. You did have your attorney read over the agreement?" He listened and nodded. "Well done. So we'll proceed with the wedding when the school term ends, late June. Would you rather I came there, or…?" He listened again. "Of course Pearl must be present. I think Bethel Farm is a good choice of locale—a small civil ceremony, justice of the peace, the two of us, close family, witnesses. By all means. Under the circumstances we don't want to turn it into more than a legality. I'll handle the arrangements and keep them simple. No, no, of course I don't mind. It's the least I can do."

He'd made the right choice in women, he congratulated himself. Miranda was eminently sensible.

"Take good care of yourself. You're not ill, are you? Good, good. Is there anything you need, anything at all? All right, then. Thank you for everything. I'm, I'm...I'm so grateful." That wasn't exactly the right comment, but he couldn't think what was.

Slowly he hung up the receiver, staring into space for a moment. Strange, how one could think an idea through with total rationality, and then when it actually transpired, feel such absolute awe.

Suddenly he couldn't keep from smiling. He had to tell someone. Everyone. He got to his feet and headed for the stairs.

Gabriel was at the dining table, eating his eggs and bacon, reading the *Times*. Larry was refilling his coffee cup.

"Miranda's pregnant," Joe announced. "We're getting married in June."

He should have enjoyed the way his father's knife and fork clattered to the floor, the way the coffee overflowed the cup and ran across the white linen tablecloth.

He would have, if he hadn't had to struggle with all his might against the silly tears that closed his throat and threatened to overflow if he so much as blinked.

THE LETTER sat on the floor where she had dropped it:

June 17/99
My dear Miranda,
So sorry to hear you're feeling poorly. I asked Tony if it was usual to go through weeks top-

notch and then become ill, and he assured me it happens regularly. Ditto being sick at night instead of in the morning. Not much consolation, I'm sure, when you're falling asleep at your desk and upchucking half the night, but at least it's good to know it's quite normal. He said to try Sea-Bands. Apparently they help some of his pregnant ladies.

Everything here is completely *abnormal;* this whole wedding thing has gotten totally out of hand. Larry's insisting on a formal dinner party the night you arrive, and sends his fondest greetings. He says his mother believed that if a woman is ill, it means the baby will be hale and hearty.

Tony's having some sort of stag for me this Friday. Dad's inviting ten of his business associates (with spouses) to the wedding. Natalie called to say that the vicar, Mr. Cavendish (who's a close friend of Elijah's), will be suicidal if he can't perform the ceremony, and she asked whether it's all right if the children are attendants. There's some huge issue about the wedding bouquet. Apparently Dierdre phoned Solange to clarify (Dad turned purple when I mentioned this, I might add). Things are very polite and cool between him and Dierdre these days, but in spite of that, she's taking an avid interest in this entire fiasco, to the point where I've totally lost control.

Miranda, I humbly apologize for all this. I tried to keep the entire wedding as minimalist as possible, as we planned, but it simply took on a life of its own. We should have agreed on an elopement.

I drove out to the farm last Saturday to double-check on your grandmother. Ronan assured me, as he did you, that she's well on the way to recovery, and she looked the same as ever, sprightly and full of life. There is a slight problem with her heart. He wants her to see a specialist in London, but as you know, she refuses. She also absolutely doesn't accept the baby's estimated arrival date of 15 January. Disappointing for her, I'm sure, as it must be for you, to miss the deadline. Ronan, on the other hand, did his best not to reveal his relief at the news that the baby won't arrive on time. He really does want in the worst way to purchase the farm. His offer, as you know, is substantially lower than that put forward by International Harvester. I understand Pearl's wish that the farm continue the way it always has, but do give due consideration to finance. You must give Harvester a definite commitment by end of August if you decide to take that route.

Tony did suggest vitamins. Are you taking any?

Glad the airline tickets arrived safely.

Do take care. I'll be eagerly waiting at the meeting point at Gatwick, but will likely speak to you before then.

Fondly,
Joe

"Soda crackers used to help me, but that was because I only got sick in the morning," Solange said chattily. "You'd chew on them before you lifted your head from the pillow."

Her voice seemed to come from far away. Miranda knelt on the tiles, head over the toilet bowl, waiting for the next bout of nausea.

It began every day about two in the afternoon and became progressively worse as the hours dragged on. By midnight she actually wondered if she'd live through the night, only to fall sound asleep around one and wake the next morning feeling groggy and frantically hungry.

"Sweetie pie, you'd better hand me those new glasses. We don't want them to fall in the toilet. I think they suit you better than any you've ever had. That rectangular shape draws attention to your eyes much more than the old ones did. Too bad you can't wear contacts. You've got great eyes. But never mind. You're gonna look fantastic. The dress is a stunner. And it's a blessing you're not showing at all yet. I always said when I was pregnant that if I could just keep the boobs and lose the belly, I'd be perfect...."

Solange, please shut up and go away. Miranda felt another bout coming on, and she preferred to heave in private.

Solange didn't budge. "I'm so glad the suit I got to get married in isn't being wasted. It's perfect for your wedding. Y'know, I sort of wish Leon would quit sulking and come over to England, too. He could even do the honors. He's a minister."

Now, that was the perfect way to make a bad situation disastrous. Miranda felt like moaning.

"But he won't. I asked him a week ago. I haven't heard from him since, so I guess that's that. Some men are really selfish. If they can't have what they want, they don't want anything. Is that a love letter from Joe?"

Miranda managed to nod. Why did Solange insist on having these conversations in the bathroom? "Gram's better, but she won't go to the heart specialist," she managed to blurt out.

"You can probably talk her into it when we get there. She'll listen to you. Did Joe say anything about the herbs Dierdre's gonna find us for your bouquet? Herbal bouquets are very in right now. They were popular in the Middle Ages. Each herb had a different meaning—lavender for tranquillity, rosemary for love and faithfulness. Did you know that, sweetie?"

Miranda shook her head and then moaned. The motion made her stomach churn all over again.

"I'll go make you some ginger tea. Ginger's for calming and settling the stomach."

Solange was finally gone. Miranda leaned back against the wall. She felt empty, dizzy, disheartened. She was getting married in six days, and there was a very good chance she'd disgrace herself during the ceremony by vomiting all over Joe's shoes. She was terribly worried about Gram; ten days ago she'd had what everyone said was a very slight heart attack. And the closer the wedding came, the more Miranda thought about what a sham the whole event was going to be.

She and Joe were deliberately deceiving everyone, and she hated it. She picked up his letter from the floor and reread it, wanting to tear it up and flush it down the toilet. *Fondly,* he'd signed it. Would it kill him to show a tiny morsel of affection for her? The nights and days they'd spent in each other's arms were as vivid to her as the checkered wallpaper she was staring at. She could remember exactly how he smelled, tasted, felt. She knew the shape of his hands, the way his toenails grew, the V-shaped scar on his back just above his buttocks where he'd slipped while rock climbing.

Fondly. She threw the letter to the side and lurched over to the toilet again as a fresh wave of sickness rolled over and through her.

As for Tony and his Sea-Bands, he and Joe could put them around their necks and choke themselves for all she cared. As if bands on her wrists would do a darn thing for this upheaval in her stomach. Neither Joe nor Tony had ever been pregnant, and neither ever would be, which at this precise moment seemed to Miranda the most unfair situation in the universe. She imagined herself in a pretty dress, standing beside Joe, making promises neither intended to keep.

No wonder she couldn't stop barfing.

"'DEARLY BELOVED, we are gathered here today...'"

The trembling voice of the ancient vicar competed with the sound of sheep from the nearby paddock, the buzzing of honeybees from Elijah's hives and a few discreet sobs from Solange.

Pearl, on the other hand, was beaming, sitting in the place of honor in the front row of chairs. She was wearing the dress Solange had brought for her, a navy-blue shot-silk shirtwaist, and a straw hat with silk roses. She looked frail, but she certainly didn't seem ill, which comforted Miranda.

The sky was a canopy of blue, and the late-June sun shone down on the wedding guests like a benediction. The heavy scent of honeysuckle combined with the perfume of the roses that climbed up and over the arbor.

"'To have and to hold from this day forward...'"

Miranda could feel the heels of her new butter-colored sandals slowly sinking into the soft grass of the garden.

Ronan had asked for the privilege of walking her from the door of the house over to the vicar, and Miranda, thinking of her own father, so long dead, had felt a stab of loss that brought tears to her eyes. But she'd been grateful for the support of Ronan's strong steady arm under her own.

During her stay at Bethel Farm, Pearl had grown very fond of him. She'd confided to Miranda that morning that she wished Solange could have fallen in love with someone like him instead of Leon. Natalie was a lucky woman, Gram pronounced.

"'For better, for worse, for richer, for poorer...'"

The one consolation Miranda had was knowing

she looked as good as she ever had in her life. Her dress was bias-cut, soft and sexy, three close-fitting gossamer layers of opalescent pink, robin's-egg-blue and cream in sheer georgette, slipping softly over one another. Solange and Dierdre had woven tiny white elder flowers into her curls, and Elizabeth had done her makeup.

She was nervous. Was the vicar really taking a very long time with the ceremony, or was it only her imagination?

"'In sickness and in health...'"

On each wrist was a Sea-Band Joe had given her, hidden beneath bracelets of fresh honeysuckle the children had braided. The girls stood just behind her, beautiful in their pink ankle-length dresses.

It was three-fifteen in the afternoon, and for the first time in weeks, Miranda felt fine. She could only pray that whatever was keeping her from upchucking would keep working.

"'To love and to cherish until death us do part,'" Vicar Cavendish droned.

At her side, Joe was resplendent in a navy pin-striped suit. His thick hair gleamed in the sunlight; his profile was strong and handsome.

"'With this ring I thee wed...'"

Joe took her hand and gazed at her with such tenderness Miranda was certain that not one of the guests could have guessed this entire wedding was a well-staged farce.

CHAPTER EIGHTEEN

"'WHAT THEREFORE GOD hath joined together, let no man put asunder,'" Vicar Cavendish pronounced at long last.

Miranda had to keep reminding herself that Joe was simply fulfilling the terms of their contract with grace and charm, that undoubtedly he would be just as affable and conscientious when the time came to divorce.

"I now pronounce you husband and wife. Joseph, you may kiss the bride."

Her heart skipped a beat, and suddenly she was in his arms. The familiar scent of woodsy aftershave filled her nostrils, and his mouth on hers was familiar and sensual.

Miranda couldn't halt the rush of emotion that filled her. She was in love with this man, she was carrying his child and now she was his wife. No matter what the reasons, for this moment in time she was suddenly unbearably happy. The tears that came easily these days gathered in her eyes and rolled down her cheeks, and Joe gently released her, removed her glasses and proceeded to ruin her mascara with his handkerchief.

"You are wonderfully beautiful," he whispered, and then their guests surrounded them.

"Long life and happiness always, my dears." Pearl was the first to give them hugs. Behind her came Solange and Dierdre, dabbing at their eyes and smiling.

Natalie, Elizabeth. Tony, Kitty. A group of Gabriel's solicitor friends and their wives.

And Elijah, gnarled and grinning. "Two's better than one, I always say," he commented, shaking Joe's hand. "When you come to a fork in the road, you should take it." He stretched on tiptoe to give Miranda a peck on the cheek. His whiskers tickled. He smelled of bay rum and mothballs, and his lovely wrinkled face radiated goodwill. "You've got a fine laddie here, lass. And he's found himself a bonny bride."

"To Mr. and Mrs. Wallace." Ronan and Gabriel filled glasses with champagne, and everyone drank, even the children. Miranda was grateful for the ginger ale Larry poured for her.

Laughter, congratulations.

Miranda only half listened. She was wondering, as she had been for days, what Joe had planned for their wedding night; after all, she was pregnant now, so there was no further need to make love to her. But everyone naturally expected them to go off somewhere together.

If only... But she stopped herself. The rules had been clearly drawn; she had no reason for regrets.

"Miss, this is from us, for your wedding gift."

Daisy handed Miranda a basket with a half-grown kitten in it.

"It's named Felicity. Mummy said that was good for a wedding cat," Lydia reported. At that moment, the kitten leaped out of the basket and went pelting across the garden with the children in hot pursuit. They knocked into the vicar, sending his champagne glass flying and earning them a reprimand from Natalie, and for a while, controlled chaos reined.

Larry and Elizabeth were putting the finishing touches on the buffet supper, set up at the end of the garden, and soon everyone had a plate of food— vegetarian in Miranda's honor. She wasn't hungry, but neither was she nauseous, which amazed her.

The toasts began. First Gabriel. He started by glibly teasing his son and warmly welcoming his new daughter-in-law.

Dierdre watched him, standing beside Elijah, and for some reason Miranda watched Dierdre. She thought she recognized in Dierdre's expression the same hopeless longing and love she herself felt for Joe, and her heart went out to the kind woman who'd worked so hard to make this wedding day perfect.

"As a confirmed and crotchety bachelor, I have no words of wisdom to offer when it comes to matrimony," Gabriel concluded. "I have it on good authority, however, that it takes enormous quantities of love. It also takes dedication, hard work and honesty, as any successful partnership does. Joe, Miranda, I wish you the best and longest of partnerships. And I wish you happiness."

Miranda couldn't take her eyes off Dierdre. The other woman's face was now pale and set, although she joined in when everyone clapped.

Next, Ronan took his turn. He began with a twinkle in his eye and an exaggerated brogue. "There's nothin' as dear to an Irish heart as a weddin', unless it's a wake."

Everyone laughed.

"Bethel Farm has witnessed many of both, I'm certain, and God willin', there'll be many more," Ronan went on. "May this day mark the beginnin' of not only a lifetime together for Joseph and Miranda, but also a time of renewal for this beautiful bit of land that puts me in mind of my dear home in Ireland."

Solange looked at Miranda and rolled her eyes. It was plain that her feelings about Ronan hadn't changed; she really didn't like him.

The speech *was* a blatant appeal to her sympathy, Miranda knew, but when she looked at Pearl, she also knew that it would have to be Ronan who bought Bethel Farm.

Gram believed, in spite of what the doctor said, that the baby would arrive before the year ended and the farm would stay in the family. Miranda knew there was no chance of that; the doctor had been positive.

A sale to Ronan at least ensured the place would be loved, its original purpose perpetuated, its beauty retained. Money wasn't always the most important factor, Miranda reminded herself.

And it was good to feel that something positive

had resulted from this most difficult day, which seemed to be going on forever. The toasts ended, and by the time the cake was cut Miranda was exhausted. When on earth could she and Joe make their escape?

As if on cue, Joe came over at that moment. He took her hand, drew her to her feet and whispered in her ear, "I'm taking you away from all this, my dear, on my white charger. Where's your overnight bag?"

"Upstairs. I'll use the bathroom. I'll only be a few minutes."

Joe followed her inside and up the stairs, and when she came out of the bathroom, he was waiting, holding her suitcase.

As they walked down the corridor toward the stairwell, Miranda became aware of raised voices coming from the bedroom at the top of the stairs. Gabriel was standing half in and half out of the room, his back to them, and it was obviously Dierdre who was hollering at him.

"Gabriel Wallace, you are a chauvinist bastard." Dierdre's voice rang out, and Miranda stopped short and looked questioningly at Joe. To get down the stairs, they'd have to pass the doorway. He hesitated, as unsure as she was about what they should do.

"You're a great one to talk about love and honesty," Dierdre was going on. "I've waited for you to marry me for years and years, and you knew I was waiting, but you weren't honest enough to either dump me or marry me."

Joe put a finger to his lips and pulled Miranda back along the corridor and into a bedroom, drawing the door shut, but Dierdre's accusations still carried to them clearly.

"You never even wanted to admit to anyone we were lovers, Gabriel. You took out other—" her voice grew wobbly and shrill "—other women behind my back, thinking I didn't know. And you even stood out there today and told everyone you're a confirmed bachelor, when at least three times a week you stay with me at my flat, in my bed. Well, I'm resigning as your secretary, effective immediately, and I'm through wai-waiting for you."

"Dierdre, wait a moment, please, my dear..." Gabriel sounded shocked.

"I...am...not...your...*dear.*"

"Dierdre, please..."

There was the sound of a slight scuffle, and then high heels pounded down the steps. Gabriel cursed, long and passionately, and then there was silence.

Miranda looked at Joe, her cheeks hot with embarrassment. He met her eyes, and she could see by their expression that he was as uncomfortable as she was.

After a few moments, Joe opened the door and peered into the hall. "They've gone. Let's get out of here before there's a murder."

Outside, word spread that they were leaving, and everyone grouped around, insisting that Miranda throw her herbal bouquet. She stood at the end of the garden, turned her back and tossed it over her head.

Dierdre, standing at the very back of the gathering, somehow caught it, and everyone cheered, but she didn't smile. She stood staring down at the meaningful bouquet she and Solange had created, her face crimson. Then she looked straight at Gabriel, walked over to him and plopped the bouquet in his hand. Everyone laughed and cheered, thinking she was teasing him, but Miranda held her breath.

Gabriel appeared ready to have a stroke. Dierdre hurried into the house, and Gabriel dropped the bouquet he'd been holding as though it had scorched him. At last he cleared his throat and said in a determinedly cheerful voice, "Do we have any rice, Ronan? Natalie?"

Everyone grabbed handfuls and pelted Joe and Miranda as they ran for Joe's car.

Miranda awkwardly scrambled in and sank into the seat. They were both silent as Joe accelerated down the drive and turned onto the roadway.

After a moment, Joe whistled, a long, drawn-out, amazed exclamation. "I have to say, he richly deserved it, but by the time Dierdre was finished I actually felt sorry for the old man. She was pretty hard on him."

"Well, I didn't think so. I feel terrible for Dierdre. I think he deserved exactly what he got."

Joe grinned at her. "Are we going to have our first argument over my father?"

Miranda smiled and felt herself begin to relax. "Of course not. And you know I do like your father."

"That's good, because he's given us a down payment on a town house as a wedding gift, and I'd hate to have to hand it back just on principle." Joe said it as casually as if the gift were a tablecloth.

"A town house?" Her voice squeaked into the upper registers. "But Joe, that's terrible. How will he feel when the baby comes and we divorce? He'll feel we tricked it out of him."

"Nonsense. I'll simply give him back the down payment. It's past time I moved out. I'll stay there afterward. In the meantime, it gives us a place to stay where we don't have to pretend at being love-birds."

His words hurt. "Is that where we're going now?"

"If you agree, yes. We'll go somewhere wonderful first for dinner, if you like. There isn't much furniture in the place, I'm afraid. I thought we could shop tomorrow. I did have a bed and bedding delivered."

Miranda tensed. Here was the issue she'd thought about all day. He'd just said they wouldn't pretend to be lovebirds. Did that mean he wasn't going to sleep with her?

"We have to make some decisions, Miranda." At top speed, Joe pulled out to pass a row of traffic, then suddenly braked and settled back in line behind a truck traveling well under the speed limit. "Sorry, I forgot about the nipper. Won't happen again. Now, about this bed thing." His eyes flicked across to her and then quickly back to the road. "What do you think?"

He's nervous, Miranda realized with surprise. So

Joe had been thinking about what their relationship would be, just as she had. "What do I think about what?" Nervous or not, he was going to have to spell out what he meant.

"About sleeping with me. I know this isn't something we discussed, but I hadn't worked it out properly. However, we *are* married. And we were compatible in that area." His voice was gruff. "Remarkably, wonderfully so. Would you consider being together the way we were before, Miranda? Having a sexual relationship? It seems ridiculous to sneak around dating other people when there's really no good reason we shouldn't be intimate friends."

Had he been dating other people? She didn't really want to know. She didn't need any more heartache than she already had. More to the point, could she stand the pain that would await her when she spent nights with him and fell even more in love than she already was?

The alternative was to deny herself what she longed for. And how honest was that?

"I think you're right," she managed, surprised at the joy and naked relief on his face.

"Good. Great." He reached across and took her hand, linking his fingers with hers and giving them a squeeze. "I don't know if I've told you, but I love having sex with you, Miranda. You're a very sexy lady."

It wasn't exactly what she wanted to hear on her wedding night. She wanted words of love, not reassurances about her sexuality. But it was the unvarnished truth, and she told herself she should be grateful for it.

HOURS LATER, Joe listened to her steady breathing. His arm was asleep where her head rested, but he didn't want to move it. His other hand was splayed on her naked abdomen, and with a sense of awe he thought of his daughter in there, growing larger and stronger every day. It was hard to imagine, because as yet there was only the slightest suggestion of roundness.

Making love with Miranda had been every bit as good as he remembered. She'd made those soft little surprised sounds that grew more and more urgent. She'd clung to him as if he was all that mattered in the entire world, and she had this way of making him feel afterward, peaceful and contented and happy in a way he'd never felt before. There was a rightness to having sex with Miranda. There was no game playing with her, no suspicion that she was perhaps comparing him with her last lover or thinking of her next. And there were no nagging concerns, either, that she was going to declare that she loved him, that she couldn't live without him. She was the perfect lover, and now she was his wife.

That gave him the most peculiar feeling. He knew it was ridiculous, considering his age, but he somehow felt as if something within him had changed today, as if life were a different proposition than it had been until now. He'd gazed at her, standing beside him on the grass as old Cavendish stumbled his way through the service, and she'd looked downright beautiful in her own understated fashion. There'd actually been moments when he'd wished it were all more than just a business arrangement.

Get a grip, Wallace. Isn't this what you always said you wanted—a sensible mature relationship based on reason?

Isn't this the answer to the whole inheritance issue? When the child comes, you'll be free. You'll have fulfilled your duty, there'll be an heir to the Wallace name and fortune and you and Miranda can go your separate ways like intelligent, mature adults. With mutual respect and good memories of each other, which was exactly as it ought to be when they'd be sharing the upbringing of a child.

And soon, he assured himself as he carefully slid her head onto the pillow and rearranged their bodies so they fitted, front to back, the infatuation he felt for her would wear off. It was just the newness of everything that appealed to him so powerfully.

Solange was flying home in a week, but Miranda was staying in England for the summer. Ronan had made it plain that Pearl couldn't attempt the long flight back to Seattle until she was stronger, so Miranda was planning to spend a lot of time out at Bethel Farm with her. She and Pearl would fly home in early September. Miranda had decided to go on teaching until Christmas, and have the baby in Seattle, as he'd agreed in their legal arrangement.

That was fine with him, he assured himself. There'd be plenty of time this summer for the two of them to be together. And there'd be ample time for them to get bored and impatient with each other, too, so that when Miranda went back, it would be a welcome relief to them both to be apart.

But right at this moment, she was here in his arms, and it surprised him how very much he wanted her there.

CHAPTER NINETEEN

SOLANGE WAS SWEATING, and she hated to sweat. She was also trying to figure out what ever had possessed her to agree to come walking with Pearl.

It was frying-pan hot out here in the sun, although not as bad as it had been in London earlier that day in Dierdre's apartment, which wasn't air-conditioned. In the three days since the wedding, Dierdre had made Solange so comfortably welcome it almost compensated for the heat.

"I saw Jacques come walking down that road right over there, and something inside me just clicked into place, like the missing piece of a jigsaw puzzle," Pearl was saying. She'd been telling Solange the story of how she and Jacques had met for the past fifteen minutes, but Solange wasn't really listening. She'd heard it all a million times before. For some reason it didn't annoy her the way it usually did, though.

She let Pearl set the pace along the pathway. Her mother was leaning heavily on her cane, and her stertorous breathing was scary, as was the bluish cast to her lips. But Pearl was determined they take this walk, and there was no point protesting; she'd never paid the slightest bit of attention to Solange's opinions.

Dierdre did, though. She seemed to think Solange knew everything there was to know about men, and it was flattering. Solange had found Dierdre sobbing her heart out in the kitchen after Miranda and Joe made their getaway. It hadn't taken much prodding to uncover what had happened, and Dierdre had begged Solange to stay with her in her London apartment. Solange had gone, relieved to get away from the farm.

Every time she was around Ronan O'Donnell, her skin crawled. There was something about him that set her teeth on edge. She hoped that Natalie would come to her senses about him before she made the fatal mistake of marrying the man.

And she had to get Pearl to come to her senses and turn around before she dropped in her tracks.

"Don't you think we oughta go back, Mother? I've had enough of this fresh air and sunshine. I need a cold drink."

"Oh, phooey. A bit of exercise is good for you. I always said you don't walk enough, Solange. But I suppose if you're beat, we could turn around now." Pearl stopped often and pretended she was looking at the view, but Solange knew better. Pearl was tired. She'd lost the vibrant energy she always seemed to have, and it was troubling.

Solange almost wished she wasn't leaving the following day, but the reservations were made. She had her shop to run. Now that she'd given up on the idea of Leon supporting her in her old age, she figured maybe she'd better start paying more attention to the business. The girl she had in there didn't know a lisianthus from a carnation.

"Miranda's baby is the answer to my prayers. I did hate the very idea of selling this place," Pearl said.

Solange held her tongue. There was no point in trying to tell her mother the baby wouldn't arrive in time, when Pearl had made up her mind it would. Pearl would just have to face up to her disappointment later on.

"You and Dierdre seem to get along real well," Pearl remarked next. "I always said you needed to cultivate women friends, Solange. I used to have dozens of women friends, but when you live to my age, they all up and die on you."

Even her mother's criticisms weren't getting to her today as badly as they usually did. "Dierdre's okay. At least she's coming to her senses about Gabriel." She'd told Pearl what had happened. "At first I was kind of worried about bringing her back to Seattle with me, but with you and Miranda staying over here, it's a blessing. The last thing I want to do is rattle around in that big old house by myself." Solange shuddered. The prospect of being alone was almost enough to make her rethink the whole Leon business. Almost, but not quite.

"What's Dierdre going to do with herself while you're at work?"

Solange shrugged. It wasn't her problem. "Get a job, probably. She's a top-notch secretary. There're always temp places that need help. And she can work for me a couple of days a week if she wants. She likes flowers.''

Pearl nodded. ''Dierdre's a real English lady,'' she declared.

That was a scary thought, but Solange figured there was at least some hope of getting Dierdre over it. ''I'm really looking forward to you and Miranda coming home in September, Mother.'' She'd been surprised when Miranda had said she wanted to teach for the first half of the school year, but that was Miranda, loyal and conscientious to a fault.

Solange had moments when she hoped the girl knew what she was doing, leaving that handsome hunk of a man here by himself. But Miranda had indicated that she and Joe had come to some arrangement that suited them.

Pearl pursed her lips and shook her head. ''I don't think Miranda will be flying home in September, Solange. Anyone can see she's crazy in love with Joe. And she's promised me she'll have the baby here at Bethel Farm, just as I did.'' Pearl stopped again and leaned on her cane. ''I always said you wouldn't have had such trouble carrying if you'd been here, Solange. There's something healing and healthy about Bethel Farm. It was just a miracle that Miranda was born healthy out there in the desert, the way you were with that heathen lot.''

Solange bit her lip to hold back the sharp retort she always made to Pearl's oft-repeated superstition. The suggestion that it had been her fault she'd miscarried drove her nuts, hurt her. But Pearl had always been oblivious to how she felt, Solange remembered.

"It's very important that this baby's born here. She's the start of a whole new generation of Irving women, and she'll be the one who decides once and for all what happens to Bethel Farm. You'll just have to come over here for Christmas, Solange, to welcome your new grandbaby."

Pearl's words were irritating. Solange had a strong suspicion that she was going to miss Miranda something awful if she stayed in England. She couldn't tell Pearl that she and Miranda had just started getting to know each other, because she suspected that had happened only because Pearl wasn't around.

"Miranda's coming out to stay with me next week while Joe's working," Pearl said next. "I want her to read the autobiography. It's all but finished."

"Am I in it, Mother?"

"Of course you are. Now, how could I write a story about my life without putting my only daughter in?"

Solange smiled and nodded, but some small part of her suspected that if Pearl could have managed it, she'd have skipped Solange and gone straight to Miranda. It had always been evident that Miranda was the daughter Pearl should have had.

"You were conceived right there under that copper beech, Solange." Pearl had stopped again and was pointing with her cane.

"Was I?" Thinking about Pearl having sex gave her a weird feeling. As far as she knew, her mother had never had a sexual relationship with anyone but Jacques, and until Joe came along, Solange had worried sometimes about Miranda. Sex was one of life's consolations for all the other things that went wrong. It was simple and fun and free, and she'd always enjoyed it fully, and she wanted Miranda to feel the same.

"I loved him with all my heart and soul," Pearl said softly.

Solange had never loved anyone like that. She didn't think she ever wanted to. There were so many nice men around; what was the point in limiting yourself to one?

"You have so much of him in you, Solange. Not your looks, but your nature. Seeing him in you has always been a great comfort to me."

Solange was astounded. Pearl had never once said that to her before. She'd always been so critical, so judgmental. That she was like the father she'd never known, and that Pearl liked her for it, was a whole new concept. It gave her a funny warm feeling in her chest.

"You know, we never would have lasted, Jacques and I," Pearl added matter-of-factly. "Different natures. But that doesn't mean you can't love."

Solange felt an unexpected surge of gratitude to her mother. She and Pearl had seldom shared confidences. Solange had never particularly wanted to hear any, but she did now. Maybe getting older made a woman more interested in her beginnings. She said softly, "You be sure and take care of yourself so you're fine to come home in September, Mother. I miss you.''

"I plan to finish my journal and keep a close eye on that girl of ours. I'll write and tell you how the baby's growing. Now, let's get back to the house and have some of that lemonade Natalie was making. It's awful hot out here.''

Not until Solange was on the plane the next day did she realize that Pearl hadn't really made any definite commitment about coming home.

JULY WAS HOT. London became a hellhole of air pollution and grime, and although the town house was air-conditioned, Miranda found she far preferred to spend the weekdays at the farm. She took the early train out every Monday morning, and Natalie picked her up at Beechford Village station after dropping the girls at school.

The thick stone walls of the cottage kept it, if not cool, at least livable, and Miranda helped with the household chores and started really getting to know Natalie and Elizabeth. Ronan was seldom there during the afternoon and evening; he had office hours in the village and afterward seemed to spend a lot of time at the local pub. If Natalie minded, she never said.

Miranda whiled away hours photographing everyone, particularly Daisy and Lydia, and of course Pearl. She read Gram's stories and laughed and cried at them; they weren't great literature, but they were wonderful chronicles of a long and busy life, the life of someone she loved. Not to mention that Gram's memories of Miranda were there. It was strange to read Gram's recollection of events and compare them with hers. Miranda found that another perspective made her rethink how she'd felt about her life, and sometimes even change deep-rooted convictions.

During July, the long lazy days at Bethel Farm passed like a dream, and Joe came every Friday night to take her back to London. All during July, and for the first two weeks in August, Miranda thought that he'd surely grow tired of driving out to the Cotswolds and collecting her. But he went on appearing at exactly the same time each Friday, and gradually she grew to expect him.

He greeted her with a hard hug and a long kiss, shared whatever food they were having for tea and chatted with Elijah about rugby scores and the garden and the sheep.

Miranda would watch him, eating as if he were starving, making everyone laugh with outrageous stories of his week as a solicitor. She loved to look at him. The heat seemed to suit him; he was tanned a deep walnut, and he usually changed from his suit into worn khaki shorts and a thin, sleeveless T-shirt that emphasized his muscular arms and strong chest. His bare feet were strapped into leather sandals, his thick unruly hair bleached golden by the sun. His dark brown eyes would meet hers, and a silent urgent message of anticipation and eagerness for the night to come would pass between her and him.

And when they were alone in the car, driving back to London through the long dusty twilight, Joe would tell her, in delicious detail, all the ways he planned to love her that night.

The knowledge that he desired her sexually made Miranda feel more attractive than she'd ever felt before, and whenever she caught a glimpse of herself in a mirror, she knew she looked as nearly beautiful as was possible for her. Like his, her curly hair was sun-streaked, and she'd let it grow longer than it had ever been, catching it up in a messy knot at the back of her head. Her pregnancy and the sun had emphasized her freckles, but she thought even that suited her. Her tanned body was changing daily, breasts swollen and deliciously sensitive to Joe's lips and hands, belly rounding. Sometimes he pressed his mouth there and talked to their baby, making her giggle by quoting Shakespeare, or reciting a nonsense rhyme, or asking if what Miranda had eaten for dinner was acceptable.

He told her repeatedly that he found her beautiful, and it made her feel utterly female, seductive, powerful. Their lovemaking was intoxicating, and when a nagging voice reminded her that she was living a fairy tale that would end in heartbreak instead of happily-ever-after, she refused to listen.

The intensity of the emotion between them wasn't only hers. She sometimes imagined that Joe was beginning to love her, although he was careful never to say it. And so was she; the first declaration had to come from him.

"KITTY'S DUMPED ME." Tony sounded determinedly unconcerned, although his bloodshot eyes and unkempt appearance suggested otherwise to Joe. "We had a blazing row. She insists it's time for us to move on to marriage and babies. Damn it, Joe, you tying the knot with Miranda got me in hot water with her."

He scowled across at Joe and motioned to the barmaid to bring another stout, ignoring the shepherd's pie they'd both ordered for lunch. "You swore me to secrecy, so I couldn't explain properly about this arrangement you and Miranda have. I tried to dance around it. I reminded Kitty it's imperative that you have an heir, that your marrying was necessity more than choice, but she laughed in my face and said that any blind fool could see that the two of you are in love. She said all the women at the wedding cried because of the way you looked at each other."

"So much for female intuition." Joe laughed and finished off his stout, but he felt as if he'd been kicked in the stomach. What exact expression had they seen on his face or on Miranda's that day that would give them that impression? Sure, there'd been something almost idyllic about their wedding if you didn't count Dierdre's outburst, but he and Miranda weren't thinking long-term about it at all.

The wedding was a means to an end, and that was that. It had gotten out of hand, what with the vicar and the flowers and the toasts, but in spite of appearances, neither of them thought in terms of a future together after the baby came.

They weren't in love, which was exactly why they got along—a huge bonus in his books. They spent hours each weekend wandering through antique shops, picking out furniture for the town house. They often ended up in musty bookstores, poring over some old tome. They went to the flicks and bought huge cartons of popcorn and laughed at the same things. He hadn't said anything yet, but the thought had crossed his mind that maybe she'd give up on the idea of going back to Seattle.

And he was unduly looking forward to tomorrow night, when he'd pick her up and bring her home.

Home. The word hit him hard. Why should the town house feel like home just because he lived there with Miranda? Sure, she was bright and sweet and funny and incredibly exciting in bed, but she was also temporary. Maybe Tony was right; maybe he was getting in over his head with her. Maybe it was past time to pull back, remind himself of the original game plan.

"How about a round of golf this weekend, Tony? Take your mind off Kitty. In fact, why don't we take off on Friday afternoon and make a weekend of it."

Tony brightened. "Sounds good to me. But I thought you and Miranda spent all your weekends together."

"We've been keeping up appearances, happy married couple and all that rot. I'll just call her and tell her I won't be up this weekend. There'll no problem with that."

"You're a damn lucky man, Wallace. I envy the hell out of you. You've got the best of both worlds."

Joe very much wanted to believe that Tony was right.

CHAPTER TWENTY

"ANYTHING WRONG, Miranda?" Elizabeth was carrying an armload of sheets, heading upstairs to make up one of the guest rooms. A couple was arriving later that evening to stay for the weekend.

Miranda put the telephone down, trying not to reveal her disappointment. "Joe's not coming up this weekend. He and Tony are going golfing." She swallowed hard against the lump in her throat.

"Stewart was a golfer. It can get to be like a disease with them. That's a bit of a letdown for you."

It was more than that. It was an abrupt reminder that she'd been living in a fantasy world. Pain swelled in her chest, and she forced down the anguish that threatened to overwhelm her.

"I think I'll go pick some of those beans Elijah said were ripe." Miranda fled out the door, grateful for the privacy of the garden.

She'd thought this weekend would be special; there was only this and one more before she and Gram flew back to Seattle. She'd planned to tell Joe that she'd written the school board and informed them she wouldn't be teaching.

She'd thought it over and decided it wasn't fair

to the children to turn them over to another teacher halfway through the term. But now she admitted that there'd been another reason for her decision.

She'd fantasized about taking Gram home and then coming back to London to be with him, having the baby with Joe there beside her. She'd actually felt he was on the verge of asking her to do exactly that.

She was a fool. Instead of wanting her with him, he'd obviously grown tired of her, and she'd been too stupid to recognize it. Furiously, she tore the runner beans from the vines and let the tears drip into the colander. A sob hiccuped out, and then another, and at last she gave in to the need to collapse on the warm earth and wail.

Somehow she made it through the rest of the day. There was peace about the farm that was healing, and by the time evening came, she'd decided what she had to do.

She wouldn't hope anymore, and she couldn't stand to be around Joe without that hope. She'd call and tell him she wasn't feeling well, and that she wouldn't be coming to London the following weekend, either. She'd spend her last days here at the farm with Gram.

But the following week, it took every ounce of courage to make the call, and then when she heard the barely disguised relief in his tone, something hardened inside her.

"It's probably for the best," he said cheerfully. "I have a rugby match on Saturday, but I could drive up Sunday and check on you. Not much fun for you, being ill, although you're absolutely right to stay out in the country. It's hotter than Hades here.''

"Oh, don't bother coming Sunday," she managed to say in a bright voice. "I'm going to church with Gram, and then I thought I'd take her out for a nice lunch, just the two of us."

"Of course, whatever you like. By the way, have you made up your mind about the sale? Harvester called again. They're pressing for a commitment."

"I've decided. I told Ronan the farm was his, at the amount he offered. Being here has convinced me I want the place to stay the way it is. Ronan will be calling you."

"I understand. And in spite of finances, I think you've made the right decision. I've become very fond of Bethel Farm myself."

There was an awkward silence, and then finally he said goodbye.

That night, Miranda couldn't sleep. She tossed and turned and tried to ignore the raised voices coming from the room where Natalie and Ronan slept. She'd heard them quarreling several times before, but tonight was particularly bad. For all his charm, Ronan had a fierce temper.

Something crashed to the floor. She heard the bedroom door slam, heavy footsteps on the stairs and a few moments later, the sound of Ronan's old Land Rover driving away.

Silence fell, and Miranda lay waiting what seemed like a long time. When there was no further sound, she got up and crept down the stairs, longing for a glass of the ice water she kept in the fridge.

She flicked on the light and saw Natalie huddled in the old armchair by the table. The front of her blue nightgown was sodden with tears, and when the light came on, she hastily brushed both palms across her cheeks.

"You heard," she said in a tear-choked voice. "I'm so sorry we woke you. It's a bloody wonder Ronan didn't wake the entire household, smashing my china bowl that way. I'm only glad there're no guests this weekend."

"You didn't wake me, Natalie. I couldn't sleep, and I needed a drink. Can I get you some water or make some tea?"

"Water's great."

Miranda poured two glasses and sat down at the table. She felt awkward. She didn't want to leave Natalie by herself, but she also didn't quite know what to say to her.

"Did you and Joe have rows before you got married?"

Miranda shook her head. "We didn't know each other very long. I got pregnant right away. We probably still don't know each other well enough to fight." That made her sad. There was so much missing in their relationship. Fighting implied a certain confidence, an understanding that when it was over, the bond was still intact. Their passion had been confined to the bedroom, while it lasted.

"I've been with Ronan just over a year now. We got along perfectly at first. He seemed everything I ever wanted in a man. But lately…lately things have changed. We can't seem to agree.''

Natalie was obviously struggling with the need to confide in Miranda without being disloyal to Ronan, but at last she gave up and blurted out, "He wants me to ask Elizabeth for the insurance money she got when Stewart was killed, and I can't do that. It's invested for the girls' educations.''

Miranda was shocked, although she tried not to show it. "He needs the money to buy the farm, is that it, Natalie?''

"I should never have said anything to you.'' The other woman looked utterly miserable. "But you'll find out soon enough anyway. He can't raise the money for the down payment. I've given him what I've saved, but it's not enough. I've told him we don't have to live here. We could be happy anywhere. But buying this place is an obsession with him." Her tear-swollen eyes met Miranda's. "Sometimes I wish I'd never met him,'' she said wretchedly.

Miranda had never felt that way about Joe. In spite of everything, she was glad he'd come into her life. She wondered if that would change as time went on.

"Do you still want to marry him, Natalie?''

The other woman hesitated, then shrugged. "I'm not sure. Especially at times like this, I think of what it was like before I knew him. We got along fine here—Elizabeth and Daddy and the kids and I. We were very happy. But I was lonely. I've never been married, you see, and I want babies before it's too late. I so envy you, being pregnant. Every time I deliver a baby I long for one of my own. I'm forty-two. There isn't all that much time left. Ronan and I have been trying, but it hasn't happened.''

''I know how that feels. I felt the same way myself not long ago.'' Miranda got up and put her arms around Natalie, trying to convey her support and sympathy. When she sat down again, she changed the subject. ''How many babies have you delivered, Nat?''

''Eighty-six. I keep a diary.''

''Tell me what delivering a baby is like.''

''There's nothing in the world to compare with it.'' Natalie's eyes lit up. ''It's the time when I feel closest to God, because I'm allowed to help with a miracle.''

Miranda posed more questions, asking about all the silly things she had wondered about but had felt too shy to broach. Natalie was easy to talk to. At last they made a pot of tea, and it was past two by the time Miranda finally went up to bed. Even then she couldn't get to sleep.

The things Natalie had said about Ronan troubled her deeply. He'd never indicated there was any problem with finances, and because he was a doctor, Miranda had assumed he must have money. His pressuring Natalie for the insurance money was unforgivable. She hated calling Joe, but this was something she had to talk to him about. She'd phone him in the morning.

She awoke to a tap on her door. Sunlight streamed through the small high window, and she felt groggy and dazed. "Come in." She fumbled for her glasses and gazed blearily at the clock. It was ten-twenty.

"I thought you'd like some tea and a fresh scone." Elizabeth smiled and put the tray on the bedside table. "Everyone's tired this morning. Natalie just got up. Pearl's still in bed. It's this heat. If the girls didn't wake me at the crack of dawn, I'd sleep, too."

"Gram's not up yet, either?" Miranda poured tea and sipped it, savoring the yeasty scent of the fresh scones.

"I've made a tray for her, as well. I'll go down and get it."

"I'll take mine into her room. We can have some of these wonderful scones together." Miranda slipped her arms into a cotton robe and washed her face at the basin, while Elizabeth brought the other tray upstairs. Carefully balancing her own tray, she followed Elizabeth along the hall.

"Gram? Gram, wake up. We're having a tea party, you and I." But there was no answer when they tapped at the door, and all of a sudden Miranda's heart began to knock against her ribs and she couldn't get her breath. She set the tray down hard on the floor, oblivious to the tea that slopped out of the mug, aware only of the increasing dizziness in her head. She opened the door, and she heard Elizabeth gasp.

Pearl was half sitting on her stack of snowy pillows, hands resting on the sheet that covered her.

She looked utterly peaceful, but in the long moment before Miranda fainted, she knew that her Gram was gone.

"I WISH YOU'D BE reasonable and let me go home by myself."

Miranda's voice was cold and angry, and Joe wondered how much longer he'd be able to hold his temper.

"You are my wife, you're pregnant and you're under severe emotional strain. You're not flying across the Atlantic by yourself under these circumstances, and that's that." He'd been through this same argument twenty times in the past two days, and he was losing his patience.

Why couldn't Pearl have requested burial in the churchyard at Beechford, as everyone had expected? Instead, she'd left firm instructions that her body be flown back to Seattle, to be buried beside her mother Cordelia, and her grandmother, Geneva.

And Miranda had been determined that she was taking Pearl home alone. Joe simply ignored her and made all the arrangements. But even now, in the last few minutes before they boarded the flight, Miranda was still resisting.

This stubbornness was a side of her Joe hadn't seen before, as was the cold reserved persona that accompanied it. He'd never imagined that grief could change someone this drastically. She'd refused to allow him even to put his arms around her, damn it, and he needed to hold her. Not for his sake, of course, but for hers. He hadn't even seen her cry once. He longed to comfort her, but she made it impossible.

"It's ridiculous. There's no need for you to come, Joe. All you'll do is fly over, attend the funeral and fly right back. I'd planned to leave soon anyway. We did agree that I'd have the baby in Seattle, you remember."

"Don't keep reminding me what we agreed upon." His voice was edgy, and he quickly controlled it. She was, after all, still in shock. "These are special circumstances. Quite apart from my own feelings about it, Dad would never understand, to say nothing of Larry." He was carrying the wicker case Larry had handed him just before he and Miranda had passed through security twenty minutes earlier.

"She has to eat," Larry had whispered, "for the sake of the child. See if you can tempt her with some of this."

Joe hadn't had the heart to explain that the executive-class steward would certainly ply them with food and drink, far too much of it. So he was boarding the airplane like a steerage-class immigrant, with enough food in the bulging case to feed everyone on the flight. And he wouldn't mind at all, if only Miranda would accept the support and comfort he was trying to extend.

Her mood would wear off, he assured himself. They'd be sitting next to each other for thirteen hours. She'd have a sleep; he'd made certain she'd be as comfortable as possible by reserving the third seat so she'd have more room. He'd ensure she was undisturbed, and then when she'd rested they could have a rational conversation.

He tried. She sat bolt upright for the first hour, so he did his best to take her mind off Pearl's death by relating the humorous instructions his father had given him regarding Dierdre. "Assure her that her job is here whenever she chooses to return. We'll regard this simply as a leave of absence with pay," Gabriel had said. "Furthermore, we won't even discuss the nasty scene at the wedding."

"Why don't you call her or write and tell her yourself, Dad?"

"I've tried." Gabriel scowled. "The woman refuses to speak to me, and my letters have been returned unopened."

Joe told Miranda that he was relieved he didn't live with Gabriel anymore, if his father's behavior at the office was any indication of his general mood. Two of the secretaries who'd been hired for Dierdre's job had already resigned.

"Your father needs to figure out what it is he wants," Miranda said tartly. "And if it's Dierdre, he'd better be quick about it. Solange told me a week ago that Dierdre's dating a businessman she worked for as a temp."

"Well, that was fast." Joe suddenly felt protective and sympathetic toward his father.

"Women will only put up with so much, Joe."

There was a warning note in her voice that he chose to ignore. He decided not to tell her right then about Kitty and Tony, and why they were a perfect example that the arrangement he and Miranda had was ideal.

There'd been a series of escalating explosions between them, with Kitty appearing at the hospital while Tony was working and dumping a load of his belongings in the middle of the obstetrical ward. Tony had then been arrested for drunk and disorderly conduct when he created a scene at her apartment building. Joe had been called to bail him out and find a barrister to take Tony's case.

Joe racked his brain for a safe topic that wouldn't upset her. "How are things out at the farm? Any wedding plans for Ronan and Natalie, now that they know they'll have a place to live?"

"Oh, heavens, I forgot." Miranda looked stricken. "I meant to tell you. Ronan O'Donnell doesn't have any money." She repeated the late-night conversation she'd had with Natalie, adding, "Ronan has a nasty temper."

Joe was amazed. "Ronan? I thought he was the soul of reason and affability."

"So did I. But lately I've seen a side of him that isn't pleasant at all. I'm sorry I ever gave him my word that he could buy Bethel Farm."

"But Pearl liked him so well." He saw the abject misery in her eyes and could have kicked himself.

"You know Gram was deaf. She didn't hear a lot of things. And she wanted the farm to stay exactly the way it is, so if it had to be sold, she wanted it to go to Ronan. I told her I'd settled on him as the buyer." Her eyes had gone blank again. "She laughed and said it was wrong to mislead the poor man, because the baby would come in time.''

"I'll contact International Harvester immediately.''

"No. I know what Gram meant now about Bethel Farm. There is something special about it. I don't want it turned into a factory.''

"Very well. I can contact real-estate people, get some photos put in *Country Life.*''

"No.'' Her chin set in a stubborn line. "Just let it be for now. Ronan may still come up with the money and he does have deep feelings for the farm. If he can't manage the purchase, I'll decide what to do later.''

"Right. No problem.'' He didn't want to upset her further, but something had been bothering him too much not to ask. "Are you sorry now that we started the baby, Miranda? I mean, it won't arrive by the end of the year, and with your grandmother gone...well, it seems rather unfair to you. The advantages to our having her will be mostly mine.''

"Don't you ever say that again.'' She turned to face him, and the fierce expression on her face made him catch his breath. "This baby means everything to me, do you understand that, Joe Wallace? You may want him for your own selfish reasons as the solution to a problem, but to me he's a miracle.''

After that, she refused to be drawn into any sort of meaningful conversation, and for the remainder of the endless flight, she maintained the impersonal, cool politeness that, although he didn't understand why, maddened and frightened him.

CHAPTER TWENTY-ONE

JOE STAYED in Seattle for four days. He insisted on taking care of all the details and being at Miranda's side every moment, and she was grateful for his support, his strong arm around her during the heart-wrenching ordeal of Gram's funeral.

In every other way, however, his presence was painful. She felt emotionally drained, desperately bereft at losing Gram, but she couldn't cry, because she knew she had to maintain an aloofness toward Joe. If she dropped her guard even a little, she'd be seduced all over again by his charm; she'd forget that it was just that—charm.

Of course Solange expected him to sleep in Miranda's bedroom. But Miranda knew she couldn't bear to be beside him during the night. "I'm not feeling well. I'd prefer if you slept somewhere else," she said the first night, and without a word Joe moved into one of the other empty bedrooms.

But on the last night of his stay, Miranda came out of a troubled doze at three-fifteen in the morning to find him standing in her room.

"Miranda, we need to talk."

He sat down on the side of the bed and snapped on the bedside light. He was wearing navy pajama bottoms. His chest was bare, and it hurt her to remember how often she'd nestled her head there, his arms snug around her, her nose pressed to that tight mat of curls.

"You've barely spoken to me these past few days, and although I understand that you're grieving, there are things that need to be discussed."

He was obviously both angry and determined.

She struggled to a sitting position and put on the glasses he handed her. He looked disheveled and red-eyed, as if he hadn't been sleeping any better than she had.

"I thought we agreed on everything a long time ago, Joe." She tried to appear matter-of-fact.

"Things change. I want you to come back to England with me."

"You...what?" It was the last thing she'd expected.

"You heard me." He sounded impatient. "There's no real reason for you to stay over here. You're not teaching. You'll be alone while Solange and Dierdre are at work. This place is isolated. I'd feel safer if you were with me. And Dad and Larry are going to wonder what's going on with us if you don't come back."

"Us?" Just for a moment, she'd thought he was going to say he'd miss her, that he wanted her with him. Instead, all he cared about was appearances. He was breaking her heart all over again, but she wasn't about to allow him to see that. The only thing she had left was pride, and she was determined not to let him know how many ways he could hurt her.

"There is no 'us,' Joe. We're going to share this baby, but we're going to do it as two single adults, just the way we planned. Sooner or later, your father and Larry will have to know that we're divorcing once it's born. Perhaps you should tell them sooner rather than later."

"I plan to, damn it all, but that doesn't change the fact that we're married right now and we have a baby coming." He reached out and put a palm on her abdomen. His voice softened. "I've decided I want to be part of the whole process, Miranda. Come home with me." He was pleading with her. His low voice dropped to a whisper. "We're good together—you know that. Why shouldn't we enjoy these next months? I want you in my bed, Miranda."

She longed to agree. Some craven, spineless part of her ached to give in to him. But the mental image of Dierdre throwing the herbal wedding bouquet at Gabriel stopped her.

Besides being father and son, the Wallace men had a lot of other things in common. They were powerful men, used to getting their own way, on their own terms. It had taken Dierdre years and a battered heart to finally understand that Gabriel wasn't going to offer a permanent commitment.

Joe wasn't offering her that, either. Unlike Gabriel, he'd never pretended he would. Joe had never been anything but honest with her. She was the one who'd lied.

And with that realization, she knew what she had to do. There was one certain way to get him to leave her alone so that her broken heart might have a chance to heal.

"I love you, Joe." The words came out easily now. "I fell in love with you that very first night we spent together." She looked him straight in the eye. "I'll come home with you if you tear up the agreement and tell me that you love me and want to spend the rest of your life married to me."

His shocked face told her she'd been right. The truth was a powerful weapon after all.

Miranda's words sent a jumble of emotions racing through Joe, amazement, confusion, a bolt of joy, and then resentment that swiftly became anger.

She'd done it again. "You lied to me, you tricked me, just the way you did in the beginning over the damn virginity thing."

She nodded. "I wanted to spend time with you. I wanted to have your baby. That seemed more important to me than the truth."

"But I told you how I felt about getting emotionally involved, and you agreed." He felt like smashing something—his fist into the wall, anything hard and hurtful. "I laid it out for us in fine print, in black and white, no misunderstandings." He drew in a breath that didn't reach far enough. "Hell's bells, Miranda, you signed the bloody contract. And now you tell me the entire thing was a lie all along?"

"Yes." She nodded again.

"You deceived me."

"I did." She made no excuses. She simply sat and watched him. He could see the outline of her nipples beneath the thin blue-and-white flowered nightgown. They'd grown bigger, darker, during her pregnancy. She was unbearably sexy. Her wild curls pressed down on the side she'd been sleeping on, and with the glasses perched on her nose she looked young and vulnerable. The contrast was intoxicating.

Angry as he was, he still knew that he wanted her. But now that she'd confessed, nothing would ever be the same between them. Love wasn't something he could do. That scared him to death, which made him even angrier.

"I don't take well to ultimatums, Miranda."

"I didn't think you would."

She sounded so sad and resigned it was all he could do not to take her in his arms. But that would mean going in a direction he'd never planned to go, and he couldn't do it.

"This doesn't change anything, not really," she said in a deadly calm voice. "You don't have to worry about me causing problems about custody, or stalking you or anything." She tried for a smile but failed. "Trust me—from now on I'll abide by the letter of our agreement. I'll never mention this again. You don't even have to see me until after the baby's born. You can communicate through my lawyer if you choose." She drew in a shuddering breath and pressed her hand to her rounded abdomen. "Right now, I need to rest. Solange said she'd drive you to the airport in the morning, so it's best if we say goodbye here."

He longed to crawl in beside her, gather her close, tell her what she needed to hear. But some demon inside him resisted. So he said a cool goodbye, turned on his heel and walked away from her.

FOR THE FIRST FEW DAYS after he left, the floodgates opened and Miranda was unable to stop crying. Dierdre and Solange tried to comfort her with cups of tea and back rubs and clusters of flowers, thinking she was grieving for Gram, missing Joe. She was, but it was all wrapped up with her love for him, and finally when Solange threatened to call him and tell him what a state she was in, Miranda had no choice but to sob out the whole sordid story to the two of them.

Neither of them acted shocked when she admitted to having been a virgin. Dierdre calmly said that she'd been almost thirty herself before she'd had sex. Solange muttered something about waste and late bloomers, adding that she'd like to wring Joe's neck. They both read a copy of the agreement Miranda had signed, and Dierdre commented that as far as legalities went, he'd done a top-notch job. The agreement was clear, concise and probably legally binding.

Talking about it helped, Miranda realized. Her tears had stopped and a little of her heartache eased.

"So do you still want him, sweetie pie?" Solange became practical. "These damn Wallace men don't seem to be able to recognize gold when they find it. My advice to you is the same I gave Dierdre. Say 'Next!' and find a guy who deserves you. Only don't marry him this time."

It was far more complicated than that. Miranda

met Dierdre's eyes, and saw a reflection of her own pain.

Solange looked at them both and shook her head. "Not an option, huh? Well, here's suggestion number two. Don't talk to him, don't write him, don't let him have any inkling how you feel. Let him stew, and when he finally comes to his senses, don't let him off the hook easy. Make him work to get you back. Make him sweat. Make him really sorry. That's what I've done with Leon, and it's worked like a charm.''

Again, Miranda met Dierdre's gaze. Why, they silently asked each other, would anyone *want* Leon back? For the first time since Gram's death, Miranda felt a little like smiling.

Joe's letters began arriving later that week, sent by overnight courier. Against Solange's advice, Miranda signed for them and read them, although with the help of the answering machine, she managed to avoid his phone calls. The women agreed to let the answering machine take all calls, because Gabriel was calling Dierdre, as well.

My dear Miranda,
I've had time now to think over what you told me, and I'm sorry I reacted so strongly. I was unreasonable, and I hope you'll forgive me. I'm very fond of you, and disturbed because of this upset between us. Until this, we've gotten along so very well—and we have the baby to think of.
I've been exceptionally busy. Something you

mentioned about Ronan made me think we really ought to find out a bit more about him before the situation goes farther. One of our investigators is looking into the matter. I'll keep you posted.

Dear Miranda, please call at any time and tell me we can go on the way we have been. No point in worrying about the future; if the dire Y2K predictions materialize, we only have now. (Joke.) Seriously, I'm inclined to believe the future will take care of itself. But I'm concerned about you, Miranda. You weren't yourself, quite understandably, and I would like to know that everything is well with you.

Affectionately,
Joe

Affectionately. Miranda was so mad at that her first inclination was to tear up the damn letter. She felt bile rise in her throat, but that probably wasn't because of Joe. She had heartburn. The baby kicked and turned, as if he were reacting along with his mother.

So Joe was investigating Ronan. Recalling her experience with Leon, she could have told him to save his energy and the firm's money. But she wasn't speaking to him, so let him go ahead and waste both.

Dierdre was at home that day. The work for the temp agency was sporadic, and she was digging up bulbs in the garden to store for the winter. Miranda went out and handed her the letter.

Dierdre read it and made a sound of disgust. She

had dirt on her nose, and she was wearing a pair of Miranda's old track pants that were way too tight and far too long. The new short hairdo that Solange had insisted she try made her appear angelic, but she was picking up some of Solange's pithier expressions.

"This is the biggest load of B.S. since the last letter Gabriel wrote me. They're obviously using the same thesaurus." She looked up at Miranda. "My dear, don't let it get you down. What you need to do is get out, have some fun. What do you say we go into the city and have lunch, pop in and say hi to Solange, maybe do some shopping."

They did, and it helped. For the daylight hours at least, Miranda was able to relegate thoughts of Joe to a back burner. The nights were a different matter. Between thinking of Joe and making forced trips to the bathroom, she wasn't sleeping much. She started napping in the afternoon. Dierdre was a great cook, and there wasn't anything Miranda really needed to do except grow her baby.

More phone calls came. Miranda played back the messages, noting that Joe sounded a little less affable with each one. A second letter arrived, and a third.

The fourth was marked Urgent, and it was short:

Miranda,
I'm losing my patience with this whole affair. It's nearly a month now since we've communicated. I think you're being unreasonable in the extreme. There are serious issues regarding

the sale of Bethel Farm that we need to discuss,
I will phone at 8:00 p.m. your time, 29th September. Please pick up.

Solange and Dierdre watched as Miranda stood
by the telephone at the designated time and listened
to it ring. The machine clicked on, and Joe snarled,
"God blast it, Miranda. I know you're there. Now,
pick up the bloody phone."

"My, my, he's a bit testy," Dierdre cooed.

Miranda's heart was bumping hard. Hearing Joe's
voice always did that to her. Would she ever be able
to listen impartially?

"I have a right to know how your pregnancy is
progressing. I'm concerned about you. Surely you
can appreciate that. Now, will you for God's sake
pick up the phone?"

He had a point. She was considering it, when his
voice turned harsh. "All right. Go on being stubborn. I'll talk quickly because this is something you
need to know. I've learned that Ronan O'Donnell is
a bigamist, a crook and a liar. It seems he's been
married twice, the second time without the benefit
of divorce, and there's no divorce pending now, either. There's some question as to his medical status
as a doctor, and—"

Miranda snatched up the receiver. "Ronan's a
bigamist? Does Natalie know?"

"So you'll speak to me about Ronan's marriages
but ignore ours?" He was furious.

"Please, Joe, just tell me about Ronan." It was
difficult to keep her voice from trembling. Talking

to him was difficult, much more so than just hearing his voice.

"I shall, but only if you promise to stay on the line afterward and discuss this problem of ours."

"Okay, I promise." It was blackmail. But on the other hand, maybe it was time they talked.

"Ronan's been dishonest about almost everything. First off, he's a gambler. He's lost heavily at cards in the past few months. He definitely doesn't have enough money to buy the farm, which is why he's been trying to get Natalie to borrow from Elizabeth. And he had no intention of making the place into a women's shelter. I've learned that he's hand in glove with a less-than-honest developer who builds shabby houses on small lots and sells them cheap. If Ronan could get you to sell to him, he and the developer would make a very nice profit."

"My God. I can hardly believe this." Miranda was stunned.

"I couldn't, either, but the evidence is all here in the report from my investigator."

"Natalie must be told."

"I'm going to drive out tomorrow and tell her personally. And I'll be there when she confronts O'Donnell. He'd better not get physical, or I'll respond in kind and plant a fist in his charming face." He blew out a breath and then he sounded a little less angry. "Now, tell me how you are."

"I'm perfectly well. Getting quite fat. The baby's absolutely wonderful. He kicks and rolls around as if he's playing rugby in there. My doctor says I'm having a very normal pregnancy."

"That's good. I'm delighted." He didn't sound delighted. He sounded cranky again. "Now. Let's see if we can't work out this little problem we have, Miranda."

Little? Her guard went up. "There's nothing to work out, Joe. We both know where we stand. Talking about it doesn't change anything. What we should be talking about is the divorce. There're only three months until the baby comes."

He swore. She'd never heard him use such foul language before. "Divorce, hell." He drew in a hissing breath. "Damn it to Hades, we'll just stay married. That's what you want, isn't it? We get along well enough. There's no real reason to divorce."

She felt as if he'd punctured her heart. "Don't do me any favors, Joe Wallace. As far as I'm concerned, there's no way I'd ever stay married to you. And you can stop calling me and sending these priority letters, too. There's no need. I'll have my doctor send you a report each month on the baby's progress, and you'll get a call when he's born."

She slammed down the receiver before he could reply.

CHAPTER TWENTY-TWO

JOE CONSIDERED ripping the office phone out and throwing it against the wall. She was driving him mad. She was the most unreasonable, bad-tempered, impossible female he'd ever had the misfortune to meet.

"Mr. Wallace wants you in his office. Immediately." Gabriel's new secretary stuck her iron-gray head in his door and was gone before he could reply.

"Yes, ma'am," Joe snapped sarcastically, his blood boiling. His father was going to lecture him yet again about Miranda, he knew it. Joe had never told Gabriel and Larry the actual facts of his marriage. When she didn't come home with him after Pearl's funeral, he'd said only that he and Miranda were having a few adjustment problems.

Larry and Gabriel had since used every opportunity to try to pry the details out of him. When that didn't work, they gave him unsolicited advice and pointed out that the fault must all be his because Miranda was a fine girl. And she was pregnant, they kept reminding him, as if he didn't already bloody know.

Well, it was time to set Gabriel straight. He'd tell him just how unreasonable and contentious his daughter-in-law actually was. Anyway, this whole damnable mess was Gabriel's fault in the first place for pressuring Joe about a bloody heir.

Arms and heart pumping, he strode to his father's office and, bypassing the martinet who occupied Dierdre's desk, barged straight in.

Gabriel jumped and tried to slide the bottle of scotch he was holding back into the drawer, but the water glass he'd just filled sat in plain view on his desk, which Joe noted was covered with messy stacks of files and forms.

"You wanted to speak to me?" Joe's voice was aggressive.

"Sit down, Joseph." Gabriel waved at a chair, which held books and newspapers and a grease-stained bag that might have been lunch at some point. "Would you care for a drink?"

Joe's belligerence faded and for an awful moment he thought Gabriel had learned that he was mortally ill. Everything pointed to it. He'd never seen his father's office look like this; he'd never in his wildest dreams thought he'd ever see Gabriel drinking in the middle of a workday, much less offering Joe a drink. And the old man looked decidedly gray around the gills.

"What's wrong, Dad?"

"Everything." Gabriel poured Joe a hefty slug of whiskey, handed it to him and tossed down the entire contents of his own glass.

"I've realized I want to marry Dierdre, but she absolutely refuses to speak to me or come home.

She's apparently dating another man. And Larry's just given notice.''

"Larry's given notice?" Joe was incredulous.

"End of December. He's buying a run-down café in Pimlico. Plans to turn it into a vegetarian fast-food takeout. Says the millennium marks a new beginning and it's time for him to move on.''

Joe was too stunned to think straight. "But where will he live?" It was a stupid question, but Larry had occupied the self-contained suite in the basement of the town house since Joe was seventeen.

"Above the shop, apparently.''

The intercom buzzed, and Gabriel pressed the button and roared, "I'm not in. Can't you get that through your head, you idiot?''

Joe flinched. That would be the end of yet another secretary. Joe figured there'd now been seven since Dierdre left.

"Did you have a quarrel with Larry, Dad?''

"Not really." Gabriel looked shamefaced. "He did mention I've been rude and impossible to please. But I've not been in the best of moods lately.''

Joe could relate to that. He hadn't been in the best of moods himself lately.

"You did try to talk him out of it?''

"Of course I did," Gabriel answered impatiently. "I don't seem able to talk anyone out of anything these days.''

Joe knew he was referring to Dierdre. What was it that made these women so irascible? Another wave of outrage rolled through him. "I just had a conversation with Miranda." *If one could call it that.*

"Did she say anything at all about Dierdre?"

Gabriel sounded so eager that Joe hated to disappoint him. He shook his head. "She was very clear about not wanting any contact with me, now or in the future."

Gabriel harrumphed. "Female hormones. Part and parcel of pregnancy. She'll come round once the child is born. Miranda is an exceptional woman. The two of you are absolutely right for each other. Be patient, Joseph. Just give her time."

"I wouldn't count on that working." The time had come to fill Gabriel in on the details of his so-called marriage.

"You see, Dad, I went into this marriage knowing it would end in divorce. I drew up a separation agreement before we were ever married."

As Joe explained about the agreement he and Miranda had signed, the plans for the amicable divorce, the equal sharing of custody for their child, the words came more and more slowly, until at last it began to dawn on him that for a smart man, he'd done some incredibly stupid things.

Memories flooded him, hurtful memories. He remembered Miranda telling him she was a virgin, how difficult that had been for her. He'd hollered at her, for God's sake.

He remembered the way she felt in his arms, the way she looked deep into his eyes when they made love, as if peering into the depths of his soul. He'd considered her special, but never unique.

He remembered the way they had laughed together, and argued, and how they talked for hours about books and music and ideas. He'd never met a woman who challenged his mind the way she did, who forced him to think, to grow.

She'd said that she loved him, and he'd accused her of being dishonest. He'd been paranoid about being responsible for her happiness, only to find that he was the dependent one.

"I love her. I love Miranda." It was a revelation.

"Of course you do. Even I knew that."

"But I didn't. I didn't realize it until just now."

Gabriel clicked his tongue and shook his head. "It pains me to admit it, but we Wallace men are not romantic heros, Joseph."

"Maybe there's a course we could take." At this moment, that didn't sound like a bad idea at all.

"It's my fault." Gabriel sighed. "I must apologize to you, Joseph. I feel responsible for your negative attitudes toward marriage. I've set you a rotten example."

"But you were only married once, to Mother."

"My point exactly. I never tried again. I was thrown and never got back on the horse, so to speak. Your mother and I were unsuited. We married hastily and should have divorced instead of going on with it."

"Why didn't you?" Joe had often wondered.

"There had never been a divorce in her family or in mine. It would have been viewed as a disgrace."

Joe considered the stack of divorce cases on his desk. Things had definitely changed.

"I've done a great deal of thinking since Dierdre left," Gabriel continued. "I always believed the failure was all mine, but I see now that it was not a matter of fault, simply of two personalities that didn't mesh. But I vowed never to marry again. Then I met Dierdre, and we made each other happy, and I still stupidly believed that marriage would ruin it. And as the years passed, I began to take her for granted. I acted the fool, and I hurt her. Hard as it is to admit, everything she said about me at your wedding was absolutely true, you know."

Joe would never hurt the old man by saying he'd known it long before Dierdre had said it. Wasn't he absolutely brilliant at recognizing idiocy in everyone except himself?

"I want Dierdre back, but I don't know how to go about it, goddamn it." Gabriel smashed his fist on the desk. "If she was here, I'd find some way to make her forgive me. I'd grovel at her feet if necessary. But she's severed all lines of communication."

"Tony says that roses help, but you must deliver them in person." It must have worked; Tony and Kitty had eloped two days ago. "It's too bad international kidnapping is illegal," Joe muttered.

Then the answer came to him.

"We'll go over there and deliver the flowers ourselves. And then we'll bring the two of them home." It was the only way. The more he considered it, the more the idea appealed to him. "It's the only thing to do, Dad."

Gabriel reflected, and a slow smile spread across

his features. "You're right, Joseph. It's inspired. We won't announce ourselves. We'll just arrive. That will give us the advantage of surprise. I'll have that new secretary make reservations. We'll fly out tomorrow." He punched the intercom button.

"Wait, we can't go tomorrow." Belatedly, Joe remembered the mess with Ronan O'Donnell. He explained, adding that he felt duty-bound to go out and give Elizabeth the bad news in person.

Gabriel was horrified to hear about O'Donnell. "Of course I'll come out with you to Bethel Farm and we'll challenge that charlatan together. We'll fly the following day. We'll take the Concorde. No point in wasting time."

Why hadn't Joe thought of that? The old man certainly had his moments.

Gabriel punched the intercom again. Nothing happened.

"Where is that bloody woman?" Gabriel leaped to his feet, strode to the door and bellowed, "Miss— I need you in here immediately." Gabriel didn't wait for a response. He slammed the door and came back to his desk.

"Whom are you addressing in that tone, Mr. Wallace?" The woman with the iron-gray hair had flung the door open and stood glaring at Gabriel, arms akimbo. "You need a course in manners, sir. Unless I receive an immediate apology, I'm leaving. And that will be disastrous for you, because I will spread the word among all the agencies that what they already suspect is true—you are rude and impossible to work for."

Gabriel opened his mouth and closed it again. He and Joe exchanged a glance, and then in a humble tone Joe had never heard from him before, Gabriel abjectly apologized.

"I THINK THE REASON I don't want to marry Leon is that I've lived most of my life with women," Solange remarked, slathering honey on the toast Miranda had just made. "Women are comfortable to be around. Men want more than popcorn and toast for dinner, and you can't lounge around in your underwear or they figure you want sex."

"Even this underwear?" Dierdre was wearing a set of what looked like men's red long johns. She'd bought them because she was cold at night, but they were so comfortable she'd taken to wearing them for lounging.

Miranda swallowed a mouthful of buttery popcorn and shoved more bread in the toaster. She'd just had a bath, and she'd put on her favorite outfit, a voluminous flannelette nightgown that had been Gram's, along with a pair of thick woolen socks. The gown was short on her, just above her knees, in a shade Solange labeled stomach-medicine pink, but it was comfortable, warm, and it made her feel close to Gram. She'd given up shaving her legs; she hadn't been to the hairdresser since before her wedding; and now that she knew Joe wouldn't be writing or phoning, she told herself she should just concentrate on motherhood.

The baby was growing. She was six months pregnant, and already the size of her belly astonished her. How could the human body adapt this way? "Did your belly button poke out when you were pregnant, Solange?" She pulled the gown tight against her to show the other two what was happening.

"Don't remind me." Solange shuddered. "But it does go back in afterward."

"Mine does that and I'm not even pregnant." Dierdre patted her plump tummy, and they were all laughing as the doorbell rang.

"If that's Leon, I'm gonna send him packing. I told him—" Solange peeked out the front window. "That's weird. It's a taxi."

Dierdre and Miranda listened, out of sight in the kitchen and curious, as Solange opened the front door.

"Good evening, Solange."

"Oh, lordie." Miranda grabbed the back of the nearest chair for support. "It's Joe," she hissed. There was no mistaking the accent, the deep-timbred voice.

"You don't have to talk to him if you don't want to," Dierdre whispered, putting a supportive arm around Miranda's shoulders.

"Is Dierdre at home this evening?"

"Gabriel. Gabriel's with him." Dierdre's hand flew to her heart. "Shit."

"What are you two doing here?" Solange sounded outraged. "You have no right to just barge in on us like this, without so much as a phone call."

"We had no choice, since all of you have given

up answering the telephone," Gabriel said. "Now, I must insist on speaking to Dierdre, if you please."

"Miranda? Miranda, where the hell are you?"

Joe was familiar with the layout of the house, and it was obvious he was heading for the kitchen. Miranda considered bolting out the back door or into the basement, but she was too late.

"Miranda?" Joe filled the doorway, his dark English topcoat open over a sky-blue sweater and gray trousers. His polished shoes reflected the light. He could have modeled for *Esquire* magazine. He had what looked like several dozen red roses clutched awkwardly in one hand. "Miranda, I need to talk to you. Please."

For one awful moment, Miranda thought about how she looked, with crumbs down the front of her nightgown, butter on her chin, not a scrap of makeup, hair unbrushed, legs unshaven—and then she didn't give a damn. He hadn't loved her looking her best; why should she care if he saw her at her worst?

Dierdre must have been feeling uncomfortable about her own appearance, because when Gabriel appeared right behind Joe, Miranda felt the arm that was still around her shoulders stiffen.

Gabriel looked at Dierdre and cleared his throat. "Dierdre, could we speak in private, please?"

Joe moved through the doorway to allow his father to enter the kitchen, and Miranda saw that Gabriel, too, held a huge bouquet of long-stemmed roses. His were yellow.

"Give me the damn flowers, you pair of idiots,"

Solange snarled. "And if you two have anything productive to say, you can do it right here around the table, but it better be good. You two have caused enough grief. The three of us have no secrets, right, girls?" She shoved her way past the men, her ivory satin lounging pajamas outlining every inch of her slender body. She ran water into the sink and stuck the flowers into it, then whirled around to glare at the two men. "Well? What are your intentions?"

Gabriel didn't glance at her even once. His eyes were on Dierdre, and his voice was beseeching. "I really would rather do this in private, my dear."

"Not a chance. This is our territory. You do things our way." Solange gestured at the chairs surrounding the old wooden table. "Sit down, girls. There's strength in numbers."

Miranda sank onto a chair, and Dierdre chose the one next to her. Solange sat on her other side.

The men hesitated, then gave in. They, too, sat.

"Miranda, there's something…" Joe began, just as Gabriel said, "Dierdre, I want to…"

"One at a time," Solange ordered. "Gabriel, you go first. You're the oldest."

Gabriel nodded. "Very well." His voice was dignified, although his face turned a mottled purple. "Dierdre, I want to say I'm sorry for the way I've acted, and I ask your forgiveness, although I know I don't deserve it." He cleared his throat twice. "If you could find it in your heart to love me again, as I love you—and my dear, I do love you— If you would consider granting me a second chance…" He stopped again. "This is damnably difficult with an audience,'' he growled. He drew a deep breath and then said in a rush, "Dierdre, would you do me the honor of becoming my wife?"

Miranda turned to look at Dierdre. Her eyes slowly filled with tears, and her face was radiant, but before she could say a word, Solange intervened.

"She needs time to think it over, right, Dierdre?"

Miranda felt Solange give Dierdre's leg a hard nudge with her own, and after an agonizing moment, Dierdre nodded.

"I'll need some time, Gabriel." She drew in a shuddering breath, and the red underwear drew tight across her ample breasts. "You hurt me very deeply. I'd have to be certain it wouldn't ever happen again."

Gabriel looked ready to explode. He swallowed twice. "I understand. But you will give me a chance to court you? You will come home with me?"

Dierdre looked across at him, and her soft loving soul was reflected in her gray eyes. It was obvious she'd never for a moment stopped loving Gabriel, so Miranda could hardly believe it when Dierdre replied firmly, "Not just now, Gabriel. I plan to stay here until Christmas. I'll give you my answer at that time."

Miranda had avoided looking across at Joe, aware that he'd never once stopped watching her.

"Your turn, Joe, and this better be good." There was a warning in Solange's voice. It was both strange and wonderful for Miranda to know her mother was protecting her.

Joe reached across the table for her hand, but Miranda refused to take his. Touching him was too dangerous. Her heart hammered against her ribs, and their baby did somersaults and headstands.

She met his eyes, and it was a mistake, because she saw something there that could make her hope all over again. She'd given that up, she reminded herself, wringing her hands in her lap and averting her gaze.

"I had this speech all prepared," he began quietly. "But all I can think of to say is that I love you, Miranda. I've been a bloody fool, stubborn and selfish, but I do know now that I love you." His voice was seductive, deep and urgent, sincere. "I love you with my whole being, and I want to stay married to you. I want to be with you when our baby's born. I want you beside me for the rest of my life." His voice trembled.

She'd waited so long to hear him say it. It felt as if she'd been waiting her whole life. Miranda pushed her chair back and stood up, smoothing the thin pink flannel over the mound of her belly.

"I'm sorry, but it's too late, Joe."

She just couldn't chance it. She couldn't stand to open her heart to him and have it battered again. Better to end the relationship, once and for all.

CHAPTER TWENTY-THREE

SHE WAS HALFWAY UP the stairs before he caught up with her.

"Miranda, you have to listen to me."

"No, she doesn't," Solange hollered from the bottom of the stairs. "You're the smart guy who called all the shots in the beginning. It's Miranda's turn now, and if she doesn't want to talk to you, she doesn't have to. I'll phone the police, if need be."

Miranda gazed down at her mother, who stood, arms crossed on her bosom, chin set. Behind her was Dierdre, looking worried, with Gabriel close behind her. He appeared shell-shocked. Miranda realized that Solange would do exactly as she threatened, and this incredible scene could only get much worse.

"It's okay, Mom. I'll talk to him." Feeling unbelievably weary, Miranda sank onto the step. Joe sat down beside her, and the group at the bottom slowly disbanded, heading for the living room.

"Call if you need me, sweetie pie," Solange yelled over her shoulder.

"Thanks." Joe started to put an arm around Miranda, but stopped when she stiffened and moved away. "Miranda, I'm at a loss. I don't know what to tell you, how to make you believe anything I say.''

"It's pretty difficult," she agreed. "Just a few weeks ago, you convinced me you didn't love me and never would. Now you've changed your mind. How do I know you won't change it back again? What guarantee do I have?"

"None. Not a damn one." He raked his hand through his hair. "I could write you up a new agreement, telling you I love you and will never leave you as long as we both shall live. But in the end you'd still have to take my word for it." His shoulders slumped and he bowed his head and clasped his hands between his knees. "I guess it's a little like this whole millennium thing. Remember when we talked about it, you told me what your Gram said? That there were no guarantees that the world wasn't going to end, that like most of the important things in life it was a matter of trust?"

Gram *had* said that. But Gram had also believed in the power of love. She'd told Miranda countless times that she knew that when her time came to die, Jacques would be waiting for her.

Oh, Gram, I hope he was. You had to wait so long.

Trust. There it was again. Gram had trusted completely, with no guarantees, through all those long years.

And up till now, Miranda had gone through her life not trusting, not taking many chances, wanting the picture to be perfect before she put a frame on it. But maybe life was like photographic film; maybe you had to accept on faith that something would show up when you developed it.

It was so hard to do. She wrapped her arms around her belly and felt her baby move. *He's your father, kid. Do we cut him some slack or not?*

Two hard kicks.

"All right." She looked at him, this handsome, difficult, charming, impossible Englishman who happened to be her husband. She loved him so very much. "All right, Joe. But you have to tell me again. You have to tell both of us. Every day, until we get sick of hearing it." Which, of course, would never happen.

He looked as if he hardly dared to hope. "You and Solange?"

"Nope. Me and our baby."

"Oh, my God, Miranda." It wasn't blasphemous. It sounded like a heartfelt prayer. He knelt on the step below her and enfolded her in his arms.

They still reached around her, she realized, but only barely.

"I love you both. I love you with all my heart and soul and strength. If you let me, I'll care for you, protect you, honor you, adore you, for the rest of my life." He cradled her head between his palms and kissed her, and then he bent his head and kissed the mound under the pink nightgown.

"You'll come home with me, Miranda?"

She nodded. Home was wherever he was. Bethel Farm was lost, but their child would at least be born in England, as so many Irvings had been. That part was certain.

But there was much more that was unknown to her—the sex of her baby, the exact day and hour of its birth, the life it would have in the new century also about to be born.

So many things had to be taken just on trust, like the certainty that there was no such thing as the Irving curse.

Other things were assured, however. Truth, forgiveness, surrender, compassion—these, along with trust, were the age-old ingredients of love, and Miranda was learning their power. It would take time and effort, but she'd learn how to use them, how to teach them, how to live them. They were the tools that she'd take into the new century, the lessons she wanted this baby, all her babies, to learn.

"Are you two going to spend the rest of the night on the stairs?" Solange sounded petulant as she squeezed past them. "There are bedrooms, you know. I'm getting out of here. I'm putting some clothes on and calling Leon to come and get me. Those two down there are drooling all over each other, and obviously the two of you are getting along. It makes me feel completely left out, but of course that wouldn't cross anybody's mind."

Solange stomped along the upstairs hallway and slammed her door. Miranda looked at Joe, and they started to laugh.

Solange was Solange. Miranda had gotten to know her mother better during the past months. Old wounds had healed; old grievances had been forgiven. She could accept her mother now for exactly who and what she was, and that was a great blessing.

It was a gift, like so much else these difficult months
had brought.

A sense of joy came over her, so overwhelming
it sent a shiver down her spine.

CHAPTER TWENTY-FOUR

"CAN I FEEL the baby kick, please?"

"Sure you can." Miranda took Lydia's palm and placed it exactly where the baby's feet were, stuck somewhere near her right ribs. For the entire week before Christmas, those feet had hammered her rib cage regularly, but now, on the afternoon of Christmas Eve, her child seemed to be sleeping.

Lydia waited expectantly, and at last the baby moved, but it wasn't the usual threshing around that Miranda had become accustomed to in the past six weeks.

"Me, too, please?" Daisy took her turn, eyes round when the baby obliged with a listless bump. "Ooooh, you can really feel it, can't you?"

"Mummy says that I was rather quiet, but Daisy moved so much Mummy could hardly sleep at night," Lydia noted in a superior tone. "What does it feel like, having a baby inside you?"

"Like a miracle." Miranda smiled at the little girls. "I get so curious, wondering what he'll look like, what color his hair is, or whether he even has any." She moved restlessly against the pillows Natalie had arranged behind her on the sofa. She couldn't get comfortable.

"Are you sure it's a boy? Aunt Natalie told me that ultrasound shows whether it's a girl or a boy. Did you have that?"

"I did, Lydia, but Joe and I decided we didn't want to know. It's so much more fun to be surprised, don't you think?"

"I suppose so." She didn't look convinced.

"I'd want to know," Daisy stated.

Elizabeth came in from the kitchen and smiled at Miranda. "Feeling a bit better? Lyd, go and tell Grandpa and Joe that tea's ready. Daisy, help Auntie Nat finish setting the table, please."

When the girls had gone, she added, "Let me stick another pillow under your feet." She raised Miranda's legs and arranged the cushion. "Sitting in a car for several hours isn't easy when you're hugely pregnant, is it?"

Miranda shook her head. "Particularly not at the snail's pace Joe drives these days. We had other drivers honking and shaking their fists at us even in the slow lane. He seems to think the baby will jar loose in the middle of the M4." They'd started for Bethel Farm at nine that morning, and the drive had taken twice the usual time.

Miranda had declared firmly that she wanted to deliver the gifts she and Joe had bought for everyone at the farm, but the truth was, she was more than a bit lonely. It would be such fun to be there on Christmas morning when the children opened their presents, she'd argued when Joe balked. Besides, even though everyone knew she was better off without him, Natalie must still think of Ronan at holidays, and she needed her friends around her, Miranda insisted.

Because for the past month Joe had given in to every one of her outrageous demands, he had loaded everything in the Bentley, muttering that it was against his own better judgment. He wanted her near the hospital and Susan Meadow, the Harley Street obstetrician he'd insisted upon, but Miranda reminded him that Dr. Meadow had assured them the baby wouldn't make an appearance until well after the New Year. "First babies are often up to two weeks late, so don't begin expecting the arrival too soon," she'd cautioned.

That was probably good advice, but Miranda didn't want to hear it. In the past month she'd grown bigger than a house and as temperamental as a prima donna; not being able to put on her own shoes or get out of a low chair were taking their toll. But secretly she reveled in the way Joe spoiled her. And he'd kept his promise: every day he found new ways to let her know how much he loved her.

Being at the farm was comforting. It was worth enduring the nagging ache in her lower back that had started in the car and wouldn't go away. And she'd been fighting off an emotional outburst for hours; this was her first Christmas without Gram, and tears were never far away. There were so many changes, so many things to consider.

The pressing issue of Bethel Farm, for one. International Harvester had extended their deadline, and she still hadn't made a decision about selling this place she'd come to love. She and Joe had discussed alternatives, but the financial and legal issues were complex. In the meantime, Natalie and Elizabeth were staying on at Bethel Farm for at least another month.

And there was the house in Seattle. Solange was moving out, into an apartment near her store, so selling the Seattle property made sense, but everything seemed overwhelming at the moment.

Solange was coming over for the baby's arrival, but not until January; she and Leon had gone on a Christmas cruise to the Bahamas and wouldn't be back until then. Solange had somehow convinced Baillie that if the world was going to end with the dawning of the millennium, a luxury cruise ship was the best place to make the transition.

Gabriel and Dierdre were also away, on their honeymoon somewhere in Europe. Dierdre had managed to hold out until the first of December, and then she'd said yes to Gabriel's proposal and flown home. Terrified of losing her again, he'd insisted they marry immediately. They, too, would be back well before the baby's arrival.

Now that she was at the farm, Miranda acknowledged how lonely the London town house had been weekdays when Joe was at the office. She'd coped by going out often. Before she got too big to waddle around comfortably, she had been able to sling her camera case on her shoulder and board the bus to spend the day happily photographing the unique faces she spotted everywhere in the huge old city. She'd usually end up at the Natural Gourmet, the restaurant Larry was meticulously refurbishing, to be plied with bowls of his hot thick soup and chunks of fresh-baked bread.

He'd made her cry the last time she had visited by showing her the small backroom he'd painted bright yellow and outfitted with a bassinet, a changing table and a high chair, so the baby would have a place of its own.

That made three lavishly equipped nurseries. Gabriel had bought an entire display area at Harrods and set it up in a sunny upstairs bedroom at his house. And Joe and Miranda had found an antique crib, a carousel lamp and a rocking chair for the nursery at the town house.

"You okay, love?" Joe and Elijah came in, bringing with them the smell of rain and a blast of cold air. Joe bent to kiss her, placing a hand on the hard mound that was her middle. "She's behaving?"

Miranda smiled up at him and nodded. She still had moments when it was hard to believe this handsome man was her husband. It had finally dawned on her that by marrying him, she'd ended the Irving curse...not that she'd really believed in it in the first place.

"Stay right here, dearest. I'll fix you a tray."

"No." Her stubborn streak had grown right along with her baby. "I'd rather come to the table."

With Joe's help, she struggled to her feet, and a pain hit her without warning, so powerful she cried out and clung to him.

It seemed to last forever, and she heard Joe hollering frantically for Natalie. When the pain began to ebb, she realized that her legs and feet were soaked, and Joe's, too, probably.

"Her water's broken." Natalie was matter-of-fact and totally calm. "Let's get you upstairs and into some dry clothes, Miranda."

"Hurry it up, because we're driving back to London right now." Joe was in a frenzy. "I should never have let you talk me into coming out here at this stage. Are you sure you can walk? Let me carry you, sweetheart." He actually tried to get her into his arms at the bottom of the staircase.

"Put me down. You'll break your back." Miranda smiled at him, her heart melting with love. "And I'm not going back to London." Now that the pain had subsided and she realized what was happening, she knew that this was exactly right. The universe—with a little help from Gram—had planned it this way: her baby was to be born here at Bethel Farm, in time to meet the conditions of the trust.

"I want to be in the room where Gram had Solange." She beamed at her husband. "I'm going to give you the best Christmas present ever, Joseph Wallace."

Elation filled her just before the next pain hit.

While Natalie was helping Miranda into bed, Joe raced madly downstairs to the telephone. "That incompetent bloody idiot of a doctor promised me this wouldn't happen until January," he barked at Elizabeth, who was serving dinner to Elijah and the children. "I'll sue her, sure as hell I will." His hands were shaking, and it was tough to fumble through his wallet and find Dr. Meadow's number. Her office would be closed, but she'd marked her home number on the card.

He dialed it, and his temper rose when a machine came on and Meadow's quiet voice informed him that she was away for two days, but that Dr. Bamfield would take her calls.

Elizabeth handed him a pad and pencil, and he scribbled down the number, muttering obscenities in a low tone so the children wouldn't hear.

He dialed again. "Dr. Bamfield is unable to take your call at the moment. Please leave your number and the nature of your request after the signal," a nasal voice intoned.

"My wife's having a baby," Joe bellowed into the receiver. "I need a doctor." He remembered belatedly to leave the number, and slammed the receiver down.

"Natalie's delivered about ninety babies. Miranda is in good hands even if the doctor doesn't arrive," Elizabeth soothed, placing a mug of tea beside him on the counter.

"It's too soon," Joe groaned. "The baby's not due until at least January 10, the doctor said."

"That's only two weeks away." Elizabeth was trying not to smile, and it infuriated Joe. "I was that early with Daisy. Nature knows what she's doing, believe me."

Joe had no faith in nature. "Tony. I'll call Tony. There has to be one bloody doctor at home."

This time a familiar voice answered. Joe blurted out a fervid "Thank God" and babbled out what was happening. "We're out at Bethel Farm. You've got to get here right away, right *now*. It's an emergency," he ordered. Without waiting for a response, he hung up, knocked over the tea and raced for the stairs.

"Hi, darling." Miranda was in a white nightdress, sitting on the side of the bed and looking so cheerful and normal that for an instant Joe felt such incredible relief it made him dizzy.

But then she made a strangled sound and bent double. Natalie helped her to lie down and rubbed her back as another contraction hit.

"This is going along quite well," Natalie had the audacity to say. "I think we'll have a baby before too much time goes by."

The contraction eased and Miranda closed her eyes and relaxed. Joe took Natalie by the arm and half dragged her into the hall.

He hissed, "How long is this going to go on?" How long could he stand it?

"That depends on a lot of things, but if everything progresses the way it should, probably not more than another five or six hours. She's dilating really quickly."

Five or six hours? Eternity. Joe gulped and tried to force down the nausea that threatened to disgrace him.

"PUSH, MIRANDA. That's wonderful. That's great…"

How could Tony and Natalie think that anything about this agony was great? She'd traveled into the dark place where the pain waited again and again, and she was weary and worn. She was dimly aware that midnight had come and gone.

There was no time to rest now; the contractions were coming one on top of the other. Whenever they eased a bit, she collapsed into the strength and security of Joe's arms. He was holding her, keeping her safe.

The agony built again. She couldn't stand it; she couldn't—

"Okay, one more time, that's it, that's it...I can see the head, lots of hair, Miranda... Don't push, don't push... Pant now, pant..."

And that was the moment, suspended in time, when she thought that Gram was there, smiling at her. *Irving women are strong, pumpkin.*

The pressure built and built, and she was going to have to push or die...

"Okay. Okay, now. *Push.*"

And with an incredible effort she seemed to have prepared for all her life, Miranda sent the daughter she and Joe had made together out to meet the world.

EPILOGUE

His DAUGHTER'S quavering cries woke him, and Joe uncurled himself from his wife's warm body and squinted at the clock.

Three a.m., the first three a.m. of the new century. He and Miranda had toasted in the year 2000 with champagne and kisses and then collapsed into bed before it was an hour old. They'd learned in the space of a week to snatch what sleep they could, when they could, because eight-pound three-ounce Jesse-Pearl ran the Irving-Wallace household.

He swung his legs out of bed and scooped her out of the bassinet, fitting her downy head under his chin and whispering to her as he walked down the hall.

"Let's change you, angel, before we wake up Mummy for your meal."

During the three days they'd spent at Bethel Farm, Natalie had taught him the intricacies of diapering Jesse, bathing her and holding her properly, plus the complicated art of burping. In the muted light from the carousel lamp he undid snaps, fastened closures, gently stuffed minuscule arms and legs back in the proper openings.

And between his yawns and her indignant squalls, he talked to Jesse, as he always did. "Happy New

Year, button. It's a whole new century, good old Y2K, and the earth is still turning, the television works, there's water in the tap. All the nonsense about the world ending was just that—nonsense.''

He wrapped her snug in a fresh flannel sheet, the way she liked, and planted a kiss on the brown silk that passed for hair.

"You're a lucky girl, you know. You're the future. You're heir to a beautiful piece of property in the Cotswolds—you can garden and raise sheep there if you decide to be a farmer. Or else there's Wallace and Houmes, if you choose to go that route. It's all about choices, Jesse-Pearl.''

Jesse was bawling in earnest now.

"Are you two having a party in here?'' Miranda smiled at them and seated herself in the rocking chair, undoing the buttons on her gown. Joe handed over the frantic baby, and in a moment her cries became greedy gulping sounds.

"I was just explaining her career options.'' Joe sat down to watch his wife nurse his daughter. The beauty of it touched him to the depths of his being.

"It's difficult to imagine what 2000 will be like, the changes that she'll be part of,'' Miranda said. "She could live to see still another century.''

That vastness was too much for Joe's sleep-starved brain to absorb at three in the morning. His universe was here, in this dimly lit room, where a woman he hadn't met a year ago shoved her glasses up her nose with one hand and cradled his child with the other. She smiled at him, and what he experienced wasn't a feeling.

It was a state of being called joy.

HARLEQUIN®
SUPERROMANCE®

Three childhood friends dreamed of becoming
firefighters. Now they're members of the same team
and every day they put their lives on the line.

They are

AMERICA'S BRAVEST

An exciting new trilogy by

Kathryn Shay

#871 FEEL THE HEAT
(November 1999)
#877 THE MAN WHO LOVED CHRISTMAS
(December 1999)
#882 CODE OF HONOR
(January 2000)

Available wherever Harlequin books are sold.

HARLEQUIN®
Makes any time special ™

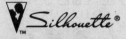

HEART OF THE WEST

Every Man Has His Price!

Lost Springs Ranch was famous for turning young mavericks into good men. So word that the ranch was in financial trouble sent a herd of loyal bachelors stampeding back to Wyoming to put themselves on the auction block!

HARLEQUIN®

Makes any time special ™

Visit us at www.romance.net

PHHOWGEN

Come escape with Harlequin's new

Series Sampler

Four great full-length Harlequin novels bound together in one fabulous volume and at an unbelievable price.

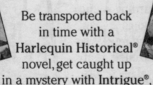

Be transported back
in time with a
Harlequin Historical®
novel, get caught up
in a mystery with Intrigue®,
be tempted by a hot, sizzling romance
with Harlequin Temptation®,
or just enjoy a down-home
all-American read with
American Romance®.

You won't be able to put this collection down!

On sale February 2000 at your favorite retail outlet.

HARLEQUIN®
Makes any time special ™

Visit us at www.romance.net   PHESC

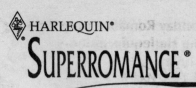
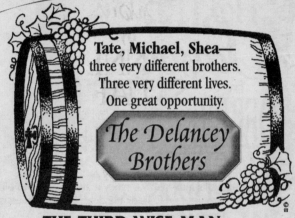
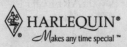

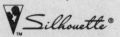